Oblivion

STEVE P LEE

ACKNOWLEDGMENTS

It can be a lonely existence, tapping away at your laptop, bringing imaginary worlds and characters to life. My Cockapoo, Peggy, constantly keeps me company – and occasionally adds extra letters, numbers and symbols to the draft. I have human family as well, and must mention the constant support of my wife, Tracey, and offspring, Alex and Kathryn.

Thanks are due, and given profusely, to Lisa at Green Cat Books for turning my manuscript into a paperback and eBook.

I try to maintain a constant presence on my blog and Facebook. Thanks go out to all who regularly gaze in confusion at my regular output and even share it to a wider audience. You know who you are

All characters and events in this publication, other than those clearly in the public domain, are fictitious and any resemblance to real persons, living or dead, is purely coincidental.

GREEN CAT BOOKS

www.green-cat.co/books

CONTENTS

DEDICATION

I would like to dedicate this novel to all the pioneering people involved in space exploration and technology. May you achieve all the success your hard work and dedication deserves; bringing the promise of a bright future for humankind among the stars.

Day 1

"Ancient and malevolent, it dwells beyond the sight of man, waiting ever long to rise again, ascend skyward in flames and scour the land! Leave, we must leave, before the coming of death." The man's bloodshot, heavy lidded eyes stared up at the faces gathered around his unkempt body, slumped precariously at the centre of a busy road junction.

"Well, I'm a woman so I'll keep a look out for it," Mint announced, hands on her hips, eyes glaring. "Get up, Tom, you're drunk - again!"

"I haven't touched a drop," Tom slurred, looking up at her, spittle mixing with a sticky gobbet of sick in his straggly beard. The liquor bottle slipped from his fingers and clattered onto the hard, resin road surface, rolled until a constable took charge of it.

"Get him up and out of here," Mint ordered and turned away. Behind, she heard her constables taking the drunk by the arms and dragging him upright.

Stalled traffic was slowly building down each road at the heart of Charlestown, drivers and passengers peering out at the scene. Mint's command vehicle was parked across one entry, lights flashing incandescent blue, the siren silenced. An adjacent road was blocked by the constables' patrol vehicle. Tom was being fitted with a puke-mask as she climbed up into the seat of her rugged 4x4 and accessed the traffic control signals on her command-pad.

. Her finger hovered over the reset symbol as she watched her men secure Old Tom into their rear seat. All four traffic control signals would remain on red until she was ready to leave. The patrol vehicle began to move, performed a slow U-turn then accelerated up the road towards the police station. Mint pushed the accelerator pedal at the same time as the reset button and set off in a different direction.

Two minutes of steady driving and waving at acquaintances saw her pull into the car park of her favourite café; Taste of Java. Several other vehicles were already parked up but her regular spot was left vacant. Her job as local police chief had its perks, being the sister of Java, the titular owner also helped. Their parents had been tea connoisseurs and chose original, but not too abnormal, first names for their twin offspring.

"Morning, Minty," Reid called cheerily from the counter as she strolled through the door. Her brother-in-law and sister were the only people permitted to address her so.

Mint assumed her usual position at her regular morning table as Reid busied himself preparing her morning coffee. Just to the side of the door, next to a large window, she could watch the outside world from this vantage point while enjoying cosy familiarity with family.

"Java not in today?" she asked as he placed the steaming brew on the table, the usual extra biscuit sat atop the normal customers' one.

"Should be in later," Reid smiled through sleep speckled eyes, "Mikey had a rough night."

"Oh dear," she looked up from stirring in a spoonful of sugar, "is he poorly again?" Her five year old nephew had only recently recovered from a seasonal stomach bug.

"A bit feverish, but otherwise he's fine. Strange really, he settled down perfectly ok last night, woke up in the early hours screaming about monsters."

"Well, that's kiddies for you," Mint observed. "It wouldn't be normal if they didn't have nightmares, not that I'd know." She remained single, childless, wedded to the job.

"Scary stuff for a youngster," Reid agreed as he returned to the counter, and accepted payment from a departing customer.

Another pair of regulars stumbled in through the entrance, bleary-eyed. They had a regular morning table too and dragged chairs out to slump gratefully down.

"Early morning runs getting too much for you?" Reid enquired.

"They are after a bad night," Penny replied.

"Ooh, it's catching," Mint called over. "Are you dreaming about the bogey-man too?"

"Something of the sort," Trent called back from opposite Penny. "We both kept waking each other up, tossing and turning."

"Hey, keep it clean!" Reid observed with a grin. "Don't go putting other customers off with details of your nightly antics."

Mint chuckled as she propped up the command-pad on the table and scrolled through the overnight reports. As usual, it had been another quiet night shift. A couple of minor vehicle prangs and red lights ignored, nothing she needed to get involved in. The two night shift constables had also installed Old Tom in a cell and loaded up their report of the incident. She switched to traffic and checked the crossroads she had just come from, nodded satisfactorily when she saw traffic was flowing freely now. Old Tom was starting to become a persistent nuisance and sooner or later she was going to have to address that issue. It might have to be sooner, she decided. This was the first time he'd taken his drunken antics into traffic; he was usually found propped up against streetlights or laying in doorways. She made a note to contact his doctor before he was released.

More customers came and went as she slowly downed the coffee and waded through command-pad based admin. She had just replaced the mug on the table when a shadow fell across her. She looked up to see Connor Granger, he looked quite anxious.

"Sit down Connor, what's the matter?" Mint kicked out the chair on the other side of the table for him to take.

Connor perched on the edge of the seat and placed a grease-stained hard hat on the table. He was general manager at the hydrogen fuel plant, five miles out of town.

"You're not going to like this," he said, his face emitting fear and concern. "You need to come to the plant; there's been a murder."

*

The thermos of coffee Reid had quickly put together for her kept rolling about on the passenger seat of Mint's 4x4, forcing her to extend a hand to stop it falling off into the footwell. She had eschewed Connor's offer to show her a photograph of the corpse and the murder scene; wanted to form initial impressions upon first sight, not in jumbled and unprofessional still-life perceptions on the short drive out. Following Connor's similarly sized 4x4 out of town on a main road, she drove past ranks of well-presented, detached houses on the outskirts until greenhouses took over, fields of grain and vegetables succeeded those until a rising wall of pine trees, bordered by rhododendrons and gorse marked the timbered zone. Her destination was beyond this outer fringe, within the forested ring, set back in a well quarried out hillside.

Obsirion II had been colonised nearly fifty years ago. The gigantic colony ships, financed and built by the British Corporation, had travelled for several years, utilising the massive and enigmatic Starjump constructs first encountered and partly deciphered at Proxima Centauri. These had opened up much larger regions of the galaxy for mankind to explore and colonise but, whom or what built them and where they are now, remained a total mystery. Mint's parents had followed in the second wave of settlers ten years after, making the twins part of the second native Obsirion generation. More waves of excited, expectant colonists had followed over a further twenty years.

The planet was a rare beauty, it already boasted life that utilised the process of photosynthesis and, as such, had an oxygen rich atmosphere. Animal life was not terribly advanced but kept well-observed, studied and allowed to evolve along its own lines by a large scientific team. Only one temperate continent had been colonised for human use, the rest were reserved for the local wildlife.

The quarried hillside Mint was heading towards had been dug out with powerful laser cutting tools to provide rocky material for the stable foundations and ground floors of the town's buildings. Upper floors were constructed from an extruded resin manufactured into prefab components and walls. The indented hillside had then been repurposed as the perfect placement for the town's hydrogen fuel plant, walled in on three sides in case of industrial accidents, enshrouded by the nascent forest and well placed to utilise natural water run off as well as the deep and voluminous local water aquifers. An underground pipeline fed out from the onsite wells, followed the road towards town then veered off to the water purification, storage and management plant that handled the town's drinking water supply and sewerage treatment. Many more towns and cities were dotted about the continent; perfectly planned with all the utilities and growth space needed, they were independently autonomous.

Mint followed Connor along the slip road and turned left onto the short access road that led to the automated production unit. Engineers might find the plant beautiful but Mint only saw a jumbled tangle of shiny pipes, pumps, generators and storage silos. The whole place appeared to be on standby at the moment, several fuel tankers were pulled up on the side of the road, waiting to receive the liquefied hydrogen load. It didn't take many people to run such a well automated place and Mint counted nine of them as she studied the small crowd assembled at the parking area out front. Adding in Connor that made ten, a number she now knew was the correct headcount of employees; her command-pad had provided the necessary details. Therefore, whoever the unfortunate victim was, he or she wasn't an employee. This already had her brain ticking over, it must have been planned and premeditated. Connor was right when he said it was murder, this would be no accident.

"Morning folks," Mint nodded to everyone as she stepped down from the 4x4. "I'll try and get this cleared as quickly as possible but I can't make any promises. Who made the discovery?"

"Connor and me," Nicky Smith stepped forward, she was Connor's second in command. "We were doing our regular morning rounds."

"Ok," Mint nodded, "is it undisturbed? You haven't gone traipsing around have you?"

"Are you kidding?" Nicky looked aghast.

"Mint didn't want to see the pictures," Connor clarified, joining them. "Something about forming first impressions on the scene, was it?"

"That's right," Mint said. "Back up is on the way but I'm not waiting for him. Nicky, can you stay here and bring my constable when he arrives, please?" She received a nod of assent. "Connor, lead the way."

Mint was aware of their eyes as she strolled away alongside Connor. The other plant employees were all well-educated, highly qualified, intelligent people but there was a potent combination of uncertainty, inquisitiveness and mostly fright in their expressions. She couldn't fault them; murders were few and far between. The original colonists, those that arrived after the initial terraforming scientists and infrastructure engineers, were carefully vetted so crime was initially very low level and petty. With the inevitable arrival of native generations and growth of infant colonists though, there came feelings of cut-off resentment, lack of opportunity and general dissatisfaction. Some of the later colonists simply paid for passage and weren't vetted; a virtual open door for anybody to travel, whether they were suitable for the local conditions or not. Obsirion II was a far flung 23rd century human outpost, a young, rugged colony despite humankind's technological prowess. It differed considerably in its rough, hard-wearing, practical simplicity from the views available in reference material of old Earth and its highly developed decadence. Wheeled transport was virtually unheard of on mother Earth. On Obsirion II, much of it harking back to tried and tested 20th or 21st century technology, it was vital, easy to maintain and produce.

The town's police station had grown over the years from a two person operation to the current twelve, of whom Mint was the senior. Her predecessor had moved on to an Inspector's post at the planetary headquarters but was still her boss. Mint had sent him a quick advisory as soon as the crime was reported to her. He wanted regular updates.

Connor led her around the perimeter of the industrial clutter of humming metal, rubber and plastic. There was a clear area, a minimum of three metres in width all the way around, covered in a layer of crushed rock fragments mixed with a resin to form a stable, non-slip surface. This was constantly challenged by a build-up of cones and needles from the surrounding pines, although a robot caretaker had kept a central walkway clear. There were areas of greater width at regular intervals, access points for maintenance work. Connor led her to the rearmost section.

Mint saw the markings on the rock face first. It rose in a backwards angled steep cliff, clearly displaying a grid pattern of weathered burning from the laser cutting lines. However, it was the fresh, deep red lines painted in queer geometric shapes around a central, upside down five pointed star that captured her gaze. A horrified, mutilated face appeared to be painted less crudely dead centre.

The body lay perpendicular to the wall, head first. Arms and legs were splayed out in a grisly mirror of the painted star, the head abutting the lower point. Mint was thankful for her strong constitution as the chest and abdomen had been cut open and peeled back with the insides mushed, as though by a blender. A veritable horde of flies was feasting upon the contents. The face had been removed. Slowly, she raised her eyes and took a proper look at the centre of the red star. It wasn't a painting after all, there was the missing face.

"I understand Nicky's reaction now," Mint muttered. She took a moment to peruse the surrounding ground; a fresh splatter of vomit was two metres away. "Yours, Nicky's or …?"

"Mine, I'm afraid," Connor admitted. Mint placed a reassuring hand on his upper arm.

"Ok, has anything been taken away, moved or touched since first discovery?"

"No," Connor shook his head, his face a perfect representation of a 'why the hell would we do that' question.

"I don't suppose you recognise the victim? Have you had any unexpected visitors recently?"

"No, on both counts," Connor shook his head again. "Do we have to stay here, can we, err, move away?"

"Yeah, no problem, I'll leave DNA sampling to the SOC constable," Mint took a few still images and narrated a short length of video before following Connor in his hasty retreat. She kept looking back, however, transfixed by the extraordinary sight.

They walked a short distance away to hide the grisly murder scene behind machinery and vertical pipework. It was also noticeable how much fresher the air became through the separation of distance. Connor visibly relaxed when they stopped and took several deep breaths.

"A disturbing sight for sure," Mint said in an understanding tone. "Do you have recording security sensors all over the plant?"

"Yes," Connor nodded, "we can access them from my office. I can arrange for you to have copies of last night's recordings, too."

"Let's have a look first," Mint replied. "At the moment, given the nature of the murder, I need to consider the whole plant as a crime scene. Overnight recordings might allow me to clear certain areas for you to get back to work."

Nicky appeared, unenthusiastically leading the SOC constable to the murder scene. He nodded at Mint as he puffed past in his overalls towing a trolley loaded with high-tech machinery.

"Take a deep breath, Roman; it's like nothing you'll have seen before," Mint called to his retreating back, received a grunt in response.

Shaking her head, she set off to retrace her steps to the front of the plant. Connor and Nicky followed closely behind, they didn't want to remain anywhere near that scene any longer than was absolutely necessary. The small crowd of employees and tanker drivers looked their way expectantly, hoping for some update. Mint merely shook her head while Nicky shrugged her shoulders. The front door was protected by a security scanner that read eyeball iris patterns and hand prints. Connor stepped forward, his head jutting out, hands raised to the sensor pads.

"I'll need a record of access for the past twenty-three hours," Mint announced when she stepped over the threshold and followed Connor inside.

Intelligent lighting turned on and off as they made their way to Connor's first floor office. He dragged a second chair behind his desk and altered the angle of the control screen so Mint could see it.

"Connor Granger, 278," he identified himself to the system. The screen sprang to life. "Access security recordings and display the entire network. Start at 1700 hours yesterday and play at thirty times normal speed."

"What time does the dayshift normally end?" Mint asked, staring intently at the multiple images flashing quickly by.

"1800 hours," Connor replied. "The plant reverts to standby mode overnight; we take call-out duty on a rota basis. It was my turn last night but I had an undisturbed sleep at home with the family."

They watched as the recording rapidly played out before them. In no time at all, the entire workforce was seen to exit just after 1800 hours. It was at midnight the static appeared on all feeds. It continued for an hour then perfect recording resumed with the gruesome murder fully visible at the rear. None of the security sensors had shown any hint of human presence or movement. They ran through individual recordings over and over again at differing speeds, forwards and backwards, but the static stubbornly remained.

"Damn it," Mint complained. "That was some seriously high-tech jamming. This doesn't make me feel warm and fuzzy at all. We'll be lucky to get anything more than DNA to analyse from the murder scene. Looks like I'll have to put in a high level request for any available recordings from satellite coverage. I'll ask my tech expert to run a diagnostic over your security feeds before that though, make sure we aren't looking at a technical glitch."

"That's highly unlikely," Connor looked personally aggrieved. "We run weekly diagnostics and the whole system's serviced every three months."

"I don't doubt it, but that's what they'll ask for before they have to jump through hoops for satellite surveillance records. I'm sorry Connor, with this lack of footage I'm going to have to keep the plant closed for the rest of today at the very least."

"Ah, come on, Mint," Connor said, "can't we at least fill up those tankers waiting out front?"

"I'm sorry, Connor. We'll have to follow proper procedure, this looks like it's gonna be a bitch of an investigation and you can bet your life it'll attract far too much media and public curiosity. I'll see what I can do about maybe clearing the areas you need to load the tankers first of all, ok?"

"Aye, it'll have to do," Connor looked less than thrilled at the upcoming public interest in his site Mint had alluded to.

*

Mint finally took refuge in her office in the middle of the afternoon, the empty thermos flask tiredly placed on her desk. As predicted, media crews had flocked to the town as soon as the story broke; messages from employees to family members had soon promulgated and caught the ever receptive ears of the news hounds. The local crew had predictably been first on the scene in their mobile truck; the hover-jets had started to arrive from further afield about an hour later. Mint gave the local reporter a soundbite as soon as she arrived but eventually had to arrange a news conference to satisfy the demands of the others, not that she could offer much detail. The name of the victim was still being withheld and she certainly didn't want to go into the gory details of the murder. That would only serve to heighten the smouldering levels of unease and fright in her town.

Why would anybody want to kill Jaicon Hewson? She scanned through his company file on her desk screen again. Mint was employed by the British Corporation, as were a majority of the people on the planet, and she had easy access to the basic records of other employees. Politics was not a viable entity on Obsirion II; for all intents and purposes the planet belonged to the company and was under the overall management of a board appointed overseer. It worked as an autonomous operation with an enclosed economy that revolved around the mining of metals and precious elements from the system's many moons and asteroids, gases from the atmospheres of several gas giant planets, and scientific research that could follow paths outside of the tight governance enacted by Earth Central. Jaicon had worked as records administrator for a large laboratory on the opposite side of town to the hydrogen fuel plant. She could see no immediate link between the two places or offer any theories as to why Jaicon would voluntarily travel to the scene of his demise. His personal vehicle had been found at his home, looking exactly as she'd expect had it been parked up after work the previous day. It was now in the underground garage beneath the police station where the SOC constable would examine it once he returned from the plant. Given the nature of the crime scene and the size of the plant, Mint did not expect that examination to take place today.

The death had already been reported on the official record, full control of the record was under request. This would block off external access and give Mint control of all relevant entries. She was desperate to receive the authority that would allow her to examine every detail of Jaicon's professional life and his history of electronic communication: business and personal. A single man of thirty-five years, Jaicon Hewson did not present to Mint as an obvious murder victim. His work was important but not vital; although she supposed he was one of a handful of people at the laboratory with an awareness of all the different projects being undertaken. A few thoughts were developing. The one she concentrated on the most centred around his access to this confidential scientific research. In his position it would be relatively easy to obtain information that other corporations or even Earth Central would pay good money for. Yes, some form of covert money-making or industrial espionage seemed most likely. If only she could have full, unfettered access to his records, his entire electronic life.

Rocking back in the chair, Mint lifted her feet onto her desk and relaxed, closed her eyes. She visualised the crime scene in her mind. The actual method of murder was not known and, unless some chemical means that left tell-tale residues had been utilised, was unlikely to be ascertained; the condition of the corpse was too messed up. This was likely to be deliberate, however sick and twisted it came across. The markings on the wall puzzled her. The SOC constable had uploaded still images to the central Police AI for analysis, something else she had to await a reply to. Why bother going to that effort though? It must have taken some time to produce the markings especially with the careful removal of the facial tissue that was then stuck to the rock face. Admittedly, the sophisticated jamming that had robbed her of visual surveillance clues gave the perpetrator, or perpetrators, a cushion of time to go about their gruesome work, but surely the markings must convey some meaning.

Constables had attended the laboratory and visited Jaicon's workspace. Laboratory records were stored in temperature controlled underground archives where Jaicon also worked from an isolated office. He had no co-workers, assumed total responsibility for record storage and access. His office was spartan in layout and appearance with no personal touches or comforts; drawers were only used for work equipment and a few personal essentials. There was nothing more for her constables to do than interview those employees who had dealings with Jaicon and review sensor recordings.

A bleeping sound was emitted by her command-pad. Mint cursed softly when she looked at the reason. It was a reminder of Tom's incarceration for drunken behaviour and public nuisance. She had completely forgotten about his arrest that morning. Taking wearily to her feet again, Mint exited her office and walked the short distance to the custody suite. Cells, of which there were only four, were constantly monitored by a medical AI that would sound an alarm if any vital signs went awry. Only one cell was occupied, Tom was sat on the padded wall seat staring at the floor. He raised his eyes when Mint stopped at the barred door.

"Death will stalk this town, horror and menace lurks unseen. Terror will be visited upon all, forced into confrontation. Ancient powers surge, regrow and manipulate. Burn, you will burn with fear and loathing," Tom's eyes swivelled here and there as he spoke, his hands repeatedly slapped the seat surface.

"Tom?" Mint was suddenly concerned for her charge; he couldn't still be drunk. Too much time had passed and the drugs automatically administered to drunken detainees accelerated the metabolising process. She checked his medical readout on the screen beside the door; all readings were within acceptable levels. "Tom, can you hear me?"

"I hear you, Mint. It's not safe here you know. You need to go, far away, Mint. You must leave. It won't leave anyone untouched; its power grows even now."

"What are you talking about, Tom?"

"It, Mint, it; the unseen dweller in the shadows. I hear it more and more and drink no longer stills its voice. Not a voice like mine and yours," Tom quietened and superficially appeared less agitated. His voice dropped to a conspiratorial whisper. "It talks inside your head, you know. Makes you see things, too; images of horror and violence. It wants you to be afraid. It likes those feelings of fright and dread."

"Ok, Tom. You just sit there, I'm going to ask a doctor to check you over before we take you out of that cell," Mint turned and walked away. Great, Tom's finally lost his marbles, she thought. It would be down to the medical professional to confirm his insanity and make the necessary arrangements; the old man was no longer her concern.

*

"I've arranged a temporary room for Tom in the hospital," Doc Davidson told Mint as he settled his ample frame into a chair on the opposite side of her desk.

"Temporary?" she queried.

"It's ok, I'm not going to release him," the Doctor reassured her. "Not unless he makes a remarkable mental recovery, anyway. No, he'll need specialist care at the main psychiatric centre in New Cambridge."

"I should've referred him to you a lot earlier," Mint said, her voice self-accusatory.

"Don't you go beating yourself up about him. I've had my eye on him for a long time, too. This sudden snap is just that, sudden and unpredictable. Forget about Tom and leave him to me. I hear you have a big job on your hands, you'll want all your energy for that."

"Too damn right! Doc, confidentially speaking, how long would it take to remove a face?"

"Ooh," Doc Davidson grimaced, "nasty crime scene, eh? Let me see, a full dermal excision of the face you say?" Mint nodded. "Well, how was the tissue on the head - cauterized or raw?"

"There were a lot of insects, Doc, but I would have to say cauterized. There wasn't much blood around the head."

"Alright, so, with a careful excision that left the facial tissue intact, I would say fifteen minutes with a decent laser scalpel. A butchered removal could be done in a lot less time. Do you have the face?"

"Mm-hmm," Mint nodded, "it was intact."

"I'm glad you've got the detective role then, not me. Why remove the face in the first place? Even with a laser scalpel it would be messy, you wouldn't come away clean from your morbid task. It's pointless to try and slow down the investigation that way anyhow, with implanted chips and DNA an identity couldn't be hidden at all."

"No, and everybody would know that. I'm starting to think it's to cause fear or maybe a calling card, a sick modus operandi."

"Yikes, let's hope you catch whoever's responsible quickly. If you're right, it's compulsive behaviour and likely to lead to serial murders with similar mutilation."

"Tell me about it," Mint looked at him for a moment, "or it could be the actions of a mind gone mad. You don't think …"

"Old Tom did it?" Doc Davidson shook his head. "No, he's far too clean and those big, old hands of his could never wield a laser scalpel with the sort of skill you're alluding to. No, Tom's final snap is coincidental, nothing more."

"Oh well," Mint looked slightly disappointed, "I suppose it would've been too neat. I think, deep inside, I already knew it was too much of a hopeful leap. I'll just have to be patient and await the scene of crime report."

"Get some sleep, Mint," Doc Davidson advised, rising from his chair. "You're going to need all your faculties working at 100% to catch this one. And do it quickly, the thrill of this crime will surely make the guilty party act again very soon. They'll want to experience that surge of adrenaline again; the ecstasy will dull quickly and prove quite addictive."

"Yeah, thanks for the advice, Doc," Mint tapped at her command-pad. "I've released Tom into your care. Make sure he's kept safe."

"You can count on it," Doc Davidson's voice drifted over from his retreating back.

Mint watched him walk away with mixed feelings. She remembered Tom from when she was younger, at school. He'd been a safe and ever present town personality. Tom had worked as the local courier, delivering packages to businesses and private homes. As she grew up she came to deal with him professionally, remembered calling at his house after his wife's accident. He'd been killed inside by the news of her sudden, accidental death and started drinking soon afterwards. He was caught drink-driving before long, thankfully by another constable, and replaced in his duties. The corporation had been compassionate with him, seemed to understand the cause and extent of his downfall, and made his dismissal an enforced early retirement with full pension privileges. As kind a move as that was, it had the unintended consequence of funding his growing alcohol addiction. He'd changed from a jovial, ever-laughing courier with a permanent smile to a drunken bore and nuisance. Mint liked to remember that earlier character, figured that was why she had cut him so much slack for so long. Now he'd be gone for good if what Doc Davidson had said held true. She felt sad about that, the town had somehow diminished. But people who meant a whole lot more to Mint than old Tom had left the town bereft before …

Mint snatched the thermos from her desk and her cap off the hook as she left her office, pulled the door shut a little harder than usual and headed for the exit. She grunted and waved her cap absently at the night shift as they bade her goodnight. They'd be a constable short tonight; a permanent guard was posted at the hydrogen fuel plant.

Java's house emitted warm, cosy tones of yellow through the large, shuttered windows when Mint pulled up outside five minutes later. Her sister had insisted on feeding her tonight, didn't want her settling for a ready meal after the busy day. Mint knocked once and opened the door. Mikey was instantly upon her, leapt into her arms.

"Aunty Mint, Aunty Mint," he cried, "come look at the pictures I drawed."

"That's drew, Mikey," Java called from the kitchen. "Don't bother Aunty Mint too much; she's had a rough day."

"Ok, Mummy," Mikey hollered back.

Mint pulled funny faces at him as he excitedly tugged at her arm, dragged her to the table where his paper and crayons were scattered liberally. Colourful pictures of houses and animals were common but Mint was drawn to one in particular. This was scribbled in black all over save for two eye shaped red ovals in the centre.

"Ooh, this one's scary," she said. "What is it?"

"Scary monster, nightbare," Mikey shouted.

"Nightmare," Java called. "M, it's an m not a b."

"Well, I don't like nightmares," Mint said with a business-like expression, "and I'm chief of police in this town, so I'll make it my top job to find this nightmare and lock it up where it can't trouble little boys or girls anymore."

"That's silly, Aunty Mint," Mikey stood with his hands on his hips and looked at her seriously. "You can't arrest a nightbare. It's hiding under the ground anyway, where it can't be seen."

"Imagination," Reid said, ruffling his son's hair. "Come on Mikey, tidy up, I need to set the table."

Java was an excellent cook, she'd learnt at her mother's apron strings when their parents ran the café. Dinner table talk was light and avoided the story of the day, until Reid took Mikey for his bath.

"People are scared, Minty," Java said. "I've done better business today than the last two days combined. Folk want to find out what I know, they need reassurance."

"I know and I'm sorry, my hands are tied; it's all caught up in corporation red tape at present. Besides, trust me, people do not want to hear the details of this. I wouldn't tell you even if I could, it wouldn't just be Mikey having nightmares."

"That bad, eh?" Java looked her sister in the eye for a long moment then broke contact. Mint always was the harder personality of the twins. "I hear Connor and Nicky found the body, Connor puked."

"He did. There's no shame, it was puke worthy. Nicky must be a tough old bitch."

"I don't know," Java shrugged her shoulders. "Nicky's always one to gossip; spread the shit far and wide. She was tight lipped apart from that nugget today, held off anyone who pried her for more details. I get the feeling she didn't want to dwell on the specifics. How are you bearing up?"

"I'll be fine, don't fret," Mint put a reassuring hand on her sister's. "It's gonna be busy but we'll get through it. Funny thing though, I feel more cut up inside about old Tom being carted away to hospital in New Cambridge than the murder."

"Alcohol finally done for his liver?"

"No, his mind," Mint looked inwards, to her first job of the morning. "He was found in the middle of the central crossroads this morning. Sloshed as usual and raving. We put him in the cell, gave him the drugs, as usual. I forgot about him all day, what with the other incident, until the command-pad reminded me. I went to his cell where all readings showed he was clean but he continued with his raving. It didn't take long for Doc

Davidson to confirm his mind had gone. It's sad; he had such a happy life before."

"Remember when he found us skipping school that day?" Java reminisced.

"Ha," Mint's face lit up. "He promised us a chocolate bar each if we let him take us to class."

"And we got it," Java smiled back. "A big bar of Velvet Smooth each."

"Lecture about taking school seriously included," Mint added. "We never did play truant again, did we?"

"Perfect students," Java agreed.

"This is getting maudlin," Mint said with a softening smile as she rose from her chair. "Let's sort these dishes so I can go home and sleep."

"I'll sort it, you go home and get your rest," Java insisted.

They kissed each other on the cheek before Mint shouted good night to Reid and Mikey. She arrived home ten minutes later, it was only a five minute drive but she was compelled to stop at a late opening shop on the way, bought a big bar of Velvet Smooth.

Day 2

Bruce awoke with a gasp, sat bolt upright in his bed. The thin summer weight sheet clung to his clammy chest and peeled away slowly. He wiped a hand across his sweaty brow and dried it haphazardly on the rumpled bedsheet. The memory of the bad dream had retreated to the deepest recesses of his mind where it refused to be accessed. It had though, left its final, breathless feelings of terror and dread as a going away present.

Bright red figures on the far wall indicated the time as 0500 hours. Weak dawn light was peeking around the edges of his window blinds, casting odd, stripy shadows against the side wall. Bruce sat for a moment, slightly leaning forwards, supporting his body with rigid arms, eyes squeezed tightly shut. It took a few minutes for his breathing to calm, his heart to cease its pounding. Falling back to the mattress, he closed his eyes and tried to return to his previous slumber; the morning alarm wasn't due until 0600 hours. Sleep, however, had deserted him and proved as elusive as the memory of his dream.

Throwing back the sheet he rose from bed and stretched as motion activated lights switched on. Padding across the floor to his homework desk, Bruce snatched up a pair of waterproof ear buds and selected his shower list on the music player. The sounds of modern rock music, probably over five years out of date owing to its arrival by high bandwidth transmission from Earth, accompanied a long, warm wash-down followed by a blow-dry. Today's clothes had been selected last night and draped on the back of his chair. Bruce stared at the t-shirt he'd chosen after pulling on his trousers and shook his head. What had he been thinking? He put it back in the relevant drawer. None of the other t-shirts took his fancy so he opened the wardrobe door and swiped through a selection of shirts. A plain, short sleeved black one pulled his eyes back. He nodded appreciatively and swung it around his shoulders. His trousers were dark; today felt like a black day, a reminder of his waking emotions. The shirt was left untucked.

Nobody else seemed to be awake; certainly none were mobile or audible when he walked past their bedroom doors and entered the spacious kitchen. He took a couple of slices from a fresh bread loaf and popped them into a toaster before examining the contents of the fridge. The fast machine spat out the toast as he pushed shut the fridge door, veggie oil spread and a jar of peanut butter in his hands. It didn't take long to assemble the peanut butter toast sandwich. Bruce heard movement in his parents' room as he trotted back to his own and closed the door behind him. Sitting on the chair at his homework table, he munched through the toast as his desk screen came to life and updated with the nightly news. At thirteen years old, the news didn't interest him as much as the weather. Today was Saturday, no school, and he was awake far too early! At least the weather looked clement, good for today's planned activity, as it should with mid-summer approaching fast. He selected a science fiction role-play game from the screen's drop down menu and donned the necessary helmet and gloves for character control.

He emerged from his room just over an hour later having traded successfully with the Glynch Empire and piloted his spaceship, Wolfstar, to another new, unexplored planet. There was no sign or sound of his parents, Trent and Penny Webster; they'd be out pounding away the miles as they engaged in their regular morning run. His year younger sister, Gretta, wasn't to be heard or seen either. He slipped his feet into a pair of self-fastening all terrain shoes, grabbed the backpack he'd prepared last night and trotted to the front door. Bruce stepped out onto the shaded terrace, grabbed his scooter and dropped down the three steps to ground level. Fitted with a small liquid hydrogen fuel powered motor, manual pedals and a charge storing dynamo these scooters were popular with the younger generation. He pushed off and pedalled onto the road in bicycle mode.

It didn't take long to reach Gabriel's house, just around the corner. Gabriel was his lifelong best friend; they'd met before reaching school age, their parents having birthed their sons on the same day at the local hospital. Bruce's parents were conventional for the town, his mother a scientist, his father an engineer, whereas Gabriel's parents ran the small town church. Bruce and his family weren't at all religious but a small fraction of the population maintained the old beliefs. With such a small local flock, Gabriel's parents also doubled up as counsellors and social workers.

Bruce propped his scooter against the exterior wall, next to Gabriel's, and pushed the front door open, calling out that it was just him. His friend popped his head around a doorway and waved Bruce over, handed him a piece of toast.

"Good morning, Mr and Mrs Parkes," Bruce called around a mouthful of toast.

Gabriel's parents waved back from where they sat at the kitchen table as Bruce was quickly ushered away by his friend. They had the other two members of their group to meet up with before a long journey.

"We're meeting them at the shopping centre," Gabriel said as they hit the road on their scooters. "Have to get some snacks and drinks, keep us going."

"Bloody five o'clock I woke up this morning. On a Saturday with no school," Bruce said.

"Too excited?" Gabriel grinned at him.

"Get away, it was - nothing, I just woke up early and couldn't get back to sleep. Got to fly Wolfstar for an hour though, much closer to the galactic rim now."

Gabriel didn't push the early wake up jibe as they discussed the immersive role-playing game. Gabriel wasn't allowed such games at home, had to play at Bruce's. All the time, the scooters took them towards the centre of town and the shopping zone. They passed the police station where they had to weave around a collection of reporters.

"Sergeant Harris is in early today," Gabriel noted as they left the small crowd behind.

"At least she's not at the hydrogen plant. If she spots us spying on the murder scene she'll be straight on to Mum and Dad again," Bruce pulled a face at his friend, remembering when they were caught trying to break the unofficial scooter speed record. If you knew what you were doing, it was possible to bypass the speed restrictor. Bruce was a burgeoning technical wizard and knew what he was doing. He'd been grounded for two weeks after the local Police chief took him home to his angry and embarrassed parents.

"No, we can't get caught, my Mum and Dad …"

"We'll not be spotted," Bruce assured him. "Do it like I said, leave the scooters on a forest road, like we've gone trekking, and no-one'll be suspicious. We are trekking after all, just to the top of that hill."

"Too right," Gabriel laughed, his mind eased by his friend's confidence. "Hey, look, Kieron and Dan are here already."

The four friends, school classmates for nine years greeted each other loudly as they propped up their scooters and piled into the convenience store. They emerged five minutes later with lighter credit accounts but backpacks brimming with food, chocolate and drinks.

*

"At this juncture, there is nothing more I can tell you," Mint said, louder than she intended. Dealing with the reporters, always clamouring for the next juicy titbit of information, was really getting on her nerves. "I have been granted full access to the relevant electronic records for the crime scene and the victim's personal accounts, communications and work records. My constables and I will be working hard today to gain a better understanding of the victim and unearth any clues. I would appreciate your patience at this time and promise to update you with further information, if and when, it is cleared for public consumption. No questions, I have work to do."

The police station door banged closed behind her as Mint stopped just inside and took a deep breath. She removed her hat and combed her fingers through her hair, exhaled in a deep sigh then made for the underground garage. The victim's vehicle was being scanned by a flock of SOC drones as she descended the stairs and headed towards her 4x4.

The little drones were hovering all around the exterior and interior of the vehicle, using lasers to map out an exact 3D model. Chemical sniffers would detect any suspicious substances. They were good; Mint and her constables would soon know exactly how many different aftershaves and deodorants the victim used. Ideally though, they might identify another presence, perhaps a perfume from a lady friend or something such. Mint wasn't holding her breath though. The constables' reports that quickly detailed his home and work life painted a picture of a loner who kept very much to himself.

Pushing those thoughts to the back of her mind, Mint found she was sat in the driving seat and started up the engine. She always found it funny how her body could work on automatic to perform some task or motion while she concentrated on a mental problem. The 4x4 surged up the ramp and into daylight. Mint had a clear view into the sky on the upward angle of the ramp with the two moons, Hare and Tortoise, clearly visible. They had quickly acquired these colloquial names as the official, scientific, names of Obsirion IIa and IIb were considered somewhat dry by the populace. Tortoise plodded around its orbit in twenty-four of the planet's twenty-three hour long days. By stark contrast, Hare completed a full orbit in ten days. Charlestown was not close to the sea, so its residents had to travel if they wanted to witness the regular high tides raised by the increased gravitational tug when they aligned. It looked like today was a local lunar alignment day.

The morning rush of traffic had subsided when Mint joined the town's road network. She half-smiled at the unforeseen benefit of the impromptu statement to the press as she turned right at the central crossroads and joined the main road heading out of town to the hydrogen fuel plant. Her 4x4 was the only vehicle headed in that direction which allowed her mind to semi relax as she drove along. Constables had been despatched to the laboratory now she had the necessary authority to access Jaicon's electronic life while another had departed for his home. The SOC constable was still hard at work at the crime scene, prompting Mint's visit for a real-time update. With such a large crime scene to process alone, he'd left the body there overnight, covered by a refrigerated cocoon. She passed the serried ranks of greenhouses and put her foot down as fields dominated the outside vista. The pine forest came into view, a forest green wall over the gently undulating hills. A group of four youngsters turned off the main road in front of her to ride their scooters up to a forest trail. Mint recognised Bruce Webster and Gabriel Parkes among their number. Again, she half-smiled as she remembered pulling them up for illegal modifications to their scooters – was that really four months ago? The Webster boy had accepted sole responsibility for the illegal tinkering. She had been impressed by his honesty and willingness to take the flak, as well as the skill of his electrical engineering. That boy would be a welcome addition to the local skillset for the corporation.

The 4x4 entered the shaded section of road that was bordered on both sides by tall, softly swaying pine trees and continued on to the left hand slip road. No other traffic was present; the plant was still a closed crime scene, the two fuel tankers had left empty, the staff temporarily appropriated by other engineering departments. She slid her 4x4 alongside the SOC constable's truck and stepped down onto the pounded rock and resin surface. The plant still emitted a soft hum as it maintained standby mode with a few auxiliary pumps working more noisily to pump out the town's water supply. Mint enjoyed the warm summer days and skipped the necessity to cover her head with the police issue cap; nobody was around for it to matter. She set off in the opposite direction to the previous day, wanted to give the other approach to the crime scene a once over. It was just as industrial and sanitised in its design efficiency as the other side and she soon rounded a corner to come face to face with the red markings on the rock wall again. The face had been removed from the centre of the star; a grim residue remained in place as a grotesque mirror of the expression it had borne. A gurney trolley stood to one side with an opaque forensic cover hiding the body inside.

"I'm happy to see you've moved the body. How's it going, Roman?" Mint said.

Roman Reckhart paused from scraping a fleck of the red material from one of the symbols into a sampling tube and turned to face his boss.

"I should be finished by midday," he replied. "It's strange; these markings aren't painted on with a regular compound. I need to run further tests back at my station lab but initial indications of its composition are consistent with the contents of the victim's chest."

"Are you saying the murderer killed and mutilated Jaicon Hewson then dipped a paintbrush in his mushed up chest cavity and painted all this?" Mint looked suitably horrified.

"Yes and no," Roman looked puzzled. "Take a close look at the markings. What do you see?"

"Just painted red shapes," Mint shook her head. "What am I missing here?"

"Brush marks," Roman stated, "it's too smooth and neat for my liking. It looks for all the world like it was professionally applied with an airgun or something similar. What's also puzzling me is the lack of the substance in the victim's hair."

"What do you mean?"

"Well, the body was sticking straight out from the wall with the head touching, yes?" Mint nodded agreement. "There was no overspill from the wall markings in his hair. That means the markings were fully dry-not just tacky-when the body was placed. There was a great deal of careful activity here with exacting attention to detail. Whoever did this is scary; completely dispassionate and detached from their task."

"Ok, I see what you mean," Mint looked around, didn't see what she was looking for, but did notice the puddle of vomit had been removed. "Is this the only place you've found any blood?" Roman nodded. "So the murder occurred right here?"

"That would be my conclusion," Roman nodded again. "However, with the obsessive cleanliness and attention to detail shown by the perpetrator to this point, I can't rule out use of a trolley, like mine or something similar, to transport the body from a detached murder site."

"Hmm," Mint mused, "it is unlikely though, isn't it? I mean, that's a whole new level of planning and increases the risk of discovery. Somebody might get suspicious if they see the trolley being transported, or simple bad luck on the perpetrator's part might cross their path with a night patrol. No, I think, unless further evidence proves otherwise, the murder was committed right here. Jaicon Hewson was brought here and the deed was done under the cover of that advanced jamming."

"I'm sorry, Mint, I disagree," Roman shook his head earnestly. "His face was removed carefully with a cauterizing tool – that's a good fifteen to twenty minutes work. Add in the actual murder, opening of the chest cavity and abdomen, blending the internal organs, exacting painting of the marks on the wall, and the final, careful placement of the body; I couldn't do that within an hour and I'll bet you couldn't."

"Thanks for the vote of confidence," Mint pulled a disgusted face as she considered the activity Roman had suggested. "I should have surveillance satellite evidence by late afternoon. We'll know more when we see what that reveals. How can I help you here?"

"Thanks," Roman held his hand out to the gurney, "let's start by getting Jaicon loaded into the truck?"

*

The day was shaping up to be exceedingly pleasant, a little on the warm side but there was no rain, not even a cloud in the sky. Forest scents from sap and pine needles drifted into the noses of the four teenagers. They had followed the main forest trail on foot after parking up their scooters but had recently veered off at a tangent. Tree trunks became more widely spaced as they trudged up the steepening incline, the bracken underfoot thickening in density as more light was able to penetrate to the forest floor. Ahead, the trees became sparser as the top of the hill approached.

"This is about the level we need to start tracking round, no more climbing," Gabriel said. He was finding a real interest in maps and satellite imagery and readily plotted out their route when the four friends decided they needed to have a look at the rare scene of an actual murder. The strange and macabre had always held an instant fascination for youngsters throughout the centuries and that hadn't diminished after mankind took his tentative steps into interstellar expansion.

"Ok," Daniel Reckhart said, "left or right?"

"Right looks easiest," Gabriel advised. "Did you manage to talk with your dad about it last night?"

"Fat chance," Daniel replied. "He was home just as I went to bed and out again before I got up. Might as well be just me and my sister."

"He's bound to be busy given his scene of crime training," Bruce said. "It won't last much longer will it?"

"I dunno," Daniel shrugged as they trampled down bracken. "Feels like ages since we last went out together. I kind of miss those days when I was younger and he'd take us to Java's for a milkshake followed by bowling or something."

"You've got us," Kieron Hall chipped in. "Look at the fun we get up to. I bet your dad never went bracken trampling with you."

"Ha-ha," Gabriel turned unimpressed eyes on him. "Do you want to navigate?"

"Oh no, master of maps," Kieron said. "Lead us on, find more bracken to trample."

Gabriel grumbled under his breath as he continued the circumnavigation of the hill. Bruce laughed quietly; Gabriel could get really touchy at times. He sensed a further thinning of the trees ahead and assessed their location, realised they must be getting close to the edge.

"Stop," Gabriel hissed. "We're close. I'll go ahead and check."

Bruce, Daniel and Kieron gathered closer together as Gabriel made slow and careful onward progress. They watched as he stopped next to a tree trunk and sank to his knees, fished around in his backpack. Gabriel produced a pair of electronic viewers and put them to his eyes. Then, he waved the others forward, motioned for them to be slow and quiet. The closer they got to him, the more it became obvious Gabriel's direction finding had been true to form. They saw the approach road first, then the car park came into view.

"Sergeant Harris is here," Bruce stopped in his tracks upon spying her 4x4 below.

"She's not going to see us up here, c'mon," Kieron urged him forward.

Bruce crouched ridiculously low as he neared Gabriel and ended up lying fully flat at the cliff edge. Once he was sure the police sergeant was not in sight he fished around in his own backpack and produced a small aerial drone and its control pad. The tiny rotors spun into life with a muted whir, lifted it into the air easily. Bruce guided it out into clear air further away from their vantage point. Everybody fixed their eyes on the control pad as it began to show the images relayed by the drone. The miniature camera provided high quality, clear footage of the ground below. They could see the outer pathway next to the quarried out hill with Daniel's dad and Sergeant Harris visible in the distance.

"I haven't got the range to get much closer," Bruce admitted. "This is on the maximum optical zoom setting already. I can get closer on digital zoom but quality will suffer."

"Hey, master of maps," Kieron patted Gabriel on the back, "go and find us a better viewpoint. We'll wait here for you."

"You'll appreciate what I can do one day," Gabriel muttered as he backed up and turned to explore the hillside.

"Go easy on him," Bruce said. "He's got us here, it's not his fault what we came to see is further away."

Gabriel grinned as he heard those words behind him. He could trust Bruce to always look out for him, but he wished he could be a little more assertive himself. Confidence had always been his Achilles' heel and, although Kieron was a really good friend, he had a habit of pricking the hackles in others. Gabriel was a constant target for his quips as Bruce and Daniel were more likely to riposte. The best he could do was to find the perfect viewpoint and show them exactly how good he was.

Retracing his steps, Gabriel came to a lower elevation and increased his pace through the bracken, no longer concerned about making noise. He couldn't hear his friends now so any noise he made probably couldn't carry that far either.

His legs began to tire after a few minutes so he stopped for a quick breather, heaved in lungful after lungful of clean, pine scented air as he leaned against a tree. Gabriel had been too embarrassed to mention his early waking from a nightmare that morning, despite teasing Bruce about his early awakening. On top of that, the day had been reasonably strenuous so far. Emotions suddenly flooded his mind, a mirror of his terrified thoughts on waking, sweating and terrified too early in the morning. He heard movement nearby and turned his head this way and that, his eyes wide, his breathing ragged again. This was just like Kieron, what a stupid idea when they needed to be quiet. There was the movement again, again, and again. It was coming from the downward slope in all directions. Gabriel felt his heart thumping heavily in his chest, a lead weight had attached to both his feet, anchored him to this spot. A low, guttural growl reached his ears, made him lurch backwards and bump into the tree trunk. Yet again, his head snapped left and right as he searched for the source. Did a shadow just disappear behind that tree? It had, there was another, and another over there. There were shadows lurking behind most of the trees down there; it wasn't Kieron being stupid. A great flapping sound came to him. He traced the source and looked up to see a huge diamond shape gracefully weaving between the trees. It was a blueish-grey in colouration with flexible side wings that lazily waved up and down. A long whipping tail stuck out from the back and two pinpricks of red marked its eyes at the front. They were staring straight at him. It was coming closer. A wide, fanged mouth opened up beneath the eyes and the growl came again. Gabriel's bladder released as he turned and ran screaming up the hill, away from the terrifying monster.

*

"Did you just hear something?" Mint suddenly straightened and craned her neck upwards, scanned the wall of rock.

"No," Roman said. His eyes followed Mint's inquisitively.

"I could swear I just heard a scream."

"You must be hearing things, there's nobody about," Roman said.

*

Gabriel bounced off a tree trunk and fell to his knees, bashed one hard against a protruding root. With tears streaming from his eyes, he regained his footing and limped up the hill as quickly as he could, his ripped trousers turning red. The growl sounded behind him again, closer. With fright inscribed clear across his face he turned panicked eyes to look over his shoulder, only to see the flying monster a mere thirty metres away, its crimson gaze still locked greedily on him. Another scream escaped his throat as he accelerated his terrified flight. He was dimly aware of his friends shouting somewhere to his right. Don't go to them, a voice warned in his mind, there may be more monsters waiting to chase them. His arms windmilled as he tore onwards, ignoring the pain in his knee, the burning in his chest. The cliff edge loomed before him.

*

"I heard that!" Roman announced, his eyes scanning the edge of the rock wall above from where the scream had carried down to them.

"There," Mint pointed.

A figure came into view above. Not an adult, Mint assessed, too short. She watched as the figure danced around in agitation with arms waving, the head alternately looking down the opposite hillside then back at the fifty metre drop.

"That's Gabriel Parkes," Roman announced, shocked. "What's he doing?"

"Looks terrified to me," Mint replied.

Another scream made its way down to them, then they heard other voices, shouting, alarmed.

*

"Gabriel," Bruce shouted. "Gabriel, what's the matter?"

The three boys had leaped into action as soon as they heard Gabriel's first scream. It was tough running through the bracken but they kept up a fast pace as they homed in on the source of the ruckus. Now, their friend was in full view, stood at the cliff edge, his trousers tattered and torn, bloody. A large wet patch marked his crotch and madness blazed from his terrified eyes. Gabriel released another piercing scream as he stepped backwards, dangerously close to the edge.

"Gabriel, stop," Daniel shouted. "You're going to fall."

"Stay away, keep back," Gabriel shrieked at them. "It'll get you too."

Bruce stopped in his tracks and looked where Gabriel had run from. Nothing sprang into sight, just trees and bracken. He followed Gabriel's gaze upwards but saw naught but branches swaying in the gentle breeze.

*

"That's my Daniel shouting," Roman said. "What the hell is he doing here?"

"Never mind that," Mint sounded concerned. "Gabriel's terrified, look at him."

"Gabriel, Gabriel!" Roman hollered upwards. "Step away from the edge, you're going to fall."

Another scream echoed down to them from the terrified boy and three more figures stepped into view fifteen metres away from Gabriel.

"What have you done?" Mint called to them. "Why is he so terrified?"

"Nothing, Sergeant," Bruce Webster shouted down to her. "We were trekking, he went off to find a trail then started screaming, but there's nothing else up here. I don't know what's got him frightened."

*

"Gabriel, step away from the edge," Roman Reckhart's loud voice drifted up from below.

"Gabriel, please, do as he says," Bruce said. He took a tentative step forward, his eyes never leaving his friend's petrified face. His own heart was beating rapidly, frightened for his lifelong friend.

"Don't," Gabriel screamed at him, "it's coming closer. It'll get you too."

"There's nothing there, Gabriel," Bruce told him as calmly as he could manage. "I promise you, you're seeing something that isn't there. Step away from the edge or you're gonna fall. Come on, Gabriel, please."

Gabriel's head continued to snap this way and that, his breathing snatched in great gulps, tears still streaming. His feet danced and slipped. Gabriel began to topple backwards. Bruce lunged forward but already knew he was too late.

*

"Oh hell, no," Mint exclaimed as Gabriel slipped. She watched in useless dismay as the boy fell, another was lunging for him in her peripheral vision, but too far away. Gravity plucked the boy's body downwards, arms still waving crazily. Mint became aware she was dashing towards where he would land; Roman a few steps in front of her. Looking up again, she saw his body bounce off the rock wall as it curved outwards slightly. He hit the rock again and seemed to gain a little handhold, paused in his plummet, then resumed. That brief moment was crucial, slowed Gabriel enough to survive his uncompromising landing on the ground, just a short distance from Roman's outstretched arms.

Mint stopped in her tracks, temporarily frozen at the sight. Blood was pooling under Gabriel's head and oozing out of his nose. One leg looked broken, its angles all wrong.

"Priority medical despatch required," Mint finally managed to force the words out into her command-pad, surprised herself by how calm she sounded. "Medical airlift needed at the hydrogen fuel plant for a thirteen year old boy with injuries sustained from a fall."

"Message received, Sergeant Harris, medical airlift is despatching to your location," a calm voice replied through the speaker.

Roman had removed his jacket and pillowed it under Gabriel's head by the time she finished the call. Mint knew Roman was trained to a much more advanced level in first aid than she was and left him to his work. She looked up and saw three pairs of eyes looking down in shock.

"You three, get away from the edge!" Mint shouted. "Come down carefully, away from the edge and meet me in the car park."

She waited until all three disappeared before checking Roman and Gabriel again, then strode away. Her own shock and horror at witnessing the terrible event had disappeared now as she attempted to gain control of the scene. Damn those kids, no doubt they were looking for ways to get eyes on the murder scene.

"Constable Fletcher," she called into the command-pad.

"Here, Sarge."

"Get to the Parkes' house. Gabriel's had an accident here at the fuel plant. Medical airlift is inbound; take the parents to hospital."

"Copy that, on my way."

Mint's purposeful stride swiftly took her to the car park where she stopped to assess the available space. Both vehicles would have to be moved to allow the hover-jet to land. She moved Roman's truck as flush to the side wall as she could, then her own 4x4. As she stepped down she saw Bruce Webster come rolling down the hillside, regain his footing, and continue at full pelt. She met him at the bottom and forcefully prevented him from running straight past her.

"Stop!" she ordered the boy. "He's injured but still alive. Constable Reckhart is first aid trained and treating him. Medical airlift is on the way."

Bruce was in a near hysterical state; he kept trying to speak but failed and turned away again and again in pain and confusion.

"Sit down," Mint said, more gently, "you'll hyperventilate and go into shock. Sit down and catch your breath."

After a few seconds the boy processed her words and did as he was told. Daniel Reckhart and Kieron Hall reached the car park and ran up to her. Mint held up a hand and pointed them to the floor beside Bruce. They obediently followed her instruction and stared at Bruce as he struggled to heave in great gasps of air.

"What's the status of that medical airlift," Mint asked calmly through the command-pad. With all three boys sat before her she finally felt in control of the area.

"This is Medlift501, Sergeant Harris," a voice replied, "we are inbound; ETA two minutes."

"Copy that, Medlift501. I have ears on you."

A low roar was building in volume from the direction of the town. Mint crouched down in front of Bruce and looked at his face, all scratched with bright red beads of blood from his mad dash down the hillside. His breathing was much calmer now and he seemed less agitated. His eyes met hers for a moment before looking down.

"Gabriel's alive, ok? I don't know how badly hurt he is so I can't make any promises, but your dad is with him, Daniel, and he knows what he's doing. Gabriel's in good hands. Now, what the hell happened up there?"

All three opened up at once forcing Mint to wave them into silence. She looked pointedly at Bruce.

"We were out trekking, you know, having a nice day out …"

"You were here with a drone, no doubt. I know your capabilities, Mr Webster; you were here to look at the murder scene. Never mind that just now, what happened to Gabriel?"

"We couldn't see much from the side of the hill where we stopped so Gabriel went to scout out a better vantage point. After a few minutes we heard him scream and ran over to find him."

"He went alone?" Bruce nodded. "Did you see anybody else up there; was it just the four of you?"

"No," Bruce shook his head. "Nobody else was up there. Gabriel looked terrified, kept staring at something behind him, down the hill. He'd run away, higher. I looked where his eyes were focussed but there was nothing to see, just trees."

"Ok, ok," Mint thought for a moment. "Was he well, had he shown any signs of illness or fever?"

"No, nothing," Bruce shook his head again. "He was excited. We all were, sorry."

"Sorry doesn't cut it really, does it?" Mint gave them all a long hard look then softened. "Look, we were all young once and made stupid mistakes. This one just happens to be a biggie. I only hope your friend pulls through with nothing serious. I suppose you all saw him fall and land?" All three nodded dumbly. "I have a trained constable you can talk to; it would normally be Mr or Mrs Parkes but they'll have other concerns. Get it out of your system, don't dwell on it or you'll have nightmares for weeks."

She noticed Bruce and Daniel flinch as she said that and gave them a quizzical look.

"I had a nightmare last night," Bruce admitted sheepishly. "Couldn't get back to sleep after, you just reminded me is all."

"Really?" Mint said. She turned her eyes on Daniel. "You flinched too, Mr Reckhart, did you have a nightmare last night?"

Daniel nodded but remained tight-lipped. The hover-jet coasted into view above and halted forward flight above the car park. Mint ducked down in front of the three boys as it finished its landing and the engines spooled down to idling speed. A pair of paramedics and a doctor jumped down from the doorway and followed Mint's pointed finger. The co-pilot hurried after them soon after, pushing a stretcher trolley.

"Alright," Mint said as she stood up, "everybody into my 4x4, come on – move!"

The three boys took to their feet and shuffled over to the vehicle. Mint opened the rear door and ushered them inside. After closing the door she wandered to the front and perched on the bumper, took a pen from her pocket and lazily chewed at its end. In her mind's eye she saw the slow motion stumble and fall all over again. Why did her memory have to repeat that? The horror of the vision washed over her once more and she cupped her head in her hands, tried to shake it clear.

"Hey, are you ok, Mint?" the pilot had crept up on her.

"I'm good, don't worry," Mint gave him a small, reassuring smile. "Not every day you see a fall like that; all the way down, bouncing off the rock. It's a sight to haunt your memories alright."

"Lucky to survive a fall like that," the pilot nodded. "What was he doing up there?"

"He was with this bunch," she jerked a thumb at her charges in the 4x4. "They wanted to see the murder scene, grim little buggers. Gabriel, the one who fell, he was terrified of something. Screaming and running, the poor lad was frightened to death. Weird thing is they all swear nobody else was up there with him."

"Playing a prank?" the pilot suggested.

"I don't think so," Mint shook her head. "They don't come across as hiding anything. I'll probably have to get satellite footage again."

"I suppose that makes your job easier, the constant surveillance," the pilot said. He rubbed his hands over his face, slapped his cheek. "Sorry, I didn't sleep well last night."

"That's happening a lot," Mint replied, turning to look at the boys in the back seats. "Nightmares, was it?" she asked turning back to face him.

"Must've been, but I'm buggered if I can remember," the pilot shrugged.

"Here they come, you're needed," Mint stood up straighter.

The co-pilot was pushing the stretcher trolley with a paramedic pulling it from the front. Walking alongside, the second paramedic held a drip aloft, while the doctor trotted along behind with Roman.

"He's in the back, with the others," Mint called over to Roman as they began to attach the trolley to the apparatus that would lift Gabriel into the back of the hover-jet.

Realising he was superfluous now, Roman backed away from his patient and walked over to his truck. He wiped his bloody hands on a rag then reached in to a storage compartment and withdrew some wet wipes. Running these over his blood-stained fingers he nodded at Mint and walked to the rear door of her 4x4.

"Out, Daniel, now," he said in a quiet, purposeful voice.

Mint watched as Daniel clambered over Kieron and stepped out. He was immediately led away by Roman, a forceful hand on his back. Mint climbed into the front seat and switched on the engine as the hover-jet took to the air. She turned to look into the back where Kieron and Bruce were staring out at the departing medical airlift. No useful words sprang to mind so she sat quietly with her hands on the steering wheel and waited. Raised voices began to drift over. Roman and Daniel were talking animatedly. Mint tried not to listen but caught snatches about 'you're never here', 'it's not like it used to be' and 'I've tried my hardest since your mother died'.

Eventually, they both ran out of accusations to hurl at each other and stomped back to the 4x4. Kieron moved over to allow a visibly fuming Daniel to get back in without having to clamber over him again.

"I still have a few bits to finish off here," Roman said through Mint's open window, his eyes boring into his son's face. "I'll see you back at the station to conclude the report."

"Take your time," Mint said as she began to reverse and turned to face the exit road. "Where do you want me to take Daniel?"

"Home," Roman called. "His elder, responsible sister will be there to watch him."

Mint heard a huff from Daniel as she pushed at the accelerator and began to move away. She had a good view of all three boys in the rear-view mirror: Daniel had his elbow on the window armrest, his chin in his hands, and a furious expression; Kieron seemed quite calm but she could discern a haunted look in his eyes; Bruce had wiped bloody streaks across his face from the scratches and looked very worried. She left them to their own thoughts as she drove up the access road and stopped at the junction for the main road. There was no traffic as she turned right to head back to town and reviewed the event again in her mind's eye. The more she reviewed it, the more she saw the boys had been truthful from their prospective. Satellite coverage would have to provide the evidence and explanation she required. What had terrified Gabriel so?

She stopped briefly to make sure the boys' scooters were suitably secured and sent a message to Roman to load them in his truck and take them to the station. The three youngsters still hadn't said a word or changed expressions when she reached the urban area and turned off to stop at Kieron's house. It took a few minutes to explain to Mr and Mrs Hall why their son was being dropped off by the police. Kieron was led in by a fretting mother while Mr Hall stood on the threshold and waved. Daniel's older sister, Hayley, was stood waiting at the door when they pulled up at Roman's home. Nothing needed to be said as Daniel stomped past her and disappeared. Hayley shrugged, put up a hand of thanks to Mint and followed him inside.

"So, Mr Webster," Mint said as she drove off, "it's just you and me now. Why don't you tell me about your nightmare?"

"Small talk to take my mind off it?" Bruce replied.

"Humour me."

"If I must, but I can't remember anything really. I woke up all sweaty at 0500, breathing hard, you know? There was a feeling but no imagery. A bit stupid at my age, don't you think?"

"The brain still isn't fully understood, even in this day and age," Mint said. "I have bad dreams, it's part of the job. Had you done anything yesterday to prompt such a dream? Played a game or watched a recording?"

"No, it was all school and homework yesterday."

"And planning for your little trip today, no doubt."

"Yeah, we did that on net comms. Look, I'm sorry. We wanted to see, you know? It's a big deal; nothing ever happens here."

"Plenty happens here, Mr Webster," Mint pointed out. "This murder is a real rarity, hopefully a one off. I don't know how much you saw although, thankfully, the body had been removed. But that crime scene is not nice; that's why I've not released any details to the media. I, for one, will be more than happy when we return to 'nothing ever happens here.' Understood?"

Bruce nodded as Mint pulled up outside his house. She spotted some gawping neighbours, craning their necks from vehicle driveways, desperate to see what was going on. Bruce had already slid out and closed the door behind him. She placed a hand lightly on his back and led him towards the door. It opened before she got there and Penny Webster's worried face appeared.

"Not speeding on your scooter again?" she said exasperatedly on seeing his dishevelled appearance and scratched face.

"No, not this time, Penny," Mint said. She turned to look at Bruce. "Are you telling all or shall I?"

"I'm sorry, Mum," Bruce started. "We went to the hill, wanted to see the murder scene ..."

"Oh, you little monster," Penny took a step back.

"I know, Mum, but ..." his throat caught.

"But what?" Penny demanded.

"There was an accident, Penny," Mint judged it prudent to step in, Bruce was close to breaking down. "Gabriel Parkes has been seriously hurt. He fell, a long way. Your son and his friends witnessed it."

"I heard a hover-jet earlier," Penny gasped. "What happened, is Gabriel alright?"

"He's alive. Quite how, I do not know," Mint shrugged. "It was a big drop but Roman was on hand to apply first aid. Gabriel's at the hospital now and in the best hands. Bruce got all cut up ignoring my advice and rushing down the hillside to check up on his friend, nothing serious there. How did you sleep last night?"

"Oh, Bruce," Penny's expression softened as she looked at her son. "I was restless, didn't sleep well at all. Why?"

"Oh, it's nothing," Mint said, turning away. "Ignore me."

Her mind was busy as she drove away, intending to go straight to the hospital. So many people having poor sleep and nightmares, could it be coincidence? She made her decision and turned left at the crossroads, headed for the station, delaying her visit to the hospital. The 4x4 was soon parked in her underground space and she cursed at a slight headache as she headed up the stairs to her office. Locking the office door behind her, she swept a couple of headache tablets into her mouth and washed them down before raising the desk screen and logging on. It was a matter of seconds before her video call request was flashed through to the regional police headquarters at New Cambridge.

"Hi Mint, how are you looking after Charlestown for me?" Inspector Pete Field's face appeared.

"Are you kidding me?" she said. "First, of all things, a murder; now I've got an accident at the same site. I witnessed it, Pete. A group of thirteen year old lads with gruesome viewing tastes hiked up the back of the hill to see the crime scene. One of them slipped and fell."

"Shit, Mint," Pete's face lost its grin. "Dead?"

"No, he bounced and slowed his fall, thank goodness. He's still in a bad way though. It's the lead up to the fall that's bothering me. That kid was terrified of something, that's what made him slip. I've gone over events again and again and questioned his friends. I don't think they had anything to do with it. I need priority satellite surveillance recordings, Pete."

"I'm still waiting for recordings from the murder night. Do you see any connection between the two events?" He could be seen tapping away at his headquarters-pad while he spoke.

"The same location is the only connection I can see at present. That's why I need the footage; if they are connected, we could have a serial killer on our hands."

"I hear you, Mint. The request has been submitted. Is there anything else?"

"Well, it's probably nothing but …"

"Go ahead, I'm here to help."

"It sounds foolish, but too many people I've spoken to over the past couple of days are experiencing restless sleep and nightmares; far too many for it to be coincidental. I want to request a clean air survey. I'm worried there may be some sort of leak into the atmosphere."

"No problem, I'll handle that for you. Keep up the good work, Mint. I'll let you know once I get results."

The screen flashed off as the call ended. Mint lifted her command-pad and checked the disposition of her constables. Everything appeared to be calm and orderly in town. She noted Roman was just leaving the hydrogen fuel plant. Five minutes later, as she was typing up her report of the morning's events, the screen came to life again and she saw Pete's face staring out at her.

"That was quick," she said.

"Yeah, well, don't get too excited; I can't send you the footage. There are some - problems, but analysts have confirmed that, other than you and Roman Reckhart, nobody else was in the area."

"What? I need that footage." she asserted.

"It was combined spectrum footage, Mint. I have it on good, corporation authority that nobody else was involved, you have to accept my word on that."

"But he was terrified, Pete. There must have been something. I was there; I saw the state he was in."

"Let's think about your other request today. Could he have been affected by this leak you suspect?"

"Oh, come on, Pete. That's a stretch. I was there, Roman Reckhart was there and three other boys were there. None of us were affected. Atmospheric leaks don't work like that. No, that boy saw something that scared him witless. I heard him shout to his friends that it was coming closer, it would get them too. That boy ran from something real."

"Or something he thought was real. Was he unwell, feverish, seeing things?"

"His friends say not, and he had scootered out from town and trekked to the hill. I don't think he'd have done that if he was unwell. Ah, this is a nightmare."

"Did the boy have a nightmare? He might have been running from a dream he was reliving?" Pete's face looked at her intently.

"Two of the other boys admitted to having nightmares last night," Mint sat up straighter, realization dawning. "Gabriel could have had one too. What would make him relive it though?"

"He could be more susceptible to whatever that leak is. I'm going to fast-track that request for the scientific team."

"Great, Pete, thanks. One more thing, get me both sets of surveillance footage. It's taking a ridiculous amount of time and this accident must be linked."

The screen went blank after a quick nod from the Inspector.

Mint sat and typed for a few moments more but couldn't concentrate on the task. She was soon in her 4x4 again, driving up the ramp with clear sky above, the two moons had moved on. It only took her a couple of minutes to reach the hospital and park up in an emergency services space, next to another police vehicle. It was a scene of calm efficiency with only an undertone of urgency when she walked into the emergency room and saw Constable Fletcher drinking coffee next to a door bearing the 'Family Room' sign.

"The boy's in surgery," he told her as she approached. "He's got a nasty crack to the skull, broken leg in three places, several broken ribs and impact injuries. All in all, he's one lucky kid."

"You didn't see it," Mint said. "I was sure he was going to die. He managed to get a grip for a second, which saved his life, slowed him down. Mr and Mrs Parkes are in here?" she pointed at the door.

"Mm-hmm," the Constable nodded and opened the door for her.

Gabriel's parents were sat next to each other, holding hands, with shocked expressions on their faces. His father was mouthing words, praying, Mint assumed. They both looked as Mint stepped in and closed the door. Nobody spoke but the two parents tracked her with sad eyes as she took a seat opposite them and leaned forward, elbows on her knees.

"I'm so sorry for what happened," she began falteringly. "I suppose it was lucky Roman and I hadn't finished up and left the scene."

"What possessed him to go along with his friends' plan like that, such a monstrous endeavour," Mr Parkes spoke first. He locked red-rimmed eyes on Mint.

"Let's not worry about that, right now, they've all had a shock," Mint replied. "Constable Fletcher has listed Gabriel's injuries for me. Has he regained consciousness at all?"

"No," Mrs Parkes said, "they say he'll live but he may have injuries to his brain from the impact and a permanent limp." She broke down in tears.

Mint kept quiet as Mrs Parkes filled the room with soft sobs, Mr Parkes' whispered offerings to God a constant accompaniment. Although she still had questions to ask, Mint had to respect their sorrow and waited patiently until Gabriel's mother had regained some composure.

"I've watched satellite footage of the accident and the lead up to it," Mint said, uncomfortable with the lie. "There was nobody else involved, his friends were a long way over the hill and ran to help as soon as they heard him in distress. Has Gabriel been in any way ill or troubled over the past few days?"

"We all had bad dreams last night, I think. Demons haunted my mind," Mr Parkes nodded his head. "I'm sure I heard him talking in his sleep, angry. Then he went to the toilet. Aside from that, he's been perfect, as always."

Mint thought back to the incident with the modified scooter. She had never notified Gabriel's parents about the incident, Bruce had admitted full culpability. She wondered about that now. Mr and Mrs Parkes were hardline Christians, strict disciplinarians, and would have severely berated Gabriel for his involvement in such an endeavour. Maybe Bruce was savvy enough to foresee the ramifications if they had become involved in Mint's response. The four boys were well known to her, not criminally, just as active young members of society, but she doubted that Gabriel's parents knew much about his extra-curricular activities. Her opinion of young Mr Webster took a step upwards as she mulled it over.

"Thank you," she finally said. "I heard him scream several times and observed him in an extremely frightened, agitated state on the cliff edge before he slipped. As I said before, the footage showed no animals or people in the vicinity, so my initial conclusion is that he maybe had a relapse of a nightmare. It's not just your household; I've become aware of an alarming number of people from Charlestown mentioning disturbed sleep, bad dreams and nightmares. My worry is that some sort of substance has been leaked, or maybe there's a natural venting incident. As such, I have requested despatch of a scientific team from New Cambridge to perform an environmental analysis."

"You think one of the research laboratories is responsible for my boy's injuries?" Mrs Parkes asked.

"I am coming to the conclusion it is likely some substance is responsible for this spate of mental unease. Whether it is natural or manmade is something for the scientific team to advise, should they discover such a substance."

"You're being very careful with your words there, Sergeant Harris," Mr Parkes stated. "Are you covering up for one of the labs?"

"Not at all," Mint adopted her forthright voice. "At this stage I have an open mind and a murder to investigate alongside this. I don't even know if the two incidents are connected in any way beyond occurring at the same site. I understand that you are angry and distressed, and I respect that. Gabriel's accident will remain just that, unless an outside cause is discovered. I merely wanted to let you know what is occurring at present and how I'm attempting to deal with it."

"Thank you, Mint," Mrs Parkes said, reaching forward to squeeze her hand. "Please keep us up to date with your investigations."

"I'll do what I can," Mint took to her feet. "Excuse me; I have a heap of things to deal with."

Gabriel's parents didn't watch her leave, they returned to their prayers.

"Stay with them and let me know if Gabriel says anything when he wakes up," Mint said to Constable Fletcher once the door had closed behind her. "I'm going to catch up with Doc Davidson while I'm here."

"Will do, Sarge," he said to her back as she walked away.

Doc Davidson was chief medical officer at the hospital and Mint knew the way to his office like she knew the streets of Charlestown. Thankfully, he was sat at his desk when she arrived and looked up in response to her knock on his open door. She closed it when he ushered her inside.

"I hear you've had a rough morning," Doc Davidson began. "I oversaw the arrival of young Gabriel, he's in a bad way for sure but he should pull through. Quite remarkable the fall didn't kill him outright."

"He was lucky, alright," Mint replied. "He got fingertips on a slight outcrop and slowed his descent. That's not what I'm here for though; I'd rather file that vision away and not relive it. This will sound like a strange statement but I'm hearing an awful lot of people talk about disturbed sleep and nightmares. Gabriel was running away from nothing, shouting and screaming about being chased. His parents had a rough night, his father says he heard him talking, arguing in his sleep before a toilet visit. Have you heard anything similar?"

Doc Davidson sat and looked at her with a thoughtful expression for a long stretch of seconds. He relaxed back in his chair and cocked his head to one side before speaking.

"I had a bad night last night," he admitted, "but I haven't heard anybody else mention it, I have been busy. How many are you talking about?"

"Too many to be a coincidence: my sister and her family, Gabriel and his parents, two of the boys with him, the airlift pilot, the Websters. I've requested a scientific team for an environmental analysis."

"Ok, good move," he nodded his head. "If you need my approval and backing, you've got it."

"No, that's not why I'm here, but thanks," Mint sat forward and locked eyes with him. "I'm thinking about Old Tom. Was he suffering too, would that explain his behaviour yesterday?"

"It shouldn't, no. When I assessed him he was sober and not exhibiting any signs of physical distress. His mind was definitely the problem; I don't think we've sectioned him unnecessarily if that's what you're thinking."

"It is. I'm soft with him, ok? I have too many happy memories of how he used to be. Is he still here?"

"No, they sent a hover-jet to collect him very early this morning. Look, I need to contact the psychiatric centre for an update; I can do it now, while you're here, if you like?"

Mint nodded and watched Doc Davidson turn to his desk screen, initiate a video link to his contact at the facility in New Cambridge.

"Doctor Tyndall," Doc Davidson began. "I have Sergeant Harris from our local police in my office. We were curious to know the current status of the patient we sent your way."

"Tom Barker?" Mint heard another voice. "I was going to call you this afternoon. I'm afraid we have a difference of medical opinion in this case. The patient has reduced mental capacity due to alcohol induced enfeeblement; however, he is not displaying any symptoms of insanity."

"How can that be?" Mint spoke up. "He was raving about some unseen dweller that would bring horror to the town."

"Let me finish, please, Sergeant," she heard the other Doctor say. "We need to run further tests and assessments to confirm our initial findings. The spanner in the works is that the team sent to collect him confirm he was displaying definite signs of insanity with proclamations similar to those you describe, but only on collection. He became calmer and more rational the further they flew from Charlestown. Now, isn't that interesting?"

"More than you know," Doc Davidson said with a knowing look at Mint. "We appear to have a sudden outbreak of restless sleep, bad dreams and nightmares throughout our town. Sergeant Harris was concerned Tom may have been affected also and sectioned by mistake."

"I share a level of agreement with Sergeant Harris at the present time," the other Doctor said. "Your outbreak sounds interesting; do you have any suspicions about its cause?"

"A scientific team is being arranged to perform an environmental survey," Mint said. "We hope to pinpoint some natural emission or chemical leak from one of the research laboratories."

"I'll stay in touch via Doctor Davidson," Doctor Tyndall said. "As I say, we have more tests to run to finish our assessment of Tom; we'll bear that possibility in mind. I'll also do some research to find out if any other cases similar to yours have been recorded. I may be able to give you a precedent to accelerate the survey."

"Thank you," Doc Davidson said. He ended the call. "I'm sorry, Mint, I may have been wrong, we'll have to wait and see. With Tom's reduced mental capacity and the effects of alcohol on his system it is possible he could have displayed more marked symptoms from your pollutant. One thing is for certain though; something is affecting people in Charlestown."

*

The psychiatric centre at New Cambridge was a sprawling, reactive glass fronted, two storey building on the western edge of the city, close to the river. Although fenced in, with security cameras in operation all day long, it wasn't a high security facility. Thankfully, cases like Tom Barker were rare. Psychiatric cases on Obsirion II arose from extended periods in space, separation from family members back on Earth or elsewhere, and plain, unfortunate illness.

Tom had walked inside calmly after disembarking from the hover-jet on arrival, the waiting wheelchair deemed unnecessary by the medical escorts. His eyes had looked around with clear interest at the new location while he smiled and said hello to everybody he met. Once inside the building he had been assessed by Doctor Tyndall who scratched his head, reread Doc Davidson's referral, and questioned the medical escorts. It seemed he had, indeed, recovered from his insanity during the flight.

After the video call with Doc Davidson, Doctor Tyndall made notes to consider the effects of external influences on the patient's mental wellbeing. He had several appointments from early to late-afternoon and returned to perform a second assessment of Tom's mental state around 1800 hours. A rarely used room was set aside for the comfort of seriously mentally ill patients with a one way window covering one wall. Doctor Tyndall observed Tom through this aperture for five minutes before entering the room. He had seen nothing abnormal to warrant concern.

Tom flew at him as soon as the door was fully open. His hands encircled the Doctor's throat and squeezed hard. A startled gurgle emerged from the psychiatrist's mouth as Tom's hands glowed with inner heat and smoke arose from singed skin. The dead body dropped from his hands and Tom stood over it, his fierce eyes staring through the open doorway. He took a step forward and emerged into the corridor. A medical orderly appeared from around a corner, intent on a medical-pad. She looked up as she detected Tom In front of her but never saw the upper-cut that lifted her from her feet and crashed her body into the far wall. Burn marks would forever scar her chin although the broken bones would mend, in time, and teeth could be replaced.

An alarm began to sound as security personnel reacted to the scene playing out on the sensors. Doors slammed shut and automatic locks clicked into place. Tom soon came to a halt before one such barrier. Stepping back he raised both arms before him, a curious shimmering in the air about his hands. There was a whoosh as the shimmering blasted from his forward thrusting hands into the barricading door. It buckled and fell from its fixtures and fittings. Tom stepped through clumsily and continued on his way. Frightened eyes stared out at him from rooms along the length of corridor but he ignored them. At the far end he contemptuously blew away another door.

"Lock down, lock down," a voice began to blare out from ceiling speakers. "There is a dangerous patient on the loose. Security teams are inbound. Do not depart from your current location. Security assesses the patient is seeking to exit the facility and will leave personnel alone if they do not challenge him."

Tom did not react to the message, merely continued on his determined passage. Several more doors fell to his inhuman power before he reached an exterior exit and stepped out into the lowering sunlight. A wall of four armoured security personnel stood waiting for him.

"Surrender now or we will use force," a fifth security officer ordered from behind them.

Tom ignored the order and stomped forwards. Two dart guns fired simultaneously from the guards on the outside of the wall, the middle two held control shields and advanced to meet their adversary. Both darts bounced from Tom's skin with little electrical fizzle sounds and visible sparks. He stood stock-still and locked fiery eyes on his assailants. The dart gun guards dropped their weapons and swept in to encircle the violent, transfixed man. Tom shrugged his shoulders, there was a loud boom, and the four security guards were launched backwards, away from him. All four were killed instantly, landed on their backs with wispy smoke trails rising from comprehensive scorch marks. Tom looked at the fifth guard who fearfully peered back, his knees quaking. With a flick of his hand, and no physical contact, Tom sent the guard flailing to the ground and marched over to the prone, frightened man.

"I am Varla Tiada," a deep, inhuman voice erupted from Tom's open mouth. "You will know, fear and feed me."

Tom turned on the spot and strode to the perimeter fence. He drew an arch in the air with one finger and a smoking, bubbling trail appeared on the fence. With a swift kick, the arch fell flat. Tom stepped through and marched away. Behind those fierce, blazing eyes the essence of Tom Barker was curled up, a prisoner in a corner of his own mind, gibbering and terror-stricken.

Day 3

Java's café was Mint's first port of call the following day. She parked in her usual spot and pushed the door open wearily, her own sleep had been disturbed overnight. Java waved equally tiredly from the counter and mechanically began to prepare the required cup of coffee while Mint sat at her table.

"Now I've fallen victim to this outbreak of bad sleep it's turned personal," Mint grumbled as Java placed a pair of mugs on the table and sat opposite her.

"Reid's dealing with Mikey this morning, he damn near screamed the house down last night," Java said over the rim of her mug.

"I've got Pete on the case," Mint said. "He's organising an environmental survey to pinpoint and seal the suspected leak."

"He's worked quickly, I reckon," Java replied. "Saw a flight of hover-jets dropping off trucks as I drove in this morning. I wondered what they were."

"Mm," Mint looked up surprised, "I didn't expect it to be that quick." She fumbled in her bag and withdrew the command-pad. Her eyes shot up in surprise when she looked at the screen.

"Bloody hell!" she exclaimed.

"What?"

"Tom, he escaped from the New Cambridge psychiatric centre late yesterday, killed five people and injured two more. There's a manhunt going on. Shit, that doesn't sound like him at all; he must have really lost it."

"Is there any danger here?" Java looked around with nervous eyes. "Do they think he'll come home?"

"I doubt it, he's one hundred miles away," Mint reassured her. "Look, you shouldn't know about this – keep it to yourself. Feel free to let everyone know about the survey though."

Mint drained her coffee, pocketed the two biscuits and stood up to leave.

"Another busy day, eh?" Java looked up at her sister.

"Looks like it," Mint nodded. "I'll have regular patrols through town today, people will be getting edgy with the murder unsolved and poor sleep all round."

She walked out of the café and wandered to her 4x4. The door was open with her foot raised to step in when she heard her name being called and turned to see Trent and Penny Webster running towards her.

"Still getting the exercise in," Mint observed as they approached.

"Got to keep it up, come whatever may," Trent puffed as they came to a stop beside her.

"Yeah," Penny agreed. "Poor sleep or no sleep, he continues to drag me out. Look, we're really sorry about Bruce yesterday. I didn't get chance to properly apologise with the shock of poor Gabriel's accident."

"Don't worry about it," Mint patted her sweaty shoulder in thanks, rubbed her palm dry on her trousers. "I should have known it would attract attention and placed sentry sensors around the exterior. That'll be a job for Roman today. I was really impressed, in a way, by their planning and skills – misplaced as it was. Bruce will turn out fine once he's grown beyond these troublesome teenage years. You should be proud of him; he really keeps a look out for Gabriel."

"It's a pity he got the neighbours chin-wagging," Trent said. "They couldn't wait to find out the details after you'd left."

"Sorry about that, unavoidable," Mint shrugged. "I'm working on the possibility there's a leak causing the sleep disruption, you'll no doubt see the environmental survey team working around town. With luck we'll have that sorted sooner rather than later. Oh, Bruce can call at the station any time today to collect his scooter."

The Webster's waved as Mint drove away. She watched them join her sister in the café then focussed on the road and day ahead. Traffic was non-existent at this time on a Sunday morning; her commute was nice and easy.

The news about Tom had shocked her to the core. She couldn't believe he was capable of such actions. Then, it dawned on her there was still no response to her request for the satellite footage for the day of the murder. She also really wanted to see it for Gabriel's accident yesterday. Why was that taking so long and why couldn't Pete fast-track it to her with his level of authority? She screwed her face up in annoyed confusion as the 4x4 dipped into the underground car park.

Something bothered her mind about the street in front of the station - it had been clear. Old Tom's escape must be dominating the news now, dragged the newshounds elsewhere. At least some good had come from it, she wouldn't miss them.

A light headache pricked annoyingly behind her eyes as she dropped to the floor and made for the stairs. Mint looked around, confused; she'd noticed a headache starting when she parked up yesterday. Was that coincidence or was something in the car park causing it? She made a slow circuit of the underground area, checking all the vehicles and storage lockers. However, nothing came to light that could account for her malady. She took the steps two at a time, a new worry suffusing her mind, and hurried to her office where she swallowed a couple of tablets.

Nobody had arrived yet for the day shift so she checked the night shift's reports, nothing to note, and accessed her desk screen. It took fifteen minutes to finish up her report on yesterday's accident. Next, she turned her attention to Old Tom's escape. There was a complete lack of detail, just the bare, matter of fact report: he had killed five people and injured a further two before he scaled a perimeter fence and disappeared. Mint found this most confusing, everybody on Obsirion II had a subcutaneous chip insert. Theoretically, it was possible to know where every person on the planet was at any given time. Old Tom certainly didn't possess the skills to remove or defeat such a device. She returned her attention to the scanty report and noted that a shoot on sight policy had been implemented, he was deemed too dangerous to approach. Sadness gripped her again but then the day shift began to arrive. She closed the report and put the screen on standby. It only occurred to her the headache was gone when she closed her office door and moved to the centre of the main room.

"Gather round, everybody," Mint called and waited for her constables to congregate. "Ok, it looks like an environmental survey team is in town. If anybody asks, they are here to determine if an industrial or natural leak is responsible for the outbreak of poor sleep and headaches. People are rattled by the murder and feelings are further exacerbated by the effects of the potential leak, so I want regular patrols mounted, make yourselves visible. Roman, after yesterday's unfortunate incident I'd like you to place sentry sensors in a one hundred metre perimeter around the murder scene. You'll all know that Old Tom was sectioned and taken to a facility in New Cambridge yesterday. It saddens me to inform you he murdered five people and escaped late in the day." A series of startled exclamations silenced her for a moment. "There is a shoot on sight manhunt ongoing. Now, I have not been given any reason to suspect he is heading for home but we must consider the possibility. Keep small firearms concealed in your vehicles and set Tom as top priority in your facial recognition sensors. Otherwise, there's no overspill from any events last night, in fact, last night was very quiet. I like that, very quiet suits me just fine. Let's see if we can maintain it. I'll be in my office most of the morning, working on the murder case; interruptions by prior appointment or in emergency only. Let's get on with it please, people."

Mint retreated to the sanctity of her office as the constables split up to go about their duties. She quickly booted the screen from standby to active and checked for progress on her satellite footage request. There was still no hint of its release so she spent a frustrating five minutes putting together a message of complaint to send via Pete. She reworded it multiple times, often having to reign in her anger and irritation at the forced delay in progress towards apprehending whoever was responsible. The poor pen she picked up to chew on was splintered by her clenching jaw and chomping teeth. Eventually she settled on a watered down version of her original text that wouldn't put her job at risk. Roman's updated SOC report was awaiting her perusal and confirmed that the geometric markings had indeed been applied with the contents of Jaicon's chest cavity and abdomen. Other than that confirmation of his suspicion, there was nothing new to add to her current, inadequate case knowledge.

Mint closed her eyes and took a few deep breaths as she mentally ticked off the known facts: the victim was positively identified as Jaicon Hewson, he had not driven himself to the murder scene, his vehicle was clean and presented no leads to follow up, cause of death was not ascertainable due to the mutilated state of the corpse, advanced jamming techniques had been used to disable the plant's sensor suite, his face had been carefully removed and stuck to the rock wall, geometric markings and a red star had been 'painted' on the rock using his blended body contents, and the body had been arrayed in a mirror image to the painted star. What was the point of the star and the markings? Mint cast her eyes over Roman's report, searching for the relevant section. There it was, he had submitted all images for review by the corporation's AIs and was awaiting a response. She checked the time of his request. It had been submitted late on the day of discovery. Why should that request be taking more than twenty-three hours she wondered?

Next, she read through all of the reports from interviews with Jaicon's few friends, acquaintances and work colleagues. Nothing stood out as suspicious to her, he was a loner, kept very much to himself, and got on with his duties in the underground library and archive without fuss or comment. There was a file that contained sensor footage of Jaicon's last day at work. Out of curiosity she played it, what was this loner like when he was alive? She put playback on full screen mode and watched his last afternoon on fast forward. It all looked rather boring to Mint as he sat at his desk and intermittently visited the adjoining rooms to file or retrieve documents. Then, she stopped and went back several hours, watched the footage again. He was rubbing his forehead a lot, as though bothered by something. Finally she returned to the timeframe that initially caught her attention and played it at normal speed. Jaicon pulled a desk drawer open, fiddled inside and then put something in his mouth. He followed this up with a drink from a glass. He'd taken tablets! Mint minimised the sensor footage and opened the report from the search of his office. There it was, headache tablets and pep pills were listed in the desk drawer contents.

Mint sat back heavily in her chair and considered that revelation. Jaicon Hewson was the person to whom she could attribute the earliest signs of headaches. Did that implicate the facility he worked at as most responsible for the leak? No, that didn't quite make sense to her. Jaicon's working environment was separated from the actual scientific work being undertaken. He was two levels underground which would insulate him from an airborne contaminant. This wasn't getting her any further she decided and stood to leave. A drive around town was called for, put her face out there to reassure the populace, see what the prevailing attitude was out on the streets.

She sniffed carefully upon stepping through the door to descend the stairs to the car park but didn't detect any change in air quality or smell. Still, contaminants could be odourless. The air started to feel a little thicker, a sense of foreboding began to build. She stopped and tutted at her sudden agitation, all this suspicion was starting to backfire on her, influence her attitude and feelings. Several deep breaths calmed her and she continued down with muted self-remonstrations.

Mint jumped when she saw the tall, dark figure stood by the driver's door of her 4x4. She stared at the motionless figure for a moment then scanned around the garage. The only other vehicle present had belonged to the late Jaicon Hewson, parked in the evidence corner on the opposite side. She took the last two steps slowly, her finger hovering over the panic button on her command-pad.

"That won't be necessary," a male voice called over as the figure turned around.

Mint judged the man to be roughly her own age, dressed all in black with equally dark hair. He smiled at her, through a neatly trimmed short beard, with a grin that, under other circumstances, would have been quite disarming.

"This is a secure police garage. What are you doing in here and how did you gain entry?" she demanded.

"Oh, let's just say I have a skeleton key," he waved a pad at her, similar to her own.

"Ok," she was thinking fast, "so you've hacked past our security. Who are you and what do you want?" Mint hadn't moved beyond the bottom step, remained a safe distance away from the intruder.

"We could go up to your office, through the door at the top of the steps, turn left, enter the main office; your personal office is on the right hand side with a window overlooking the town school. Correct?"

"We could do that," Mint was nonplussed by his detailed knowledge. "But, something tells me you want to stay hidden; otherwise we'd be having a different conversation in my office right now."

"That's good," he nodded appreciatively. "I said you were capable, I'll revise that assessment upwards."

"What's going on here? Are we going to get to the point?"

"Of course, Sergeant Mint Harris," he placed both hands in his trouser pockets. "You have a murder to solve and suspect Gabriel Parkes' accident yesterday is connected somehow. Shall I continue?" Mint replied with a slow, deliberate nod. "You also suspect there's some natural emission or industrial leak that's affecting the local population and causing disturbed sleep, nightmares. Don't look so surprised, I work for the corporation too. My job is somewhat differently security related and nebulous than yours though. If you really feel the need to know I work for Department 44, although, if you ask about it 99.9% of people will tell you there is no such department."

Mint's command-pad emitted a little ping. She looked at the screen to see an image of the man before her with a security clearance that hit atmospheric levels compared to hers.

"I need you to carry on as normal, Sergeant Harris," he continued. "I have been ordered to investigate your murder and other, unusual goings on, shall we say."

"You're closing down my case?"

"Running parallel up to now, except yours ends and mine continues. I've accessed all of your reports and sensor data."

"You've blocked the satellite footage!" Mint came to a sudden realisation.

"You wouldn't understand it if you saw it," the man turned and began to walk towards the exit ramp. "You'll see me around town. I won't get under your feet as long as you keep clear of mine."

Mint watched as he walked up to the ramp and only then spotted the black 4x4 parked halfway up. With growing concern she watched as he climbed into the vehicle and drove away. She was back in her office in less than a minute, the desk screen activating as she impatiently drummed her fingers on the desk. Pete Field wouldn't be at his desk today but she had a home connection.

"I hope this is important," Pete was in his dressing gown, sat at a table.

"What's Department 44, Pete?"

"I've never heard of it."

"That's bullshit, Pete, I deserve better than that. I've just been told to drop my murder investigation by a guy from Department 44 with a security clearance beyond anything I've seen before."

Pete's face stared at her from the screen as a text message began to appear, she could see his fingers moving on his command-pad. The text read: *'Ok, let's make this secure. I'll call you in two minutes when I'm in my study.'*

Mint huffed when the connection was closed and sat staring out of the window to calm her nerves. Her foot began to tap on the floor and she kept turning to look at the screen every few seconds, anxious for the return call.

"Department 44 does not officially exist," Pete said as soon as the call connected. "Forget the name. They are real though, and they have power and resources. I knew access to the satellite footage was being blocked as soon as I authorised your original request. I'm sorry, I couldn't tell you. The best advice I can give you is to go along with what the agent has suggested. Don't obstruct them, just maintain law and order in Charlestown."

"This is bollocks, Pete." Mint wasn't entirely sure she was hearing right. "The events of the last three days are all interconnected: the murder, Old Tom being sectioned, the Parkes' boy's accident, the contaminant, and I learned this morning that Tom's escaped from the psychiatric centre and killed five people. I figure Tom's going to make his way back here if he isn't stopped beforehand. I need to know what the hell is going on if I'm to do my job and protect these people."

"I realise you're in a tough position, Mint, I really do," Pete's expression didn't change. "Continue with your job and ignore those investigations. That's an order, Mint."

The connection was terminated as abruptly as before, leaving Mint to stare aghast at the blank screen. Pete had never treated her like that before. She sat as though paralysed; her eyes not focussed on anything and remained so for many minutes as she went through the last three days in her mind. Coming to her time at the hospital yesterday, she remembered her request to Constable Fletcher and finally broke from her statue-like pose to consult her command-pad. He had responded but only to tell her the boy hadn't awoken yet; he was in an induced coma to assist in healing his internal injuries. Finally, her thoughts arrived at the present when Mint remembered assigning Roman Reckhart to place sentry sensors around the murder scene. As she'd been removed from the murder case she wondered if Roman had been impeded in his task. She quickly requested a connection with his pad.

"Are you turning telepathic?" Roman's face appeared agitated, filling the pad's entire screen. "I'd put half of the sensor spread in place before these corporation security goons insisted I stop." He moved his pad to show a couple of large, burly men against the backdrop of industrial machinery. "That's only half of the story, though. Mr and Mrs Parkes have arrived; insist on seeing the scene of Gabriel's accident. I was just about to call you."

"Ok, Roman," Mint ran a hand through her hair, thought quickly. "I've had a few surprises myself since morning roster. I'm coming out to you. Stay where you are, don't try to finish the sensor spread, just help keep the Parkes' away, ok?"

"Copy that, Sarge," Roman said and disconnected.

*

Mint cursed the busier traffic as she sat in line at the junction. She had momentarily considered activating the blue lights and siren but decided against such a move. Tension was already building in the town and she didn't intend to add to it. Bright, morning sunshine spiked through the windscreen, it was another pleasant summer's day, although Mint's mood didn't match it. The lights finally changed to green and she found, to her surprise, she was the only driver taking the road out of town towards the hydrogen fuel plant. Tom's dramatic, murderous escape had definitely pulled away all the reporters – unless Department 44 was in some way responsible for their disappearance. Her right foot pushed the pedal down, took the 4x4 to the exact speed limit through the urbanised area then accelerated once she reached the ranks of greenhouses. A pair of signs blocked both sides of the road where greenhouses transitioned to agricultural fields. Mint slowed down to swerve onto the grass verge and neatly bypassed the signs. They bore the biohazard warning symbol. Off road drive kicked in when a wheel momentarily spun in thick mud.

The side road leading to the plant was obstructed by a very recently familiar vehicle that she couldn't drive around; it formed an effective roadblock in the confined space. Mint stopped her 4x4 and turned off its engine. Climbing out of the door she paused and reached into a compartment beneath the steering wheel, pulled out her police pistol in its belted holster. Something inside was sending warning signals to her brain but she couldn't tell what the stimulus for that was. She swung the belt around her waist and buckled it, settled the weight comfortably on her hips.

Mint tried to peer through the black tinted windows of the Department 44 agent's 4x4 roadblock but couldn't see a thing. She discovered it was locked upon trying the door handle. On a whim, she delivered a solid kick to a rear tyre but the action didn't dispel her sense of irritation at the unfairness of the whole situation. Sunlight dazzled her where it glinted from the polished metalwork on the plant, visible a good one hundred metres further along the road. Mint began a determined walk but stopped almost immediately when she caught a hint of movement to her right, among the trees.

"Who's there?" she called.

Further sounds of movement reached her ears: a rub against bark, a shuffle in the undergrowth. Glad of the reassuring weight on her hips, Mint's right hand dropped to rest on the butt of the gun. The sounds of movement had ceased again. Only now did she become aware of the lack of any natural noises. There was no chirruping of birds, scurrying animals, whirring insects, or breath of wind.

"This is Sergeant Mint Harris of the Charlestown Police," she called again, slightly louder. "Who is in there?" There was a long wait, devoid of any reply or further sounds. "I warn you, don't mess about – I am armed."

The noises came again in a rush, louder. It sounded like someone, or something, was crashing around amid the trees yet, try as she might, Mint could see nothing. She prided herself on standing her ground, though the urge to retreat had been strong, her fear level elevated. Silence descended once more. Mint's eyes searched the tangle of undergrowth and tree trunks. Nothing appeared, nothing moved, no further sounds reached her ears. Even the natural sounds of local wildlife remained stubbornly absent. She seemed to be isolated in this place. The hum of plant machinery had been silenced too. Mint released the stud holding her gun secure in the holster and, with her fingers reassuringly wrapped around the handle, began a slow sideways walk towards the plant. She had made another three metres when she distinctly saw a dark shadow move furtively from the cover of one pine tree trunk to another. Before she knew it, the pistol was drawn and held in a two handed grip.

"That's enough now. Step out slowly and reveal your identity,"

The shadow moved again, closer but indistinct, her aim tracked it to the next tree. She made out a definite human shape but no details, just a darkness of imperceptible gender. A breeze blew in where there had been none before and, with slightly wild eyes, Mint watched leaves and the supple stems of ground hugging vegetation swish and sway. The moving air was crazy; it was like a small parcel of wind was weaving in an unplanned, random route that never travelled more than fifteen metres away from her. As she watched in consternation, Mint even wondered whether some small creature, invisible beneath the greenery, was embarking on an insane rampage. She dismissed the thought as she could hear the air moving; it sounded like a much more powerful and impressive gust. Tentatively she lifted one foot and took a small step forward. A hand grabbed her right shoulder. Mint jumped, lurched instinctively away from the unexpected contact. She spun with the pistol still held in shaky, sweaty hands to face the new danger. The man from Department 44 stood there, one arm held out in supplication, the other raised to his face, a finger to his lips. Mint saw he had no weapon in either hand and relaxed slightly.

"What the …" she began, but he shushed her and began to back away, beckoned her to follow.

Mint heard the wind again, even louder now and, disturbingly, directly behind her. She hurried forwards to get away from it. Mint turned once she reached the agent and began to take small backwards steps until she felt the unyielding form of a tree trunk on her back. The agent continued his reverse and signalled her to do likewise. Once they were a tree deep into the forest he crouched down and motioned for Mint to come close and copy him. Mint stepped in and sank to her haunches. Somehow, though she didn't remember doing it, the pistol was holstered; her right hand was securing the stud.

"What the fuck is going on?" she hissed at the agent.

"Honestly?" he looked at her with inscrutable eyes, his voice quiet. "I have no idea. It's been doing that, on and off, for the last fifteen minutes - started not long after the Parkes' showed up."

"You're not telling me they're doing this are you?"

"No," he replied quickly, still in a whisper. "It does seem too much of a coincidence to ignore though. Come on, down to the plant. I've been trying to get to grips with whatever's occurring over there since I left you, without success. However, luckily, it has shown no intention to cross the road and enter the forest this side."

He began to walk through the trees in a slow sideways motion, his eyes constantly scanning the far treeline. Mint followed, confused and anxious for answers. She did feel more relaxed, less agitated now she was in company but a certain level of instinctive fear would not be budged. The agent didn't appear scared or unsettled by the strange goings on. He was mystified for sure, but seemed only curious and intrigued. Shadows started to flit from tree to tree across the road and the wind followed them. Mint had to split her attention between the enigmatic phenomenon across the road and keeping her footing in the tangled undergrowth. Then, the shadowy movement stopped and the wind ceased to track their passage. It was as though they had reached some barrier beyond which it could not, or would not pass - yet.

"It does that every time," the agent said, no longer in a whisper. He stepped out onto the road and began to jog towards the plant. "Come on," he called over his shoulder, an arm waving.

Mint stepped out too and stared back at the rustling undergrowth, now a good ten metres away. She saw a shadow move again but it was distant, less threatening. She turned and jogged after the newcomer, caught up with him in the car park. Roman's truck was parked on the other side, next to another black 4x4. She could see the constable and two other men stood next to Mr and Mrs Parkes who were sat on the ground.

"I asked you to keep away, yet here you are," the agent said. "Never mind, I guess you came to help your man, maybe to remove those two. I'm Aaron by the way."

"Whatever," Mint said. She was staring back down the road but nothing was visible. Her breathing was steadily relaxing, her chest no longer heaving quite so visibly. She could still feel her heart thumping but that also seemed to be calming. "Are you going to tell me anything else about what just happened?"

"At the moment, no," Aaron held up a hand as Mint opened her mouth to reply. She bit back on an angry retort. "But, only because I can't explain it, yet," he continued. "There's something odd going on here, all over Charlestown, but this plant seems to be the epicentre of it all."

"That doesn't make much sense," Mint looked confused. "This plant can't be the source of the contamination, there's nothing here."

"There is no contamination," Aaron said in a matter of fact voice. "I've gone along with your incorrect assumption so far only because it's useful; but the people of Charlestown will continue to believe that party line because you will continue to support it. I need your help in this. This area will be the centre of my investigation and I do not need citizens, like Mr and Mrs Parkes over there, blundering in."

"I'm not used to being ordered about like this in my home town," Mint squared up to him. "However, strange things are afoot, so I'll do you a favour and go along with your cover story. I need you to be straight with me, though."

"I admire your attitude, no quarter given or taken," Aaron nodded. "Ok, you're much more impressive in real life than the corporation's record suggests."

"Come on then, open up." Mint insisted, butting in.

"Alright, alright; we'd been watching the area around Charlestown for a little over a week before your murder took place. Satellites began to return anomalous energy readings that increased every time they passed overhead. We couldn't pin it down to any particular place, just a patch of fuzz that seemed to centre on Charlestown. Data built up and clearly indicated a reserve of energy in some unknown form, concentrated in a storage reservoir of another unknown form we presume. We believe there is an, as yet unknown, connection between this energy, the murder, Gabriel Parkes' accident and your outbreak of nightmares and headaches."

"You've been watching us for a week?" Mint looked around in exasperation, her voice rose. "You could have warned us. If you had eyes in the sky you could have prevented Jaicon Hewson's murder."

"Yes, we could have warned you – but about what, unknown energy readings? What type of warning do you expect we could have issued? No, that's not going to stick. But, yes, we could have told somebody about Mr Hewson's strange behaviour that night. Instead, we watched as he walked from Charlestown, past the greenhouses and fields. We had no indication or reason to suspect he was in danger. Ok, his long night-time walk looked unusual but not criminal. Oh, but we perked up when he arrived here alright. We watched, confused and frustrated as a cloud of static covered this entire site, obscured the plant and Jaicon Hewson from our view. For an hour we watched as different satellite feeds continued to show that static. Then it cleared and the only change was the body, right where you found it. We've gone over that footage many times and there is no indication that any other person or animal was in the vicinity. What happened to Jaicon Hewson did so without the hand of a physical third party."

"Hang on; look at what you're talking about. Surely what you're suggesting is impossible," Mint stopped and collected her thoughts. "You're telling me that energy murdered Jaicon Hewson? I've a long way to go before I buy into that proposal. However, I'm willing to believe there may be some connection between what we just encountered back in the forest and Gabriel Parkes' accident. If he was presented with those moving shadows and strange winds it could well have terrified him sufficiently to account for the ensuing fall."

"You're just going to have to trust me about the Jaicon Hewson case. I agree with you to an extent about the Parkes boy. We saw a huge increase in the energy levels when Tortoise and Hare aligned yesterday, the amplified gravitational tug definitely added to the energy reservoir. But, I don't know whether Gabriel encountered what we just saw, there's no evidence to support that possibility. However, I'm working on the theory it got into his head, just like it's been doing all over town. Except it was more powerful here, targeted straight into a weak point. I also believe the energy readings we detected from space have been radiating out from this point and affecting brain waves. That's the cause of your nightmare epidemic."

"It's underground," Mint burst out. "It has to be, there's nothing visible here apart from what there should be. The energy has to be coming from a hidden source - an underground source. That's why Jaicon Hewson was affected first. He worked two levels below ground all day, five days a week. Hell, I've been developing headaches in the station's underground parking area."

Aaron considered her assertion, his keen eyes never straying from her face. Mint found the look somewhat disconcerting. His grin may be engaging but she found his intense stare perturbing, his ice blue eyes seemed to burrow through her own. Allied with his tall frame and black clothing, it all added up to an overall impression of menace. Nevertheless, she stubbornly maintained eye contact, some inner feeling told her it was an act on his part, a test maybe.

"I agree," he suddenly smiled. "I'll have to run a thorough check on the records of construction and boring at this site, find out if the drilling ever pierced any cavities."

"Should be easy enough with your security clearance," Mint said. "Let's not forget what just happened back there though. What theories are you working on for that? Was it real or planted in our heads, like what you believe happened to Gabriel?"

"Your guess is as good as mine," Aaron shrugged. "At present I'm erring on the side of real, maybe a manifestation of the energy. There may even be somebody or something hidden amongst the trees. Satellite coverage is being constantly fuzzed over this site now so we have to rely on the Mark 1 Eyeball. Come on, let's collect your citizens and get them away from here."

Mint walked beside him to the small collection of people. Roman flashed a thankful, welcoming grin when she arrived. Mr and Mrs Parkes turned in unison to see who had joined them.

"Ah, Sergeant Harris," Mr Parkes struggled to stand but was firmly held in place by one of Aaron's men. He cast him a baleful glance then looked back at Mint. "What is going on here? We demand to see the scene of our Gabriel's accident."

"No, Mr Parkes, I'm afraid that can't happen," Mint asserted. "This is a closed off murder scene and no longer falls under my jurisdiction. Another ... agency is responsible for that now," Mint glanced sideways at Aaron. "There is also reason to believe the contaminant or natural leak originates from this area," she continued. "My corporation colleague here has full authority at this plant; I am only here out of courtesy and to return you to town."

Roman frowned upon hearing that statement from his boss, then looked inquisitively at Aaron. The Department 44 agent made an upwards flick with one finger. "Let them stand," he said to his men.

"Demon!" Mr Parkes cried out on clumsily gaining his feet. His eyes were wide and staring beyond Mint and Aaron.

Mint spun around to follow his stupefied gaze; Tom Barker had just stepped out of the trees and stood staring at them.

"A demon stands before us, in the very light of day," Mr Parkes stated. He had reached under his shirt and brandished a small, golden cross. "Begone, foul spawn of Satan, thou bringer of nightmares and suffering."

"Mr Parkes," Mint turned to look at him, "that's just Old Tom, he's ill, not a demon."

"Your eyes are being fooled by the hellspawn," Mr Parkes spat out, his wife nodded at each of his cries. "Deceiver, you may have fooled these unbelievers but I see your horns, your cloven feet and the hellfire that surrounds you."

"Tom, it's me, Mint," she started to slowly approach the old man. "I've heard what you've done but I know you're ill and you didn't know what you were doing. Come with me, back to the station. We can find somewhere safe where you can be looked after."

Tom's eyes moved from a solemn stare at Mr Parkes to take in Mint's slow approach. He watched her take several steps then raised his left arm, palm outstretched, as if to halt her.

"Come on, Tom, what do you say?" Mint continued, her voice gentle, mollifying. "Orders have been issued to shoot you on sight, but I don't want to do that."

Tom's head lolled to one side, as though contemplating her words, then his left arm tensed and the hand pushed towards her. An incredibly intense blast of air slammed into Mint's chest. She was lifted from her feet and thrown three metres backwards to land flat on her back gasping for breath, winded. Roman was immediately at her side, lifted her shoulders to aid her breathing.

"You see, you see," Mr Parkes shrieked. "The demon reveals his ungodly powers. Pray to the Lord for forgiveness; beg for absolution from your denial of Him. I will wield my heavenly father's power to deliver you from this beast."

"Open fire," Aaron shouted to his men.

They swiftly swung assault rifles from their backs and aimed at Tom. The old man turned his attention to them and began to walk forward. Mint noted the tattered state of his clothing, the redness of his skin and the sores across his face. Six shots sounded as each of Aaron's men fired three rounds in a semi-automatic burst. Tom's arms weaved an arc of blurred air in front of him and he stopped walking. Everyone watched as he stood there then opened his fisted hands and tilted them downwards. Six metallic objects fell to the ground. Tom's head dropped, he looked at the bullets for a moment then his head snapped back up with an expression of blazing anger. His eyes seemed to emit an inner light. Both of his arms flung forwards in a lightning quick action. The armed men were lifted from their feet by the force of his energetic blast and hurled through the air to slam into the front wall of the plant's reception area. Aaron went for his holstered gun.

"Don't," Mint wheezed at him. She was standing again, hands held out before her, palms outwards, showing Old Tom she was unarmed. "Whatever that is, it isn't Old Tom. Nobody do anything. Mr Parkes, stop!"

Gabriel's father completely ignored her as he continued a steady, measured pace towards Tom. He had snapped the chain around his neck, the cross was now held at arm's length as he muttered prayers, his eyes locked on the demon he saw before him. Mrs Parkes followed, her arms tightly gripping his free arm.

"Mr Parkes stop," Mint called again, as loud as she could. Her left hand was beckoning Aaron to join her and Roman. "Stand your men down, Aaron."

She was too late. The assault rifles chattered as they spat out round after round, on full automatic this time. Tom didn't move as the bullets hammered into him, fell away blunted as though they had struck a solid wall. His arms powered forwards once more. Mint, Roman and Aaron stared on horror-struck as visible orange energy, like tendrils of fire, streaked across to the men and burned gaping holes into their chests. They stood and juddered as the fiercely blazing bolts spread out to slowly consume their flesh and bones. The assault rifles dropped from dead hands as the bodies glowed and disintegrated. Ash fell in piles to mark their passing.

"Your hellfire will not harm me for I have the Lord Almighty on my side, and my path is righteous," Mr Parkes began to shout again after stopping to witness the extermination. His steady advance continued, brought him to within three metres of Tom. The old man turned his menacing gaze away from the remains of the two men and focussed on the preacher. "I am not afraid as these others are," Mr Parkes continued. "I will face you down and fling you back to the underworld, where you belong."

"The Parkes' aren't hearing you," Aaron whispered urgently to Mint. "Make for the road while Tom's distracted." They commenced a slow, careful movement away from the confrontation.

"The Lord is my shepherd and you are Satan's wolf," Mr Parkes intoned. He had stopped two metres from Tom, his arms held aloft as he called on his deity. "Hear me, Holy Father and help me cast down this abomination."

Tom turned to face Mr Parkes squarely; his eyes aglow, fiery red, for all to see. He cast them downwards and made a contemptuous upwards scan of the figures of Mr and Mrs Parkes before him.

"Begone foul demon …"

"I am Tiada Vejour of the Varla K'dyamon," the figure of Tom finally spoke. The voice was impossibly deep and came from an open mouth that did not move. The three would be escapees halted at the speech. "Cease your babbling for your words are an insult to me and my power. I am ancient beyond your ken, from realms beyond your pitiful knowledge. You have arrived at my refuge by accident or by the design of my fellow Varla; though it matters not how, you have come and I have fed. My powers grow to levels I have not felt for uncounted aeons. Soon my resting body will rise and you will know fear and I will feed anew."

"Never, foul demon from the pit," Mr Parkes shrieked. "You will leave this world, return to the fires of damnation. I will cast you down and my Lord's power will arise. The world of men will kneel to the will of God once more."

"Your cries to your deity are puny, though I judge from your fervour and bravery that you truly believe this fallacy. Very well, I shall enjoy the fear and terror I instil in your quaking bodies, feed from you as I engulf your primitive mind and present your hell to you."

"Move," Aaron whispered forcibly as he began to step backwards and retreat towards the road. The figure that was once Tom began to circle the Parkes', gazing alternately at its victims and the three retreating figures. It flashed wicked grins their way, tossed its head and boomed out a deep, resonant laugh.

Mr and Mrs Parkes clung to each other in abject terror. His cries of righteous delivery had now ceased. Their eyes were opened wide, mouths gaping, faces contorted in pain. Often they could be seen squeezing their eyes shut, only to open them again, wide and terrified. Strangled whimpers escaped every so often. They sank to their knees, embraced and toppled over. The figure of Tom Barker stood on the far side of the prone couple and glared straight at Mint, Roman and Aaron. They stopped as one, as though commanded to witness the next act.

"Sweet and pure," the voice was audible velvet. "My strength grows, unstoppable. Now perish in the flames you so adore."

Sheets of fire erupted from the bodies of Mr and Mrs Parkes. Screams carried to the watchers briefly but were swiftly cut short. Mint raised her arms to shield her eyes from the blazing light and felt a wave of heat strike her. The flames subsided as swiftly as they arose to leave piles of ash at the feet of the still figure of Old Tom. Its eyes remained locked on them for a frightful minute. Mint felt powerless, utterly helpless and open to the whim of whatever possessed the body of the once loved old man. Then, with a sneer, the figure turned and walked towards the plant with arms outstretched. Mint felt a crackle in the air, a huge upswell of energy. She turned and ran. At any moment she expected to be cut down, but pumped her legs as hard as she could and concentrated her eyes on the black 4x4 blocking the road ahead. She was dimly aware of Roman and Aaron running with her but the fear in her breast kept a selfish wish for her own salvation at the forefront of her mind. Great gushing sounds of moving air reached her from behind. Then came the grind and crash of rending metal. Her foot slipped on a branch and she tumbled, rolled until her shoulder struck the black 4x4 and she came to a halt. She was lying with her back to the vehicle, eyes pointed down the road. The hydrogen fuel plant was gone. In its place a great cloud of whirling debris could be seen, a single figure stood silhouetted at its edge, arms held aloft.

A hand grabbed her shoulder. She stirred and looked up to see Roman. He hauled her to her feet and grabbed an arm, began to pull her around the roadblock to her 4x4. Mint stared back down the road but saw nothing except a huge, rippling cloud of dust; the figure was gone. She turned at Roman's insistent tug and dashed to her 4x4. Roman jumped up to the passenger seat as Mint climbed in the driver's side and pushed the engine start button. The vehicle was already reversing when she slammed her door shut. Mint's neck complained as she strained her head around to guide her frantic backwards flight to the main road junction. She turned to look back at where the plant used to be but saw only billowing dust. Aaron's 4x4 was following hers, two metres away.

Tyres screeched as she reversed onto the main road and spun the steering wheel to point the nose of her 4x4 towards Charlestown. Aaron's vehicle flashed in front of her and accelerated along the road. Mint quickly cancelled reverse and powered up through the gears as she raced to catch up with him.

*

Bruce felt a heavy, slowly sinking weight in his stomach as he peered at his friend through the window in the hospital room's door. Gabriel was still asleep, a kindly nurse had informed him he was in an induced coma to assist with the extensive healing his body required. He knew there was very little he could do for him but felt like he needed to be here to watch over his friend, have a companion close by now that his parents had left temporarily to 'sort some things out.' Bruce didn't think the look in Mr Parkes' eyes meant he was leaving to do housework.

"How is he?" Bruce jumped; he hadn't heard Kieron's approach.

"They've put him in a coma to accelerate the healing process."

"Shit, that's a lot of tubes!" Kieron exclaimed upon taking a glance into the room.

"How did you get on with your dad last night?" Bruce asked Daniel. The other boy was looking on silently.

"Didn't see him," Daniel shrugged. "Locked my bedroom door when I got in. He was off early again this morning."

"Got your scooter back yet?" Bruce didn't know how to discuss or attempt to help his friend's situation so he stuck to safer ground.

"Yeah, we're parked up next to yours outside. Are you staying here all day or coming with us to see what's going on?"

"What do you mean?" Bruce looked from one to the other.

"There's a shit load of trucks moving around town," Kieron said. "Got science team written on the side."

"Really?" Bruce frowned. "Could be for the murder?"

"I thought you were the clever one," Daniel admonished him. "They're all over town, that can't be connected to the fuel plant."

"Ok, ok," Bruce held up his hands. "I didn't see anything when I came in, mind you, I wasn't looking. Come on then, let's go and see what they're up to."

They trooped off along the corridor. Bruce cast his eyes backwards once or twice and saw a nurse enter Gabriel's room as soon as they departed. It wasn't busy in the hospital on a Sunday morning and they soon dashed out of the front doors to their waiting scooters.

"Let's go to my place first, pick up some things," Bruce said as they fired up the little engines.

"Race you!" Kieron shouted as he shot off first.

"No way," Bruce muttered.

"Scared of Sergeant Harris?" Daniel asked.

"A little, although she was ok when we were alone in her 4x4 yesterday," Bruce admitted. "But, I don't think I've got too much goodwill left to waste with Mum and Dad. I have to be careful."

They hit the road to follow in Kieron's wake. It didn't take long to navigate the light traffic on their nippy scooters and they were soon in the residential belt. Kieron was waiting, grinning smugly, when they stopped outside Bruce's house.

"You'd best wait out here, I don't want to give them any cause to ground me," Bruce said.

"Is Gretta home?" Daniel craned his neck to try and see through the windows.

"She should be," Bruce replied. "That's another reason you're waiting outside."

He dashed up the driveway and through the front door, checking his friends were staying where he left them as he closed the portal behind him. Lights shone under the study door as he rushed past, bringing a smile to his face. His parents were working; they'd be unlikely to hear him. The backpack was still where he'd placed it on returning home yesterday. Bruce looked around for anything else that might prove useful. He spotted his optical viewers and put them in the bag. His eyes scanned past his data-pad on the table and, after brief consideration, he swept it up and into his pocket. Next stop was the kitchen where he grabbed a bottle of juice and some biscuits before rushing out again, with a slower, more careful transition past the study door. His parents would be suspicious if they heard him leaving the house again so soon.

He swung the backpack over his shoulders as he walked back to his scooter and grinned at his friends. "We'll try the road to the fuel plant first," he said. "Best to see if there's more activity out that way initially."

Bruce thought he heard a shout from the doorway as they motored away but purposefully kept his eyes forward. He cast his gaze backwards once they'd turned a corner but couldn't discern any pursuit. Traffic was still very light when they turned onto the main road and non-existent as they headed out of town.

"Nothing unusual so far," Bruce observed as they rode past the last house, three abreast across the wide road.

"I told you," Kieron called, "they're all over town. There might be some further out."

Tall greenery, bending under the weight of fruit and vegetables, could be spied through the glass of the greenhouses as they hurried along. Every so often they'd spot an agriculturist tending to them but they never looked out at the passing boys.

"What's that in the road?" Kieron shouted, pointing ahead.

"Looks like signs," Bruce said.

"What's that symbol?" Kieron asked as they approached and saw them more clearly.

"Biohazard!" Bruce stated.

They pulled up at the signs, engines idling.

"Someone ignored them," Daniel said. He pointed at tyre marks in the grass and mud to one side.

"Going out of town," Bruce added. "Mud tracks over there where they took to the road again."

"Come on, let's follow," Kieron urged. "I bet they've gone to the plant."

"No," Bruce wheeled his scooter to the side of the road and propped it up on its stand.

"Aw, come on, live a little," Kieron complained.

"No," Bruce shot back, more assertive. "I'll have no life if we're caught. This is as far as I'm going. I've got plenty of tech to look from a distance."

"Suit yourself," Kieron revved his engine. "You coming, Daniel?"

Daniel powered his scooter down and propped it on its stand in response.

"Bloody cowards!" Kieron called over his shoulder as he moved away.

Bruce shook his head at Kieron's characteristic recklessness, and retrieved the optical viewers from his backpack. Resting the bag against his legs, he put the small device to his eyes.

"See any of them?" Daniel asked.

"No, there's nothing moving but Kieron, the daft sod's really going fast."

They stood for a minute scanning the far horizon where the hills began to roll and fields gave way to forest. As Bruce watched, Kieron rapidly decelerated. The unexpected move puzzled him but he could discern no visible cause. His friend continued onwards, albeit at a much reduced pace.

"What's he seen?" he muttered as he cast his eyes over the trees.

"Was that smoke?" Daniel suddenly pointed to the rise of a hill.

Bruce concentrated his viewers where his friend indicated and saw a diminishing wisp of black. "It was," he confirmed. "I reckon that's where the plant is. Whoa!" Another rolling cloud of smoke arose and rapidly dissipated. "Something's burning; the smoke's black but there's not much of it. Wait a minute, what the hell is that?"

"It's gone all hazy," Daniel said. "I can see that without viewers. The sun's glinting off something inside."

"Here, use these," Bruce handed over the viewers. His other hand fished the data-pad from his pocket and he quickly set it to record on maximum zoom. "I see Kieron's turned back." Their friend was rapidly returning to them.

Bruce watched as Kieron turned his head and pointed back down the road. He seemed to be shouting but the distance was too great to hear his words. The haze had now become a swirling cloud of dust, pieces of metal and other debris.

"Fuck me!" Daniel exclaimed in alarm. "It's like those tornadoes we learned about from Earth, but there's no storm."

"There's a couple of 4x4's just charged out onto the road," Bruce said, excited. "I don't know about the front one but that looks like Sergeant Harris' 4x4 trying to catch up. Is she chasing someone?"

"Whereabouts?" Daniel changed his view. "Ah, got them. I don't know. It's not one of the vehicles we saw earlier. She's caught up, driving alongside now. They're talking through the windows. Hey, my dad's in there with her."

Bruce continued to record the approaching vehicles, reducing the zoom to take in the full sweep of events in the distance. He ignored Kieron as he stopped next to them and cast frightened eyes over his shoulder, the scooter engine still running.

"It's getting lower," Daniel had turned his attention back to the swirling cloud of debris. "It's gone!" He dropped the optical viewers from his eyes and turned his attention to the road. "They've seen it, too, slowed down."

The approaching vehicles had reduced the urgency of their flight and were no more than one hundred metres away. Bruce took the optical viewers from his friend and stowed them in his backpack. He continued to record, holding the data-pad somewhat unsteadily as he shrugged the bag onto his shoulder. The two vehicles swerved around the signs on the opposite side of the road and stopped.

Sergeant Harris was first out, with Daniel's dad stepping out a moment later from the passenger side. They stood staring at the distant wooded hillside as Bruce watched them. He noted that Sergeant Harris was covered in mud and dust, her uniform dishevelled, her face streaked. Both were a little out of breath and appeared jittery, on edge.

"Are you ok?" Bruce asked, walking over.

"Mm," Sergeant Harris smiled at him. "I'll be ok, thank you Mr Webster. Curiosity got the better of you again, eh?"

"Daniel, are you alright?" Mr Reckhart rushed over to his son and embraced him fiercely.

Sergeant Harris stepped alongside Bruce and they stood side by side for a while as the father and son stood together. Daniel's eyes started off scared, mellowed to a confused look, and, finally, a couple of tears came.

"What's happened?" Bruce asked. His mind was racing over possibilities, but some sort of accident had definitely befallen the hydrogen fuel plant.

"At this time, I really don't know what to make of the previous twenty minutes." Sergeant Harris shook her head.

"My men are inbound," Bruce heard a shout from behind and turned to see a tall man dressed all in black had emerged from the other vehicle. He had a pad of some sort in his hand and was staring intently at Bruce, his data-pad in particular. "I don't suppose you have any recordings on that pad of yours?"

Bruce looked up uncertainly at Sergeant Harris.

"It's ok, he's with me," she assured him with a nod.

"Yeah," Bruce held the pad up and began to retrieve the footage as Sergeant Harris and the other man came closer to look over his shoulder. "Here it is."

The data-pad was expensive and provided the quality of recording expected for such a price tag. Daniel's dad cuffed his son softly at his obscene outburst but everybody watched the footage in silence until it showed the two vehicles draw up to the barrier and it came to the end.

"Transfer that over to my command-pad please. Good job, Mr Webster," Sergeant Harris patted him on the shoulder.

Bruce smiled as he enabled the transfer then scowled as another pad hacked into his and copied the recording.

"Thank you," the tall man said as he turned away.

Kieron grabbed Bruce's arm and pointed down the road, towards town. A small convoy of trucks could be seen rapidly approaching. They watched as the trucks pulled up at the side of the road and stern looking men and women began to emerge.

"They've all got guns," Kieron whispered. "They are definitely not scientists."

"No," Bruce whispered back. He was now watching Sergeant Harris and the tall man. They were deep in conversation and kept turning to look and point at him.

"Right, you three, come here," Sergeant Harris summoned them.

They all looked from one to the other then walked over, shepherded by Daniel's dad. The tall man in black locked his ice blue eyes on Bruce. It was a steely gaze, full of authority. Bruce couldn't hold it long and turned his eyes to Sergeant Harris who seemed to be friendlier.

"There has been an incident at the hydrogen fuel plant," Sergeant Harris began. "We do not know what caused it and have launched an investigation. As far as we know, the people gathered here are the only witnesses. That puts you three in an important position. We do not wish to spread fear and panic, so we need you to keep quiet about what you saw, ok? You will have to provide a witness statement at the station so we're going to put your scooters on the load racks of these two 4x4s and take you with us."

"I've put a password protection on your file, Mr Webster," the tall man added. "Only I know it and I will not unlock that footage until we are ready to go public."

Bruce nodded dumbly and followed the adults to the 4x4s as some of the tall man's people passed them with their scooters, lifted them onto racks on the back of the vehicles.

*

The three boys had been sullen since arriving at the police station and that demeanour had not changed when they rode their scooters up the exit ramp out of the car park half an hour later. Mint and Roman had taken the three witness statements themselves. Another constable was on station duty but she didn't want to involve the rest of her staff at this point. Trying to reconcile what had happened in her own head was difficult enough at present without trying to describe it to, what would undoubtedly be, a dubious audience with unanswerable questions.

She returned to her office where Roman had just arrived with hot cups of tea. Aaron remained in a seat against the wall, his chin cupped in one hand, his elbow resting on one knee.

"You look thoughtful," Mint observed as she sat down and nodded thanks for the drink to Roman.

"Just trying to come to terms with what I think happened," he stirred and looked at her with those piercing eyes.

"What do you mean?"

"What I mean is: did it actually happen as we remember it, or were we fed visions?"

"I see what you mean but I think you're wrong. Much as I'm still trying to rationalise it, there are a few things I can think of with relevance."

"Go on," Aaron urged.

"Ok, let me ask you a question first. Was the activity restricted to just those shadows and strange winds in the woods before what happened in the car park?"

"It was," Aaron nodded his head. "My people haven't encountered phenomena elsewhere. They were performing a sweep around Charlestown; I was at ground zero, so to speak."

"That's what I hoped you'd say. In that case, I believe it did happen as we all remember it. Old Tom was the carrier of whatever is responsible. The man I know … knew, was incapable of killing people and certainly couldn't summon whatever power was used to throw me backwards. Am I safe in assuming he displayed similar powers in his escape?" Aaron nodded but remained silent. "Thank you," Mint continued. "So, I'm going to say the bulk of this energy, entity, maybe entities, whatever it is, was possessing Old Tom. A vestige remained here to continue the nightmares and can be attributed to Gabriel's accident, him being so close to ground zero, as you call it. Bruce Webster's recording confirms elements of what we saw. We may not know a thing about what we are dealing with but I would imagine that planting fake images on a digital recording requires different capabilities to planting them into human consciousness, although we can now safely blame it for the static," she looked at Roman, who could only shrug his shoulders. "Bruce Webster and the other boys were completely invisible to Old Tom's point of view, yet their eye witness testimony and the recording corroborate elements of the destruction of that plant as we saw it."

"Or, what we're dealing with is so powerful it can manipulate recorded data to make us think that way," Aaron countered.

"If that's the case, we're beaten already," Mint replied. "No, I prefer to apply the simple, logical explanation. Logical, huh? If our eyes were not betraying us, what logic can explain what happened back there? Even if those events weren't real and we were fooled into seeing and believing they actually happened, what logic can explain ability such as that?"

"May I use your screen?" Aaron asked, taking to his feet.

"Be my guest," Mint pushed her chair backwards with her feet, scooted rearward on the little wheels, allowed him to reach the screen.

Aaron logged her out and entered his own credentials, careful to keep them from Mint and Roman's view. He navigated through a number of screens and security levels and finally stood back as a recording began to play.

"This is the collected and edited together footage of Tom Barker's escape from the secure facility at New Cambridge," he announced.

Mint looked from his face to the screen, pleased the secretive man was opening up and sharing evidence and details. She shook her head as the deadly events played out, aware of Roman shuffling uncomfortably beside her.

"Exactly the same powers," Mint said. "I remember studying Tom back at the car park. Between this footage and the car park his clothes degraded and his skin became visibly blighted, poxed. Plus, do you have any idea how he covered one hundred miles overnight? Surely nobody would have given him a lift and I'm not aware of any missing travellers should he have hijacked transport. No, that energy was used somehow and it left a lasting mark on his skin."

"Ok, Sergeant Harris," Aaron leaned against the window sill after connecting the screen to space surveillance; it currently displayed the waiting pattern for satellite overflight. "You're proposing that some entity has possessed Tom Barker and is responsible for everything that has occurred recently. It can apparently split, send most of itself one hundred miles away but leave enough behind to continue causing nightmares and make Gabriel Parkes fall off a cliff edge. I'm struggling."

"She could be on to something," Roman finally spoke up. "My memory isn't what it used to be but I recall Old Tom saying 'I am Tiada Vejour of the Varla K'dyamon,' or something like that. Does that mean this entity's name is Tiada Vejour and, if so, what is this Varla K'dyamon? Its race, perhaps?"

"It spoke about feeding from us," Aaron continued the thread. "There was no physical consumption of the bodies, it didn't take anything from any of us, but it still intimated it was feeding from us."

"Energy," Mint said. "It's feeding off energy. You mentioned the conjunction of Tortoise and Hare, Aaron. The energy reservoir increased that day and it's been increasing for days, feeding off … what, brain wave or emotional energy? Is that possible?"

"Perhaps it's time to ditch some of our concepts of what is possible," Roman said. "What we've witnessed has never been seen before as far as I know. We're like primitives seeing high technology for the first time and accrediting it as magic. This thing is way out of our league."

"When you say it all like that, it makes it plausible," Aaron agreed. "There are other mysteries the corporation has attempted to investigate unsuccessfully into which these events give me some further insight and understanding." They all looked from one to the other, Mint and Roman hoping for further details that were not forthcoming. "I have to begin the process of turning my presence here from investigation into a possible first contact situation. We may have an alien intelligence."

"You think so?" Roman said, incredulous. "I'd say, if that's how we're approaching this, we have gone beyond the point of first contact, and this situation is decidedly unfriendly. What, exactly, do you intend to do?"

"Not become emotional and irrational, for a start," Aaron stared Roman down. "I agree with you, this is unfriendly contact, but, could it be a misunderstanding? I need to review recent events to see if there was a trigger point. Maybe an event that led to an unveiling we are wholly unaware of."

"You do that," Mint said, standing up. "Use my office and work quickly. Roman and I will be out in the town, making sure it remains calm. I could do with a dose of normality after this morning."

*

Bruce split from his friends without a word and went straight home. His parents were in the kitchen with his sister when he walked in. Without a word, he grabbed a piece of fruit, a drink, and some biscuits and retreated to his bedroom. Shrugs were shared all round as he stomped out but he was left to his own devices.

Once at his desk, Bruce stared at the data-pad and tried to access the recording he had made. Sure enough, the tall man had password locked it. Carefully placing the data-pad in its recharging cradle, Bruce booted up his desk screen and ordered it to connect with the pad. He liked challenges and was determined to crack the password. First of all he put a commercially available decryption application to work and left it running in the background. Hours spent alone in this room had not been squandered; he had taken risks to establish his technical prowess. He accessed another file and the screen split into a grid of separate views, connected to the traffic surveillance cameras.

After concentrating on the changing views for five minutes Bruce came to the conclusion that all of the mystery 'science team' trucks had abandoned the town centre. He could only presume they were near the biohazard signs, where he had last seen them. He cancelled the connection and idly played with his optical viewers while he remembered what he could of the people who emerged from the trucks on the edge of town. They didn't look scientific at all; their movements were regimented and ordered, like a security or military team from his computer games. The guns he had seen reinforced that assumption. When they left the scene in Sergeant Harris' 4x4 he had looked back and noticed preparations being made for a more permanent roadblock.

A ping sounded from his screen. He looked up to see the commercial decryption application had failed. Bruce wasn't surprised; he was rapidly realising the tall man and his people were much more interesting than an environmental analysis science team. For a frustrating half hour he attempted to manually unlock the file. At one point he made progress but the password immediately sent a signal and received a response. It was a semi-intelligent program, not just a password lock. His eyebrows shot up in surprise, this affirmed his suspicions about the tall man.

Ok, he decided, I'm not going to break through to gain access to my footage. That seemed the end of it; he'd have to await removal, if ever, of the offending password. Flopping onto his bed, Bruce stared at the ceiling in consternation and howled inside at the unfairness of it all. He felt a sense of resentment enter his head, a rage descended on his brain, how dare that man do this to him? No, this wasn't the end, not by a long way! New footage was what he needed and he had an inkling of how to get it. Jumping up from the bed he returned to the screen and activated his shortcut to the traffic surveillance cameras, his movements abrupt, jerky and angry. Once the grid pattern appeared he took the hack back a step and scanned through the list of available applications. It took him ten minutes to hack into the greenhouse surveillance system.

*

Mint and Roman had walked silently from her office, both considering the rapidly unfolding situation into which they had been unwillingly thrust. Neither spoke until they were in Mint's 4x4 and heading up the exit ramp.

"What's your plan for now?" Roman asked.

"I don't have one!" Mint snapped. Silence followed her outburst. "I'm sorry," she continued. "This is hard; hard to believe, hard to process, hard to deal with. I'll head down to Aaron's roadblock first and find out if anybody has been turned back yet."

"Do you trust him?" Roman looked away after asking the question.

"Not entirely," Mint replied, noting Roman's reaction. "I sense you don't."

"Sometimes he seems alright. Other times, I feel like he's still holding back on something."

"Like what?"

"I can't put my finger on it, not just yet," Roman shook his head.

"I guess we don't have any other options at the moment anyway," Mint turned onto the main road out of town.

"Who is he exactly?"

"Aaron?" Mint glanced at Roman who replied with an inquisitive nod. "Some sort of agent for a secret corporation department I'd never heard of. I wouldn't have believed him if Pete hadn't confirmed its existence. One thing's for sure, he's got a security clearance way above anything I've come across before. He's got powers and access rights beyond my imagination."

"He accessed that footage from the New Cambridge facility easily enough. That was some scary shit. Did you see he had the screen awaiting footage from a satellite overflight?

"I did," Mint nodded. "He's already admitted he's responsible for preventing my access to the surveillance footage from the murder night. He tells me there was nobody else involved; they watched Jaicon

Hewson walk to the plant then the same static recorded by the plant's sensors obscured their view. Afterwards, the body was there, as we found it."

"Nobody else in the vicinity at all?" Roman looked at Mint who shook her head as she pulled up at the side of the road, just shy of the roadblock. One of Aaron's people began to walk over to them, a stony faced woman. "So the murder, the symbols, everything were all down to that energy. Hold on, that's it, I still don't have the AIs report on those symbols. Do you think he's holding back on those?"

"Keep that thought," Mint opened her window. "Any problems?"

"I'm not authorised to disclose operational matters to you, Sergeant Harris," the woman replied.

"Cut the authority and jurisdiction bullshit, ok?" Mint snapped. "I have a town full of people to think about. Has anybody tried to drive down this road?

"Two vehicles stopped about one hundred metres away and turned around." The response was curt, delivered dispassionately.

"Thank you, that wasn't too difficult now, was it?" Mint didn't attempt to keep the sarcasm from her voice. "What about the plant, anything else happened?"

This time there was no response, the woman simply turned and walked away.

"Yeah? You have a nice day too," Mint accelerated hard and spun around. "Seems clear he doesn't want to share everything after all. He's being very careful with what he wants us to know. I'm not comfortable at all with that. Tell me about those symbols."

"I put a request in for the AI to review all databases," Roman said. "If anything else was remotely similar I asked to receive the details. It shouldn't have taken the AI more than an hour but I've had nothing."

"You've chased it up?" Mint looked over at him.

"Of course," Roman sounded offended. "Twice."

"That'll do for me. I think you're on to something, he's hiding that result from us."

Silence followed as Mint turned onto a residential road and slowed down. They both looked out at the neighbourhood houses but their minds were distant, caught up in the twists and turns of the last few days.

"He seemed awfully quick to take the first contact alien route," Roman finally spoke up.

"You don't think everything that's occurred is strange, alien?" Mint questioned, somewhat taken aback.

"No, no, I don't mean like that," Roman apologised. "I mean it was almost like that was the explanation he was pre-disposed to. He's holding back on us, what if he has some evidence of alien connections?"

"You think your symbols may be that evidence?"

"I do …"

Roman was interrupted by a beep from Mint's command-pad. She drew up at the side of the road and took the device from its cradle. Her eyebrows raised in recognition.

"Speak of the devil," Mint pressed the communication button. "Aaron, how can I help you?"

"We've got a problem. Somebody's hacked into the greenhouse surveillance sensors, cleared a pathway through to bypass the roadblock."

*

Bruce ran as fast as he could. He didn't know exactly how long it would take for his meddling to be discovered but he thought, even on a Sunday, it wouldn't be much longer than an hour. His chest was heaving and aching, sweat dripped from his brow. It was too warm a day to be charging through the lines of greenhouses.

The abrupt transition to fields could be discerned in the near distance. His path had been carefully plotted to lead him into a wheat field where he would have some cover. Several times he thought he passed the figures of working agriculturists within the greenhouses but he hadn't stopped to find out. The advantage of his hacked surveillance blackout was time critical.

He powered past the last greenhouse and twenty metres into the field before he collapsed, flat on his back, the wheat gently swaying all around him. It took several minutes for his breathing to relax, his chest to cease monumental heaves as he flooded his lungs with air. Then, he was on his feet again and moving. Automated agricultural machinery was visible in the distance. It would detect him easily enough and avoid accidents, but Bruce was more worried such an encounter would be transmitted. He had to avoid the automatons at all costs.

Sweat was trickling uncomfortably down his spine where his backpack sat. He'd brought food and drink to keep him going should he manage to find a good position to spy on whatever was occurring at the hydrogen fuel plant. For a moment he wondered why he was so intent on investigating what he had witnessed. He'd been warned away by Sergeant Harris and the tall man, and they had both seemed scared and out of breath when they reached the roadblock. If it had affected them so badly, how was he, a thirteen year old boy, likely to react? Then the determination and anger hit him again, he deserved to know – a murder, then his friend's accident, and finally, what he'd seen earlier today.

Bruce clenched his jaw and started a slow, steady jog across the field. Time was passing and he had none to waste. He must get there quickly.

*

"I've got fresh footprints here, headed inwards," Roman's voice came through the command-pad. Mint had dropped him off to search the town side of the band of greenhouses.

"Thanks, Roman," Mint replied, "follow them through. I've just arrived at the roadblock."

"I've sent a patrol already," the same stern-faced woman told Mint as she stepped out of the 4x4.

"Good for you," Mint didn't hide her irritation at the woman's attitude. "My constable has just located fresh footprints heading into the greenhouses from the residential side. It looks like one of my citizens is responsible, so I'll deal with this, without pointing guns at anyone."

Mint stomped past the open-mouthed woman, pushed her way through a pair of armed guards at the roadblock. She didn't look back as she started to follow the last line of greenhouses where they bordered a field of vegetables. It took a good deal of willpower to resist the urge to check behind and find out if guns were being pointed at her. She could see a two person patrol in the near distance, making slow progress. As predicted, they had assault rifles held ready for use. She trudged on through the mud but stopped when she heard a voice call her name. Turning, she saw Aaron running to catch up with her.

"You've made quite an impression on my squad leader," Aaron said when he arrived. She was disappointed to note he was not in the least out of breath.

"I expect a certain level of courtesy," she shot back.

"Ok," he held his hands up. "These are armed troops, the closest thing this planet has to an army. They aren't used to this kind of work."

"And what exactly is this kind of work?" Mint stopped and rounded on him. "There never was going to be a scientific survey, was there? You knew what you were looking for, or thought you did, before you even got here, didn't you? Tell me about the symbols."

Aaron looked at her with those piercing eyes for a long time but Mint was fired up, rose to the challenge, and refused to back down. He grinned, a small lift of one side of his mouth. His response had been considered while he re-appraised the figure before him.

"They match symbols discovered, but not translated, on the Starjump constructs," he stated.

Mint opened her mouth to respond but shut it again. Her prepared response was no longer relevant. Shuffling her feet uncomfortably, she searched desperately for an appropriate reply.

"What?" she managed, fully aware how wholly pathetic it sounded.

"Don't worry," Aaron laughed, broke the tension. "We were stunned when the AI produced that match. We're dealing with the builders, maybe something else that worked with them, or discovered them, like we did. We don't yet know if the matching symbols were added to the constructs at a later time or inscribed on construction. There's a priority message heading to Earth."

"That'll take years," Mint pointed out.

"Indeed," Aaron smiled. "That's why I'm here to assess and attempt to control the situation. We're isolated and vulnerable. Do you understand the importance of my mission here now?"

Mint nodded dumbly. She was preparing to speak when a loud ping sounded from Aaron's command-pad. He looked at the device and frowned.

"It's a message from my team back in New Cambridge," he announced. "We finally have an asset overhead. It's tracking a heat source making its way through the fields towards ground zero. They're sending a high magnification image."

Mint stepped up beside Aaron and looked inquisitively at the pad. The zoom was extremely good and showed a figure with a backpack dashing across a field.

"One of your younger citizens, judging by the scale markings," Aaron pointed out.

"Bruce Webster," Mint decided.

"Really?" Aaron looked dubious.

"He had a backpack like that yesterday, and earlier today," she nodded, firming up her suspicion. "He's also the only youngster I know who could have hacked into the surveillance sensors."

"Ok, I'll go along with that, let me just check something," Aaron tapped away at the pad's screen and finally tutted. "Resourceful boy, this Bruce Webster of yours. He managed to evade enough security protocols on the password lock I attached to his file to force it into reactive mode. If he can do that, your local security systems are easy pickings for him. Let's go get him."

Aaron turned and began to run back to the roadblock without waiting. Mint had to sprint to catch up with him and only managed to do so when he stopped to issue orders to his squad leader. She followed him to his 4x4 and stepped up to the passenger seat.

"I'm not used to being on this side," she said, a quiver of fright in her voice.

"Scared?" Aaron looked at her as he fired up the engine. "You should be, because I'm terrified. But at least we have an idea what's waiting out there, your Bruce Webster is going in blind."

"Floor it then, Aaron," Mint said, more controlled. "We need to cut him off before he enters the forest."

Tyres screeched as the 4x4 shot through the gap that opened in the roadblock. Aaron kept his foot hard down on the accelerator while Mint leaned forward to scan the fields for their quarry.

"All clear at treetop height," Aaron noted. "If anything's going on in there it's not as destructive now. I don't know whether to take that as a good or bad sign."

"I'll tell you what's a bad sign," Mint said, "I can't see Bruce at all. He's either gone to ground or he's in the trees already."

Aaron tapped away on his command-pad, secure in a cradle on the dashboard. It pinged to confirm his message had been sent.

"We'll know in a moment," he said.

The pad pinged again. Aaron looked at the response and turned concerned eyes on Mint.

"He's in the trees."

*

Bruce had used his optical viewers to confirm it was Sergeant Harris who turned up in the first 4x4. He'd also seen the arrival of the tall man in his 4x4 and watched as he caught up with the local police chief. They'd talked for a short time and looked out across the fields. Bruce definitely got the impression he was the reason for their sudden appearance. He was in amongst the trees now and didn't fear discovery too much. They seemed keen to find him though, ran to the 4x4 and pierced the roadblock.

The 4x4 was making a fast approach along the road and Bruce realised he was at risk of being intercepted so close to his destination. He edged back into the forest and turned to continue. For some reason he just couldn't quite grasp, it seemed imperative he record new footage of the site of the incident. There was a purpose to this mission, the folk in town needed to know what was going on. Yes, it was absolutely essential that as many people as possible got to see what was going on here. He began to jog between the trees, somehow never managing to trip on the tangled undergrowth.

*

"Not a thing," Mint said, exasperated.

They had just driven, quite tentatively, to a point a little shy of the access road and reversed, much more quickly, to the treeline. Aaron revved the engine, let it return to idling speed then revved again.

"We have to try the slip road," he looked at her with slightly wide eyes.

"Are you mad?" Mint was caught between duty and fright, and selfishly found she favoured the latter.

"I don't want to face whatever's down there as much as you, but that boy is totally unaware of what he's about to encounter," Aaron appeared to be building up his own courage, from a very low start. "Is that a fate you want him to face alone?"

"No," Mint bit her lip, the word had slipped out.

Aaron accelerated hard, as though to go slower would give him too much time to reconsider his actions. The 4x4 veered off the main road and onto the slip road where Aaron applied the brakes. Mint noticed thick black deposits of tyre composite where she had performed a reverse manoeuvre at stupid speed earlier in the day. Aaron followed her eyes and half-smiled.

"There's the physical evidence," he said. "We got away from it earlier."

"It was busy then," Mint pointed out.

"There he is," Aaron cried.

Mint's head snapped left to see Bruce stepping out of the treeline, a long way down the road. His head turned to look their way and he began to run away from them, towards ground zero.

*

His legs ached awfully, today had been too energetic. However, Bruce knew if he was caught by Sergeant Harris and the tall man they'd carry on keeping the townspeople in the dark about what was happening out here. He didn't really know what was going on but he felt, deep inside, he would discover the secret if he could only reach the site of the hydrogen fuel plant.

Looking back over his shoulder as he ran, Bruce saw the 4x4 had started to chase him, thought he could see more vehicles behind. He looked forwards again and tried to run faster. The fuel plant was there, in all its glory of shiny steel panels and pipes. He began to slacken his pace when he remembered shiny bits of metal in the dust cloud he'd witnessed from afar. How could the plant look so complete after an event like that? Yet, when he next raised his eyes he spotted broken pipes and layers of dust and debris; it must be the exertion, making his sight less than perfect.

A great engine roar sounded behind him. Bruce turned wide eyes to see the 4x4 bearing down on him, evil-looking spikes reaching out from its bumper to impale him. With a terrified shriek he accelerated once more.

*

"It's in his head, it must be," Mint shouted to Aaron from her precarious lean through the open window. "He's not acting like he can hear me at all. Come alongside, I'll try to grab him."

She felt the 4x4 accelerate and looked beyond Bruce, tried to estimate the distance to the yawning chasm where the hydrogen fuel plant once stood. She didn't like the result of her mental calculations.

"We're not going to make it," Aaron had reached the same conclusion.

"I'm not giving up," Mint yelled back.

*

It was right there; just a few more strides and Bruce could escape through the door, inside the plant. He looked over his shoulder and knew the 4x4 couldn't catch him now. A victory grin lit up his face as he reached for the handle and felt the ground disappear beneath his feet. The screech of tyres sounded from behind as he fell, his eyes only now seeing the pit into which he was descending.

*

"No!" Mint screamed.

Bruce had just run straight over the edge. Before her unbelieving eyes, he'd just run on and fallen, never realised what was happening. Aaron spun the wheel and jammed the brakes on. The 4x4 slewed to a stop several metres from the pit, sent a shower of gravel and assorted debris

94

tumbling over the jagged edge of ground. They both stared, open-mouthed at the great rip in the ground next to them; a yawning chasm with bare, jagged rock walls, descending beyond view.

"What the fuck?" Aaron whispered in disbelief.

Bruce's body floated into view, legs kicking and arms windmilling as though still falling, yet his body was rising. He began to rotate, still moving as before and spun around several times before settling horizontally, arms and legs still active.

Another figure began to appear. Mint knew it was Old Tom from the tattered and torn garments hanging in strips, but the face was quite unrecognisable. All the flesh had now melted away, exposing red raw internal tissue. Gouges ran across the face, muscles and tendons in stark, full view. Teeth were hanging loose, the tongue hung down below the jawline.

"My new host body has arrived," the resonant, deep voice boomed out again. "The body I have been forced to inhabit was easy to infiltrate, the owner weak and addictive, but this puny flesh and bone was worn and tired even before I channelled my powers. It has fared poorly. I know how to shield one of these pathetic human bodies properly now and shall ensure maximum usage of the next. This adolescent will suit my purpose for much time to come. Your bodies, however, are not required here at this time. Begone; I shall not suffer your presence, return to your habitation so I may feed as you cry out in terror."

The almost skeletal hand waved and the 4x4 skidded sideways, spinning and rocking all the way back to the end of the road. Suddenly coming to a halt, inertia caused the 4x4 to teeter on two wheels before it slammed back down upright, shaking Mint and Aaron violently.

"Fuck, fuck, fuck," Aaron slammed his palm against the steering wheel with each curse.

"I think we should move," Mint cried.

Aaron followed her gaze to see a roiling cloud of dust and debris approaching. The rear tyres spun, caught traction and the 4x4 shot back towards Charlestown.

*

Bruce stared down the long, dark tunnel to the light at the end. It was focussed on a body, horribly mutilated with all the internal muscles and organs on clear display. One moment he had been falling into an endless pit, the next he was in this tunnel, staring at the body. It had been upright at first, although he couldn't be quite sure about the accuracy of that. A body in that state couldn't stand on its own; the owner would be very dead. He knew for certain it had fallen, remembered watching the splat of blood and gore as it crumpled into a heap. There was no sound to accompany the vision, though. That was strange, why couldn't he hear anything?

"You are held prisoner inside your own mind," the deep, overly baritone voice came from all around. Bruce wanted to spin and turn, seek out the speaker but found himself paralysed and trapped. "Ha," the malevolent voice laughed at his panic. "Your fear and terror would be sweet if only I could extract it for nourishment. Instead, as the new possessor of your physical form I can only revel in your entrapment. Time will come for feeding eventually, I have work to do. Here, I shall place your essence into a dream room where your inevitable slide into insanity and despair will be forestalled."

Bruce found himself in his bedroom. He ran to the door but it was locked, wouldn't budge no matter how hard he tugged and hammered at it with his fists. Turning, he rushed across to the window and opened the blinds. A blank, bare wall faced him. It felt incredibly real and unyielding to his probing fingers and frantic pushes. This was his prison, then. His own room, with no entry or exit. Bruce flopped onto his bed and wept.

*

Mint saw Roman waiting as they drew near the roadblock. Aaron's people rushed to create an opening and closed it once they had driven through. She stepped out as soon as the vehicle stopped and turned to stare back at the forest.

"We are in deep, deep shit," she said to Aaron as he exited the vehicle, his face equally as drawn and frightened as hers.

"No Bruce," Roman stated.

"It was in his head," Mint turned sorrowful eyes on him. "We had no chance. How do I tell his family?" Her bottom lip began to quiver and tears trickled from her eyes.

Aaron watched as Roman drew her into a consoling embrace, looked away when her eyes found his. He reached into the 4x4 and withdrew his command-pad, stared at the screen for a time. It was still logged on to the surveillance feed and showed nothing but the now familiar static fuzz over the site. He tapped the screen several times and frowned at the new display.

"I'm sorry to break you two up but this is important," Aaron said to Mint and Roman. "The area of static over that site has increased in breadth. I can only take that as a bad sign."

"It's a bad sign alright," Mint drew her frame upright and placed a hand on Roman's arm, nodded her thanks. "It's getting stronger, that's why. You heard what it said: return to your habitation so I may feed as you cry out in terror, wasn't it?" Aaron nodded. "It's feeding off our emotions, the gravity of the moons, whatever. It can infiltrate our minds and influence our dreams, our waking thoughts, just like it did to Bruce. It wants us to be afraid; it grows in power from us."

"I agree," Aaron nodded again. "But why now? What's triggered it to reveal itself now? Charlestown has been here forty-eight years, why has it waited 'til now?"

"Who cares?" Mint replied, louder than she intended. Aaron's people turned inquisitive eyes on the pair.

"Because if we can ascertain that, we may find a weakness, a way to fight back."

"You are kidding, right?" Mint was incredulous. "We have nothing to go against that. We don't even know if we can cause it physical harm. Hell, it may not have physicality outside of the bodies it possesses."

"Soon my resting body will rise and you will know fear and I will feed – that's what it said earlier," Aaron said calmly. "And now it's opened up that hole. Who knows how deep that is? It could have been slowly gaining enough power since we arrived on this planet to work its way up to the surface. I have to believe it has a physical form that we can combat. If not, as you've said before, we're finished here. So, what do you want to do, give in and cry, or join me and try to beat it?"

Mint wiped her sleeve across her eyes and looked from Roman to Aaron. She let out a little half laugh with a shrug and put both hands on her hips, squared up to Aaron. "I have a town of over seven thousand people back there," she stated. "Do you think I really have a choice?"

"I already know you haven't, I was waiting for you to realise that," Aaron replied. "I need you. Or rather, I need the Police Sergeant I first met who didn't get emotional. Is she still here, can I count on her?"

"You're a hard-nosed, tough son of a bitch, Aaron," Mint said, her face set. "Do you never get emotionally involved?"

"I find it easier to get my job done when I don't allow myself to do so."

"Well that's good for you. I need to be emotionally involved to work with my people properly. It's not a weakness, it's essential as a human being," Mint poked Aaron in the chest.

"Welcome back," he grinned. Mint reacted with an annoyed frown. "I need your people to get everybody off the streets and into their homes, can you do that?"

"How soon?" Mint held up her command-pad.

"Given that thing's growth, sooner rather than later; half an hour?"

"It'll be tough but I can work on that," Mint turned to leave.

"No, you and Roman stay here. You're resourceful, I may need you. Issue the order and control events from here."

"That's not a good idea," Mint argued. "My constables won't understand the order and if they can't explain it the citizens will get scared. That's going to be a lot of fear to feed you know what."

"We have to work with what we've got and how we can. Be creative, issue the order."

"This is Sergeant Harris," Mint spoke into the command-pad. "We have an emergency venting situation out at the hydrogen fuel plant. I need Charlestown's streets cleared; everybody is to return home and remain indoors until given permission to leave. You have thirty minutes. Constable Fletcher, report back once that order is carried out, not before."

"Thank you," Aaron turned to his own command-pad. "I don't know how that thing is with electronics so I'm going to order a gravity strike from an orbital platform. Drop it right into that hole, see if we can blow the sucker out of Oblivion."

"Out of Oblivion?" Roman queried.

"Yeah, my pet name for this planet, Obsirion II becomes Oblivion, get it?"

Mint and Roman exchanged a worried look as Aaron tapped away.

*

The British Corporation boasted a proud history of self-reliance. Space-based technology was one of its biggest successes; it exported its specialist knowledge and capabilities. The Lightning name for aerial vehicles traced its lineage all the way back to the 20th century, its latest incarnation being a wholly space based, ugly but effective system. It combined powerful surveillance instruments with active response systems for dealing with errant space based objects. It had also been used a handful of times to make strikes on planetary targets.

Aaron's order was swiftly approved by the Obsirion II overseer, fortuitously in the midst of a visit to Space Station 1. The three person crew on the boxy spaceship detached it from its docking umbilical and fired quick spurts from its manoeuvring thrusters to set the correct heading and drift a sufficient distance away from the command structure before initiating a sustained burn from its main engines. Crews worked on rotational shifts to ensure a quick reaction was possible to newly detected threats. This enabled the orbital asset to deploy within fifteen minutes of Aaron's order. A message was pinged back to his command-pad as soon as the main engine burn was initiated, reported an ETA above the target in forty minutes.

*

To assist in mounting an effective operation, Mint had split communications with her on-duty constables between herself and Roman. She had tried really hard to maintain a professional demeanour, to keep the inevitable tones of fright, worry, and trepidation out of her voice. Whether it had worked or not, she was not entirely convinced, however, the mission had been completed successfully, albeit ten minutes later than planned.

"All streets confirmed clear, Sergeant. Charlestown is silent." Constable Fletcher reported over the command-pad.

"Copy that, Constable Fletcher," she finally allowed herself a tight smile. "Set up a regular patrol pattern to ensure it stays that way."

"I'll stay at my current rank, thank you," Roman grinned across at her. "Don't ever ask me to take the Sergeant's exam."

"I'm not planning on going anywhere," Mint replied. "If we get through this, you can count on it."

"Who's going where?" Aaron asked. He had arrived at the 4x4's window at the end of the conversation.

"Roman," Mint's smile disappeared as she turned to look at the Department 44 agent. "He's just confirmed he doesn't want my job."

"In this situation, who would?" Aaron replied. "Time to deployment is now set at fifteen minutes. Are your citizens off the streets?" Mint nodded. "Look, you two have proved very capable, you've both held up remarkably well to a rapidly developing state of affairs. How would you react to a job offer from me?"

"I'd probably say yes, if not for Hayley and Daniel," Roman said. "I don't see them enough now, let alone if I was working away for days on end."

"Really?" Mint shot him a quizzical look. "I'm flattered, I really am," she turned back to Aaron. "But, I don't know. Ask me again, if we survive. Anyway, I've been thinking, what's to stop this Varla, whatever it is, from feeding off the kinetic and chemical energy of your weapon?"

"We still have no real idea of its abilities," Aaron shrugged. "Bullets didn't bother it so I'm trying a much bigger stick. What I'm hoping for is direct obliteration, if not, closure of that chasm to trap it underground while we work on Plan B. If it does suck up the energy, at least we've increased our knowledge of the enemy."

"What's our exposure to the blast at this distance?" Mint asked.

"The warhead is set to detonate at fifty metres below sea level or on impact if the chasm proves shallower than that," Aaron stated. "We haven't gone nuclear, although it is a high-yield chemical explosive compound. We'll feel the shockwaves in the ground and may get a level of buffeting from atmospheric blast waves should the detonation be shallow; nothing more."

"Somehow, I'm not reassured," Mint said quietly to Roman after Aaron had wandered away. "Did you really mean that about the job offer?"

*

One hundred and eighty kilometres above the planet, the Lightning arrived above its target and set velocity for a brief period of geosynchronicity. The missile had been programmed to target the exact coordinates of the recently destroyed hydrogen fuel plant. Its pylon mounting rotated downwards and stopped.

A green light confirmed 'ready to go' status on the weapons officers control console. She flipped back the cover to reveal the launch button and jabbed at it with her finger.

The missile detached and fired a two second burn from its engine. It entered a ballistic trajectory, movable fins awaiting an atmosphere to operate against before they could refine the missile's flight.

*

Mint and Roman opened the 4x4's doors and stood on the bodywork to watch for the approaching weapon. Aaron had just shouted confirmation of a successful launch. It was another bright day, forcing them to shield their eyes from the glaring sun with one hand whilst the other clung to the roof. All around them Aaron's team also stood and looked up. They had all donned dark sunglasses.

Mint could feel her heart beginning to pound again and wondered if the Varla was receiving another good feed from her fraught emotional state. Could it really be this easy? If what Aaron was revealing was indeed the truth, these Varla K'dyamon had been around a hell of a lot longer than the human race. Would one really succumb to their weapons technology? She looked across at Roman who didn't notice her glance and continued to regard the sky with scientific interest.

"Here it comes!" Aaron's squad leader spotted it first and pointed.

Mint followed her finger just in time to see a streak of silver slash a path through the sky and disappear behind the treeline. She waited. They all waited. Nothing happened.

"Was that a dud?" Aaron called into his command-pad.

Mint couldn't hear the response but did see Aaron's expression harden. He looked her way and began a slow, perplexed stroll over.

"Time for Plan B," he announced. "The missile was fully functional and reporting 100% efficiency and accuracy until it reached sea level. At that point contact was lost, you know the rest."

"Evacuate my town," Mint said, her tone brooking no refusal.

Aaron nodded and turned to stare at the distant tree fringed hillside, temporarily defeated. Mint's expression softened as she considered the weight on his shoulders and was about to attempt a reassuring comment when he straightened suddenly. She followed his gaze and stumbled off her slim perch on the 4x4's door shelf. She had spotted a small figure arcing through the sky, headed their way. Mint righted herself as the body of Bruce Webster landed gently on the road, just beyond the roadblock.

Aaron's people responded quickly, ten assault rifles were trained on the thirteen year old body. Bruce's face showed no signs of the malady that afflicted Old Tom's skin, his eyes stared, hard and steely. He flicked from one soldier to the next, a contemptuous smile on his face. The evil look on what should be an innocent face was horribly incongruous.

"Lower your weapons," Aaron ordered. He stepped forward with Mint and Roman flanking him. "They'll be no use."

"You sought to destroy me," Bruce's mouth opened but didn't move as the voice boomed out. "Why would you make this pathetic attempt? You already knew your primitive weaponry was incapable of harming me." His gaze locked on Aaron who suddenly clutched at his head with both hands, as though in pain. Mint and Roman grabbed hold of him, prevented him from toppling to the ground. Their arms strained as they took his weight.

Aaron was released as Bruce's eyes settled on a trooper to one side. He began to dance on the spot, slapping at his body repeatedly until he sank to the floor in a foetal position, hands covering his head, whimpering softly.

"Enough!" Mint shouted. She surprised herself with her calm demeanour. "We know what you're capable of, we've seen it before." Bruce's eyes swung to her and she saw her parents stood in front of her, large as life. Mint recognised the clothing they wore and sank to her knees, tears streaming down her face. That last day, their final day, the day their life force was crushed out of them by the falling tree.

"Stop it!" she screamed. "They're dead. They're not in front of me."

Bruce's face contorted as the vision in Mint's eyes changed to show her parents' vehicle approaching a forested stretch of road. She moaned as the tree began to topple, weakened by a local bacterial form that infected xylem and rotted tree trunks from the inside. Mint's head dropped to her resting knees where she cried, soft and low.

"It's not real," Roman shouted at her, still supporting Aaron. "Your parent's died eleven years ago. It's in your head, fight it."

"I can't" she sobbed. "It's too strong … too strong."

"You've proved your point," Aaron stammered, straightening up unsteadily. "You're powerful, you can affect us however you like. I get it. What do you want from us? Can we not live side by side?"

Bruce's gaze flicked back to Aaron. Mint was released from her torture. Aaron locked his eyes on the thirteen year old figure twenty metres away. He held his hand out for Mint, helped her stumble up from the road surface but held the stare without losing focus. The seconds stretched on as Mint wiped her eyes dry, streaked dirt across her face.

"You bastard," she spat out, her voice filled with hatred. "You know you're more advanced than we are, powerful and ancient. We're insignificant, still taking little baby-steps compared to you, yet you delight in mocking us, using us, toying with us …"

"You are as nothing in the great scheme," the voice cut her off. "Insignificant indeed but necessary; you expel such energy that I desire. I yearn to feed upon you, restore my magnificence to long remembered heights. I will arise and attain dominion once more."

"You feed off our energy, ok," Aaron said. "Our sensors showed you received a great meal from the moons when they aligned. Why can't you leave us alone, let us carry on while you feed off that energy until you can leave? Better still, travel to a volcano and feed off that."

"Do not presume to dictate my actions. I will do as I please to regain my long lost majesty. You are low in my reckoning, no more significant than the cattle and chickens your species once reared as food animals. I can and will continue to expend inconsequential examples of my power to receive a sweet meal of prodigious size. Here, have your missile back."

They all gazed with open mouths and terror flooding their insides as the missile rose at speed from behind the treeline and spiralled through the sky. It stopped, to a collective gasp, and hung in the air ten metres above them.

"Sweet indeed," the voice exulted as the emotional energy flooded over it. "I want more!"

Bruce's body rose into the air again and floated to the missile. Arms stretched out, and the Varla cradled the much larger missile, eyes wandering over the fear-filled faces beneath.

"Yes, so much sweeter," it said and hurtled off towards town.

Mint watched the figure recede into the distance and stumbled slightly as she attempted to regain some composure. The voice of the Varla came again, as though it was directly overhead, not several miles distant.

"You have tried to destroy me and failed," it said. "Now I hold your weapon of destruction to use as I will. How would it affect your little Charlestown, I wonder? I shall leave it here. When I release it to drop and erase you, I have yet to decide. It could be in ten of your seconds, five of your hours, two of your days. I will enjoy reaping your response until such time as I grow bored, or my appetite is sated."

Bruce's body flashed across the sky once more to descend from sight behind the distant hill. Nobody watched though. All eyes were fixed on the missile as it hung, suspended in the sky, two hundred metres above the centre of Charlestown.

*

Bruce had been forced to watch the descent of the missile. His body's possessor had been aware of the weapon as soon as it entered the atmosphere. The screen in the facsimile of Bruce's bedroom sprang to life to show it plummeting through the air. Bruce tried turning away but found that whichever way he turned his view was always towards the screen. This Tiada Vejour that had possessed him, whatever it was, had powers and abilities far beyond Bruce's understanding, with an evil intent to match.

Despite the contempt that Tiada Vejour radiated at the military strike against it, Bruce still winced when the weapon reached ground level, expected a violent resolution. The Varla K'dyamon had found that amusing.

Flying through the air had been partly exhilarating. Bruce had chided himself for enjoying it and tried to look away again, unsuccessfully, when the mind tortures began. Tiada Vejour seemed to grow somehow as a result and Bruce listened carefully to try and understand what was occurring. Instead of being frightened now, a prisoner in his own brain, he was trying to treat it like one of his computer games – a fully immersive one. So, he thought, energy, in all its forms, is your food. You're growing stronger as you absorb it. You aren't fully charged yet though, are you? I can feel that, I may be a prisoner here but I can pick up what's occurring. Is that a weakness to use? Except, he thought, energy makes up everything. It's the universal constant, never lost, just changed in form and dispersed until concentrated again.

He became aware his body was flying once more and quelled his thoughts; he didn't want the Varla K'dyamon to get wind of his plan to gain greater understanding of his captor.

*

Finally, something exciting is happening in Charlestown - that was the first thought in Kristopher Manson's mind after the unexpected declaration boomed inside his head. Once the pain subsided, he had dashed across the main room in his third floor apartment to stare out of the window and obtain visual confirmation of the impossibly hanging missile.

Kris had followed orders from the local police and left the boring and tedious refuse collection tasks of his job happily. He wasn't always so pleased to see or hear from the fuzz. His corporation record displayed three convictions, each leading to community service sentences. Of course, if all the crimes he was responsible for had been discovered, he would be dragging his heels in the corporation prison just outside New Cambridge.

He was only twenty-five years old and hated life on Obsirion II. Why had his parents found it necessary to join this ridiculous colonisation experiment? Life on Earth looked so much easier and pleasurable than this drudge. Human technological advance had progressed so well, yet here, on the fringes of civilisation, they enjoyed very few of its benefits. He was damned if he should work himself bored and broken to build a planetary habitat where people would only get to enjoy the Earth-style life in another hundred years; he might not even be alive then. Kris had enquired about migration to Earth but was informed it was not possible at this time; maybe in another twenty years, if his record remained clear of fresh convictions.

The only comfort he took from his wasted life on this backwater arsehole of a planet was the small group of acquaintances he met up with regularly. Like him, they resented their unlucky home by birth and were counted amongst the 'persons of interest' by the local police; most had a number of convictions for petty offences. Sergeant Harris and her cronies knew them all by sight, so they rarely managed to spend unobserved time together in the town's limited range of cafes and public drinking houses. The Taste of Java café was definitely out.

No, Kris had to arrange get-togethers at home apartments. His was the location of their next meeting, supposedly tomorrow. They never achieved much, just drank, let off steam and fantasised about a better life. That, in itself, drove him to angry bouts of frustration. His friends recognised the warning signs when such a fit was building and steered clear of him; he had inflicted injuries to more than one of them. He wondered how many would be able to join him tomorrow; this missile threat would no doubt lead to a curfew.

"I feel your sense of contempt and disillusionment, your desire for more than this world can offer," that same voice rumbled in his head. Kris's hands reached up to cover his ears from the pain it caused. "I can offer you an outlet, perhaps departure from this place eventually. Power and authority can be yours."

"Fuck off," Kris said, although he didn't know if that was the correct way to reply. "You want to kill us all. Your voice hurts inside my head."

"Pain is good, pain confirms your existence," the voice boomed again. "But, as I have need of you, I will acquiesce to your need for painless communication. Is this more to your comfort?"

"Much better," Kris agreed, the voice had reduced to a tolerable level and he was intrigued, nobody had ever said they needed him before. "What do you need me for?"

"I will need strong followers like you to do my bidding, keep the local population in check, ensure they perform as I require. You will have authority over those you despise, your choice of home and the petty items you desire. In time, as my power grows, you will travel, maybe even leave this planet. I sense you are willing to accept my proposal. Even more, you know of others who feel as you do."

"That missile will still kill me when it falls, why should I agree to your offer?" Kris had to admit the offer was tempting.

"I am Tiada Vejour and I alone will choose who lives or dies. You have this one opportunity to join me willingly and receive my rewards. Make your choice."

"Ok," Kris had already come to his decision. "One thing, I want Sergeant Harris and her constables dead."

"Sergeant Harris opposes my plans, it will be necessary to exterminate her and others before the end. Here is what I want you to do."

Kris' mind received the instructions from the Varla K'dyamon. A sly smile slowly spread across his face.

*

Empty streets at this time of day, 1330 hours, were an eerie prospect for Mint and Roman as they trundled slowly along the main road. Of course, the missile hanging motionless above the town centre was scarier still. Every so often a curtain or set of blinds would twitch as a citizen observed them passing by. Mint's mind was in turmoil now. The reconciliation of what had occurred over the past three days no longer consumed her conscious thoughts. She had demanded Aaron arrange evacuation procedures for the townsfolk but had to doubt the wisdom of that move now. How would Tiada Vejour react to its source of nourishment being carried away? It could easily allow the missile to drop; the brief wave of intense terror created, along with the energy from the chemical explosion, would provide it with a colossal meal.

A police vehicle cruised across the main road in front of them, headed into another residential side road. After Tiada Vejour's speech, Mint had called all her staff and permitted her married constables to return home and attend to their families; the single officers had all agreed to remain on duty. It pleased her to still drive through empty streets in the administrative and business area at the centre of town. There wasn't even a crowd waiting outside the police station. Just Penny, Trent and Gretta Webster.

Mint left Roman to park her 4x4 and drew Penny into a sobbing embrace when she ran up to the frantic parents.

"We tried, we really tried," Mint said. "But the Varla K'dyamon had got into Bruce's mind and we couldn't reach him in time."

Trent tried to speak but his voice failed him. Mint and Penny remained in the embrace and drew in Gretta for a few seconds.

They finally separated and walked in together while Mint relayed the previous events of the day. Roman was already busy brewing up steaming mugs of coffee which he carried over and distributed when they took seats in the main office; Mint's personal office was too small for all of them.

"How do we get our son back?" Trent asked, getting straight to the point.

"I don't know, and I can't and won't give you false hope," Mint shook her head. "We are so severely outmatched here, I don't even know if I can save the town's population. But, if we can find a weakness I want to hurt that son of a bitch and hurt it bad."

"Not if it hurts my Bruce," Penny suddenly looked up from wiping her tearful eyes.

"No, of course not," Mint stretched out a reassuring hand to cover Penny's.

The command-pad, placed on a desk next to Mint, emitted a soft ping and buzzed noisily. She looked down at it to see an incoming call from Pete Field.

"Excuse me," she said. Mint pushed her office door closed before she answered. "Pete, how much do you know?"

"Aaron has filled me in. Do you still want to go ahead with an evacuation?"

"I don't know, Pete," Mint replied. "We have no way of knowing how this Varla K'dyamon would react to that. I've reconciled myself to the expectation it will drop the missile eventually."

"Aaron's flying in a specialist team," Pete told her. "He wants to see if they can disarm the missile remotely. What do you think?"

"I think we are massively outmatched, Pete, that's what I think. I don't see what we can do. This thing manipulates energy at will, who's to say it can't make the warhead detonate even if the electronics are tampered with?"

"Ok, I'm sorry, Mint. You're in a tough position, for sure," Pete said. "We're putting together a multi-disciplinary team here in an effort to brainstorm resolutions for you. How about putting your citizens underground? That may help mitigate the effects of the explosion."

"No way, Pete. This thing started underground. Jaicon Hewson worked two levels below ground and he's the first person I can pinpoint as being affected. I wouldn't want to congregate crowds, anyway, too much energy to attract the Varla."

"You have to make an announcement, let people know what's happening. Otherwise, you will end up with people gathering, demanding answers."

"Yeah," Mint sighed. "That'll be my next job. I have Trent and Penny Webster here at the moment."

"You're holding together well, Mint. Aaron's expressed his gratitude for your work. I'll leave you to it."

"It doesn't feel like it," Mint whispered to herself as Pete closed the connection. She stood from where she was perched on a corner of her desk and turned to look into the main office. She could only see Roman out there. "Where have they gone?" she asked as she joined him.

"Not home unfortunately," Roman replied. "Too many reminders of Bruce there, apparently. We talked briefly about Gabriel and how he's been orphaned. They've gone to visit him in hospital."

"Ok, I wish they'd gone home, but I understand. Roman, I need you to access the emergency broadcast channel, set it to activate all receivers and play on repeat until acknowledged."

"No problem, Mint," Roman took to a seat immediately and began to access the system. "Do you want Charlestown Media Broadcasting involved?"

"No direct involvement," Mint shook her head. "Just send them the recording."

"As you wish," Roman smiled at her. "It'll be ready in a couple of minutes; you might want to sort out your script."

*

"Citizens of Charlestown, I've had dealings with many of you, for those I have not met yet, I am Sergeant Mint Harris, your local chief of police. These are strange times in the short history of Charlestown and by working together and following official advice, I am sure we can navigate our way through and come out the other side. No doubt you are all aware of the weapon hanging above the centre of town; I believe Tiada Vejour made quite certain of that."

"This all started with the murder of Jaicon Hewson, a crime I have confirmed today is attributable to Tiada Vejour. Who, exactly, is Tiada Vejour? I cannot give you the definitive answer you are hoping for, however, I can tell you the British Corporation is treating our interaction with it as an alien first contact event. Sadly, it appears to be hostile to humanity. What do we know about it so far? I wish I could admit to more knowledge, an in-depth appraisal of our adversary, but sadly that is not the case. Tiada Vejour has told us it is 'of the Varla K'dyamon' but we don't know for certain what that means. It could be its race. It feeds off energy, in all forms, as far as we can tell. That includes emotional energy and brain waves, and is the reason for the missile hanging above our town. It is there to sow fear and panic, foster feelings of dread and terror. It is perfectly normal, sane and rational for you to feel that way, but I need you to fight those feelings as hard as you can."

"At present, Tiada Vejour is a non-physical threat although, as you have been made to witness, it can manipulate energy and even get into your heads, it is the cause of the epidemic of nightmares. Bruce Webster's body has been temporarily possessed and I promise to you all we will work our hardest to get Bruce back, free from possession, alive and well. Evidence points towards the physical body of Tiada Vejour being far underground, in the location of the hydrogen fuel plant. That location is out of bounds and must not be approached. The authorities in New Cambridge are aware of all local events and assure me they are working on a solution. I ask you to remain at home, stay off the streets and keep your communications open. Remember, this entity feeds off your fear and other emotions, try to remain calm."

*

"Nice broadcast," Aaron said as he stepped into the main office at the police station.

Mint stared at him, his access all areas capability no longer troubled her, she simply wanted to assess his demeanour after that two word welcome. Was he being facetious? She didn't detect any hint of flippancy.

"It may not be perfect," she replied, a note of defence in her tone. "People will be scared and we don't need that, it'll only feed the Varla K'dyamon. If I don't broadcast there'll be widespread fear, if I do, I have to explain and there'll be widespread fear. We're in a shitty situation and that's the best I could come up with."

"Relax," Aaron turned those ice blue eyes on her, pierced her mask. "I agree, you have to broadcast and, as it happens, I like what you said. I need a central base of operations and want it to be this station. Are you happy with that?"

"I can't stop you," Mint held up her hand, the instant response had slipped out. "I'm sorry, ignore that. It makes sense. Our people need to work together if we're going to try and achieve some resolution to this that doesn't involve that missile dropping."

"Good, thank you," Aaron smiled; a different expression to the disarming grin he'd utilised earlier in the car park. Mint wondered if that was the real smile of the man. "You'll have all the necessary technology and connections here, it saves a hell of a lot of time," he continued. "Let's get our people working together, coordinate the response. I'm flying in two more tactical units to help out. They're bringing some weapons specialists and an actual science team with them; we need to get proper readings and insight into how this thing works. The specialists will attempt remote contact with the missile, try to nullify it. I'm putting your evacuation on hold for the time being, we don't want to force Tiada Vejour into further acts."

"You said the markings on the rock wall match some markings from the Starjump constructs," Roman said. "Are we at a level of cooperation

113

where I can study the two sets side by side?"

"I'll take any help at this stage," Aaron nodded at him. His command-pad rose for a moment while his fingers worked at the screen. "There, I've temporarily granted you access and sent a message with the file location, knock yourself out."

"Thanks," Roman grinned. "I'll be in the lab if you need me."

"Getting him out from under your feet or a real proposition?" Mint asked after her SOC constable had disappeared.

"He has an analytical brain," Aaron replied. "If he can come up with anything, I'll be eternally thankful. Now …" his command-pad emitted a loud chiming alarm. "What now?"

Mint shuffled around to see his screen. It showed a hover-jet overflying the greenhouse belt.

"We have a media hover-jet from New Cambridge making an unauthorised entry to restricted airspace," the voice of Aaron's squad leader came through loud and clear. "It has refused to respond to all communications."

"Fire a warning shot, I'm not playing around with these people," Aaron said, his voice hard.

"Aye, sir."

"What if that doesn't dissuade them?" Mint asked.

"Then I escalate," Aaron replied.

"Constable Fletcher," Mint called across the room. "Patch into New Cambridge media broadcasts; let's see what they can see."

Aaron strode across the room to watch the relevant screen, Mint matched his pace. The view was on a high zoom setting but currently showed nothing more than a close up of the treeline. Mint looked back at Aaron's command-pad to estimate the hover-jet's position. It had edged out over the fields, still advancing.

"No response from the hover-jet to the warning shot, sir," the squad leader reported.

"Standby, squaddie," Aaron said. "Let's see what they're seeing."

"Can you jam their transmission?" Mint asked.

"Mm-hmm," Aaron was concentrating on the screen.

A break in the trees could now be made out where the access road cut through. Slowly the hover-jet advanced, crept the view along the road towards the car park. The body of Old Tom slid into view, making the footage judder for a brief time. Then, digital zoom kicked in until picture quality started to suffer. The old man's skin had totally fallen away; his body looked oddly flattened as the inner contents sagged and spread out, their support system diminished. A clawed foot appeared making the picture jump and jiggle once more. The digital zoom was rapidly drawn back to reveal a host of demonic figures. Their well-muscled bodies ranged from bright reds to deep burgundies above which grotesque faces were festooned with horns, jagged spikes, sharp teeth and blazing eyes. They all carried evil-looking guns loaded with various, vicious projectiles. A plethora of wickedly curved knives, tridents and spears were strapped to their backs. Behind them the chasm yawned into view, flames belching from a lake of molten orange-red ooze. A thick, grey-black cloud, shot through with fiery flickers and deep shadows boiled up from the surface.

"Jam that transmission," Aaron ordered.

They watched the screen as it flickered once, but the alarming vision remained.

"I said jam it!" Aaron shouted.

"We have! Our jamming is being negated," a voice cried back over the command-pad.

"It's using them," Mint pointed out. "This sort of footage will swell people's fear."

"I know … squaddie, take it down," Aaron sighed.

Mint clenched her jaw. Could she make such an order? Hurried shouts echoed out of the command-pad followed by the sound of bolts being driven into the ground. Mint leaned in close to see a three metre long mobile laser cannon being mated with the tripod recently bolted down. The squad leader took charge, grasped the control levers and swung the weapon on target, a long power cable snaked out of the back. In the distance, the hover-jet appeared unaware of the drama playing out, the doom imminent. A bright bluey-white beam lanced out to connect momentarily with the flying craft. Destruction was swift; with an audible rumble and crash, the hover-jet disappeared in a great explosion that spread wreckage far and wide.

"Confirm destruction please, squaddie," Aaron ordered.

"All eyes saw it destroyed, sir," the squad leader replied. "We are no longer detecting transmissions and nothing is showing up on the sensors."

"I understand, thank you, squaddie."

"The screen's gone blank too," Mint pointed out the obvious for Aaron.

"It had to be done," Aaron looked squarely at her. "Tiada Vejour was scoring hugely from that footage. At least we know it can meddle with technology now. Those demons must have been plucked straight from Mr Parkes' imagination and planted in that view."

"Unless they were real," nobody had seen or heard Roman join them. "Varla K'dyamon, eh? Those last three syllables are very similar to demon aren't they? Or daemon as they used to spell it."

Mint and Aaron stood and watched silently as Roman returned to the lab.

"Fuck me!" Aaron exclaimed at last. "I told you he was analytical. Oh, I want him on my team. How could we not have picked up that connection before?"

"Whoa," Mint held her hands up. "Slow down, back track – what?"

"Ok, sorry, but this could be huge. The first Starjump construct was discovered when we sent the initial crewed deep-space mission to Proxima Centauri, yes? Now, that star is only four light years from Earth, give or take, and those machines are suspected to be millions of years old. Tiada Vejour must have travelled to Oblivion from the local one. If Roman's suspicion bears out, it suggests the Varla K'dyamon have similarly been to Earth."

"And provided the root for the ancient belief in demons and devils," Mint picked up the thread.

"But more than that, we're still here," Aaron grabbed her by the shoulders. "Maybe not this one, but humans have encountered the Varla K'dyamon before and survived."

Mint took a moment to process that and slowly started to perk up. It was, perhaps, the only piece of good news she had received all day.

*

It was hard. Like no project Bruce had ever attempted before. Tiada Vejour was totally ignoring him now, intent on feeding and making its plans. Every so often though, it would show him an outside event. The most recent had been destruction of a hover-jet. Bruce had noted the media name emblazoned on its side and guessed it was broadcasting images of the former hydrogen fuel plant. He soon understood the necessity for such violence; Tiada Vejour had sucked in an increased meal of energy until it was obliterated.

Bruce could feel his captor's energy reserves growing. He didn't know how, couldn't understand the mechanism, but he sensed the possession maybe had a feedback loop that also gave Bruce access to Tiada Vejour. Trying to keep that reverse connection secret was his top priority, followed by learning as much as he could about the Varla K'dyamon. It was an arrogant being, of that he was certain. He could feel its disdain for humans, but also its need to feed off their energy. That reliance on the 'primitive species' made it angry and drove its level of ferocity and inflicted torture whenever it had to deal with people.

Bruce's success so far had included the revelation that Varla Tiada, that was how it liked to refer to itself, had been aware of humans since first colonisation, fifty years ago. It had used up some of its low reserves of energy to influence construction of Charlestown above its deep subterranean resting place. After that, it had slowly fed off human energy while intermittent gluts of gravitational energy charged it when alignment of the two moons occurred sufficiently nearby. Growth in the town's population had been welcomed and initiated a period of burrowing through the rock strata, headed for the surface. Varla Tiada had halted in a cavern just one hundred metres below the hydrogen fuel plant, a void the boring operation for the water pumps had missed by a matter of metres. Bruce had then experienced the memories of its instigation of nightmares and headaches, watched as Jaicon Hewson became a pawn to its will but stopped before the murder.

This was as far as Bruce had probed so far and he braced to continue. A flood of power came over his mind; he could sense how Varla Tiada had grown in capability since the burrowing operation. It was still just the Varla's essence at the planet's surface, its body remained below. The time was not yet right for that to arise. Bruce had felt the power grip his mind several times and it wasn't any less uncomfortable this time. He waited as the discomfort receded and strove to detect any indication Varla Tiada was aware of him examining its memories – nothing. He probed forwards, beyond the murder, and felt the influx of energy as the Varla reached out to deliver headaches and influence alpha and theta brain waves to deliver terror to slumbering minds. A split occurred when Old Tom was flown away in the hover-jet; Bruce chose to remain with the portion left behind at Charlestown.

Then, he became aware of a tap into the mind of Gabriel Parkes. Bruce watched that drama play out from this different point of view and grew angry when he sensed the Varla feed off his own reaction to Gabriel's behaviour. Bruce was now fully aware of the shadows and sounds, the flying monster that pursued Gabriel, in his mind only. Then, Gabriel fell, and Bruce felt the thrill in Varla Tiada as his friend tumbled, bounced, and landed in agony. Afterwards, Bruce could feel Constable Reckhart and then the doctor and paramedics working on his injured body, the trolley to the hover-jet, arrival in hospital and finally, blissful sleep. Not death, just a deep unconsciousness.

Bruce's mental eyes snapped open. He wasn't as connected to Varla Tiada anymore. He'd followed a separate thread to Gabriel. The Varla K'dyamon, in its split state, had never closed its connection to Gabriel's brain and, in its arrogance and drive for more energy, did not know it was still open. Bruce concentrated hard to follow the same pathway again and arrived in Gabriel's drug blurred consciousness.

"I'm here, Gabriel," Bruce said. He didn't know if this was the correct way to contact his friend but it was worth a try. "You must wake up and tell everyone I'm still here. I'm alive but held prisoner by Tiada Vejour."

He didn't sense any response or recognition from Gabriel and pulled back. He didn't want to risk the connection for too long. Maybe, if he could just initiate two way communications with Gabriel, he could help the people of Charlestown fight this thing.

Day 4

A strange calm had befallen the police station following the destruction of the media hover-jet. Mint and Aaron worked closely afterwards, drew up patrol patterns, merged the two newly arrived tactical squads into their coverage, and deployed the weapons specialists and scientific analysis team. Time had flown by until Aaron had found Mint at her desk, the screen still lit up, her head on her desk, sound asleep. He shook her awake, embarrassed and made a persuasive argument for her to go home and get a proper rest. Mint had complied – eventually.

A shower had revived her but after climbing into bed, try as she might, she just couldn't fall asleep again. A call from Java had proved a welcome distraction and she arose with no intention of attempting sleep again. It was, weirdly, a calm, sisterly conversation; Java didn't ply her for up-to-date information. When the conversation ended, Mint dressed in a fresh uniform and drove through the night dark Monday morning streets. A police cruiser had mistakenly flashed its blue lights at her before recognition dawned. She continued her journey after a brief chat with the constable and extinguished her 4x4's headlights as she entered the illumination of the underground car park. Mint had taken painkillers before leaving home and jogged up the stairs, ignored the slight tingling behind her eyes.

The main office was orderly and quiet. She noted Aaron was in her office, fast asleep with his head on her desk. She issued a soft grin and left him alone. Roman was still working in his lab. On impulse, Mint withdrew her command-pad from a pocket and placed a call to her sister, she knew Java was having trouble settling down.

"Hi, Java, it's me again," she said, unnecessarily. "It's a twenty-three hour rolling shift here at the station. How would you feel about bringing in some refreshments?"

"Give me forty-five minutes," her sister answered enthusiastically and disconnected.

Mint replaced the command-pad in her pocket and sauntered into Roman's SOC laboratory.

"Have you had a break?" she asked.

"Fresh uniform," Roman turned and waved his hand in a flourish down his frame. "I headed home while you were asleep in your office and had a power-nap. Checked up on Hayley and Daniel, had to bring Dan down; he blames himself for Bruce's possession, silly kid. Been back here about twenty minutes, nothing's changed."

"Yeah, it's odd how quiet things are," Mint sat down next to him. "I don't like to think about it being the calm before the storm for … well, obvious reasons. It's so hard not to feel a looming presence, darkness at the edge of your thoughts and consciousness. Still, work will help. Have you made any progress?"

"Not much," Roman grimaced. "I've looked at the matching symbols from the Starjump construct and I can see it's a two dimensional geometrical glyph system of writing. Repeated elements are visible in multiple markings but there's no key to allow a deciphering process to run."

"So, you agree with Aaron then?" Mint asked. "The Varla K'dyamon are connected in some way to the Starjumps and visited Earth long ago."

"It's looking increasingly likely," Roman said. "I don't think their visit was within written history though. The AI can't find any relevant stories in the Earth knowledge databases. It's more likely to have been handed down through verbal history, fireside stories and the like. Fascinating, but no help in our current predicament. I'm just about to take a break from the symbols and run a side-by-side analysis of energy readings from orbital assets and visual recordings."

"I'll leave you to it, then," Mint stood with a hand on his shoulder. "Sounds tedious and boring to me but I'm sure you'll relish the challenge."

Mint closed the lab door as she left and sat on a nearby seat. She occupied her mind for half an hour with mundane admin before she grew irritated with it and scanned around the office. Several new screens had been set up, one of them showed the tactical situation around Charlestown with real-time locations of all personnel. Three people, presumably the weapons specialists, showed up on the roof of the town's municipal administration building. The missile was also represented on the map and displayed a 'warhead live' status. Mint tried to dismiss it from her thoughts. Another marker showed a pair of hover-jets at a landing area in the laboratory zone, their status read 'available for interception.'

"I don't want to risk more media aircraft making unexpected calls," Aaron said through a stifled yawn behind her.

"How do you do it?" Mint asked.

"Do what?"

"Live with the ramifications of your order to destroy that media jet earlier," Mint clarified.

"I use that detached side of my character you don't like," Aaron answered. "Do you deny that the order was necessary? They ignored our communications, the warning shot, and broadcast what I can only call propaganda from Tiada Vejour."

"No, I don't suppose I can," Mint admitted. "I couldn't bear that guilt, though. It's not that I don't like that rational, almost callous, part of you – it's just I don't understand it, I can't comprehend that lack of empathy."

"You have the safety and security of seven thousand people in this town to maintain, yes?" Aaron waited for Mint to nod agreement before he continued. "I have a job similar to that for over four million colonists. I have to compartmentalise my feelings and deny them as and when necessary. We're many years away from practical, physical assistance from Earth and have to rely on the resources available here and now. I'll admit I haven't been faced with a situation that comes anywhere close to this one, but I have to do my job regardless. I don't know how to counter

Tiada Vejour's capabilities, yet, but I have to believe there is a solution, some way to fight back, and wait for it to materialise."

"Catering!" Mint's reply was forestalled by Java's shout upon arrival. "I've got flasks of coffee, tea, hot chocolate and synth-bacon rolls."

"Your idea?" Aaron's eyes lit up with hunger.

"Family connections," Mint smiled. "I'll handle the human touch around here."

"Aunty Mint, Aunty Mint," Mikey ran at her with arms outstretched, passed Aaron as he approached Java.

"How's my little nephew?" Mint swept him up. "This is your first time in here isn't it?" Mikey was turning his head this way and that to see everything in the room. "This room is where we're working to make Charlestown safe again."

"No more nightbares?"

"We'll do our best, Mikey." Mint jumped him up and down in her arms until he collapsed on her in fits of giggles.

"Java says this is your special coffee," Aaron placed a mug on the desk next to her. "Hello there Mikey, what's that on your jumper?" he placed a finger on the boy's chest and tweaked his nose when Mikey looked down. Then, he poked him repeatedly, evading Mikey's defensive arms until the boy collapsed on Mint's shoulder in more unstoppable giggles.

"You have a heart after all," Mint looked at Aaron askance.

"My boy's just a little younger, back with his mother and baby sister in New Cambridge."

Mint didn't know what to say in reply to that bombshell. The coffee provided an excuse, kept her mouth busy while she processed that bit of news. Perhaps that's the secret to his drive, she thought. With a family to protect he could adopt a no messing attitude and steamroll to the conclusion he, and the corporation, deemed necessary. Mikey wriggled and she was forced to put the mug back on the desk.

"You didn't have me tagged as the family type – more the bachelor, wedded to his work?"

"That's very true," there was no point hiding the truth. "Go back to Mummy, Mikey."

They both watched the five year old charge back to Java and tuck into a plate of biscuits mistakenly left unattended. Java was busy serving a pair of constables and some of Aaron's people.

"I'll go and call some of the patrols back in to get their share, arrange a delivery to the roadblock," Aaron said.

"Aaron," Mint called to his retreating back. "I'm sorry. I've been a bit harsh on you, it wasn't deserved."

"Hold that thought," he replied. "Keep it for later."

*

It must be over three hours since his last connection to Gabriel, Bruce thought. He wasn't yet disheartened by his failure to elicit any direct response from his friend; he could sense the drugs in the other boy's system. Bruce reached out tentatively to assess Tiada Vejour's current status. It was distant, still in the local area though, so probably down with its physical body. Bruce had visited that monstrosity earlier, at the bottom of the chasm. It was large and very alien to his mind with peculiar biology. Still, if the Varla was preoccupied, that worked in his favour. The connection to Gabriel came easily to him now, like a shortcut on his desk screen.

"Gabriel, It's me again, Bruce. You must wake up when you can and tell people I can communicate through you."

Bruce waited but no obvious reply came to him.

*

"It's happening again," the male nurse told Doc Davidson over his medical-pad.

"The same increase as before?" Doc Davidson asked, taking to his feet and rushing out of the office.

"Stronger," the nurse replied.

*

"Gabriel, I'm back again. Sorry, I have to keep checking where Tiada Vejour is, I don't want to be discovered down this pathway. I know what happened to you now; I want to help people fight this thing. I need you to wake up to do that."

Bruce waited again but retreated to his bedroom with another failure ticked off.

*

"These brainwave patterns are definitely increasing alongside a slight increase in the rate of his heartbeat," Doc Davidson said. "He should be stable in this coma. Is it related to activity from the Varla K'dyamon?"

"No, I don't think so," the nurse replied. "I've reviewed the readings that coincide with the arrival of the missile yesterday, that blanket message sent to all people in town. They're of a similar nature and pattern, but the signature shows significant differences, enough for me to say the reception is of a similar energy but with a completely different ... I don't know how to describe it, intent?"

"How so?"

"It sounds ridiculous but I'd compare it to a data-pad call. The missile reading was shouted, blatant, forceful whereas, these other readings are like a whisper, a softer message coming through."

"Tiada Vejour ... Bruce," Gabriel mumbled quietly on the bed.

Doc Davidson and the nurse both turned to stare in surprise at their patient. Gabriel's head had also rolled slightly on the soft pillow. The nurse turned to interrogate the latest reading on the numerous monitors Gabriel was attached to.

"Not the same," he said. "This isn't another occurrence. More like the early stages of waking from sleep. That shouldn't be possible in this induced coma."

"No, it shouldn't. Keep reporting back to me, I'm going to contact Sergeant Harris."

*

Mint stared at the time, 0415 hours, then back at the caller's identity on her command-pad. Aaron wandered over and took a glance at the screen.

"Best you answer him," he said.

"I don't need more bad news, Doc," Mint said into the device.

"I don't know how to categorise this news," Doc Davidson sounded tired. "I wouldn't say it's bad, though. We're getting some strange readings from Gabriel Parkes. Brain activity, similar to that recorded when Tiada Vejour communicated, keeps occurring at irregular intervals. Don't worry; I don't think it's the same as when he was manipulated before the fall. It's softer, less piercing, and quite an enigma in all truth. This shouldn't be able to happen in a drug induced coma but Gabriel just moved his head and mumbled – he said Tiada Vejour, then Bruce."

"Something the Varla has planted in his head?" Aaron queried, leaning forward to speak into the device.

"I don't think so," Doc Davidson said after a moment. "It's too irregular for a biological virus or some such. I'd expect to see an exponential increase in strength, duration and rapidity which isn't the case. No, this is something else."

"I'll come over," Mint said.

*

Tiada Vejour had returned a short time after Bruce's last communication attempt. He had sat demurely in his facsimile bedroom as the Varla examined its energy store, felt the swell of satisfaction with its progress. Next he had been taken into space as the Varla extended itself outward and studied the orbital space stations. After the initial rush of space travel, Bruce had recognised the Varla's distracted concentration and returned to his bedroom. He sat on his bed for some time and searched for any indication of detection, but the Varla remained distant. Seizing the moment, he connected to Gabriel.

"It's me again. Tiada Vejour is growing stronger; it's studying our space stations at the moment. Gabriel, you must wake up and tell everyone what I know."

*

"Here we go again," the nurse sprang up.

Mint and Doc Davidson crowded round to look at the monitors. It was all gobbledygook to Mint.

"Vejour," Gabriel mumbled, "getting stronger."

"Is it in his head again?" Mint asked, alarmed.

"I don't think so," Doc Davidson said, stroking his chin. "It's still like a whisper in his mind."

"Space stations," Gabriel mumbled again.

"What?" Mint perked up. "That has no bearing on his previous connections with the Varla."

*

"Come on, Gabriel," Bruce continued. "I don't know how much longer I can evade Tiada Vejour's notice. I need you."

He waited but felt nothing and retreated to his bedroom.

*

"Bruce," Gabriel mumbled, "needs me."

"It happened again," the nurse confirmed. "Fresh spikes, immediately before the boy spoke."

"So, we have a definite correlation between the affected brain patterns and Gabriel's abnormal activity," Doc Davidson mused. "This is fascinating."

"Is it causing him pain?" Mint asked.

"No," Doc Davidson shook his head. "There's no active pain response in his brain waves."

"I wonder ..." Mint paced for a moment. "How well healed is he, could you safely revive him?"

"There's no medical imperative to awaken him. I'd signed off on a further twenty-three hours in this induced coma late yesterday. Why do you ask?" Doc Davidson raised his eyebrows at her.

"I think he's still in contact," Mint said. "Somehow, don't ask me how, I think he's patched in to the Varla. He's already told us it's getting stronger, he knows its name, he can't possibly know about Bruce, and he's mentioned space stations. He's got an open back door into the Varla's activity."

"That may be so," Doc Davidson replied. "However, Gabriel's medical condition is my paramount responsibility. Your suspicion is possible but is it probable? Either way, there is no medical imperative to stop his IV feed just so he can act as a spy; I'm not going to revive him on a whim."

"Ok, Doc, I understand," Mint said.

She patted him on the arm and left the room. The corridor seemed much longer as she slowly trudged along its length, her mind endlessly repeating what had just happened. Reaching the entrance, she turned a corner too sharply and tripped on a chair. Cursing, Mint righted herself and dropped onto the padded cushioning.

Gabriel had provided her with intelligence about the Varla; it was interested in the space stations, but why? She slapped her hand on the seat beside her. If only she could speak to Gabriel, carefully tease more information out of him. A thought came to her that she ruthlessly suppressed. She couldn't do that, it wasn't ethical; but, seven thousand people were dependent upon her. She slapped both hands either side of her face, ran them up to comb her fingers through her hair, grasp and tug. Her teeth clenched as she tugged and fought an inner battle. Tears rolled down her cheeks as she lifted her command-pad and put a call through to Aaron.

*

Mint was still in the seat when Doc Davidson found her ten minutes later; slumped over with her tear streaked face in her hands. He didn't speak for a moment as he stood and stared, then he prodded her shoulder.

Mint sat up as though she had been struck. Her eyes lifted to Doc Davidson's face and she knew.

"I'm so sorry," she sobbed. "You have Gabriel's best interests at heart, I know, I know, I know. But, I have a town full of people to consider …"

"I'll admit I was angry before I saw you," Doc Davidson squatted uncomfortably in front of her and took her hands. "I understand what you're going through, I really do. I can't forgive you though. It's done. Gabriel should be awake within the hour."

"Thank you," Mint followed his face with her eyes as Doc Davidson stood. "I could have applied for the authority to make the order myself, but I took the coward's way. Aaron's much more used to doing it than I am."

Doc Davidson was gone before she finished. He probably only heard the first few words as he disappeared around the corner without looking back. Mint sat up straight and wiped her eyes. It was done now, there was no going back. She looked at the command-pad still resting on her lap and lifted it in trembling fingers. It took several attempts before she finally managed to place a call to Penny Webster.

"Hello, Sergeant Harris," Penny answered quickly, her voice slightly hesitant and expectant.

"Hi, Penny," Mint's voice cracked and she had to clear her throat before she could continue. "I'm afraid I don't have any news about Bruce but there has been a development with Gabriel at the hospital. It's early, what? 0500 hours, ok, I'll take first watch anyway."

"Mint, what are you talking about?" Penny asked.

"Sorry, Penny," Mint gave her cheek a little slap. "I'm running on adrenaline and there's so much going on. Gabriel's being woken up and we want him under twenty-three hour watch. I need your help, please."

"No problem, when do you want me?" Penny replied instantly.

"Say, 0800 hours?" Mint suggested. "I have other people to contact for help, we'll arrange a rota."

"Get on with it then," Penny said. "I'll see you in three hours."

*

Mint left Gabriel to the watchful attention of the nurse after he awoke her from dozing in the chair. She had asked him to wake her either just before 0800 hours or whenever Gabriel awoke. He was now under instructions to record anything Gabriel said should he wake up before Mint or another came to continue the surveillance. Despite Doc Davidson's advice, Gabriel had not woken up yet, although his vital signs confirmed he was in a natural sleep now, not the drug induced coma. At least there were fewer tubes attached to him.

She arrived at the hospital entrance just before 0800 hours to catch her first sight of the new day's light and the arrival of the individuals she'd invited to form Gabriel's round the clock surveillance team. Penny was with Trent and Gretta, Roman had accompanied Daniel, and Kieron was on his own. Roman handed out the police issue data-pads Mint had requested as they walked from the car park to meet her in the little entrance room.

She had explained the situation when she called each of them to ask for help, which rendered initial introductions and outlines unnecessary. Mint led them through the corridors to Gabriel's room and showed them, through the door window, the still slumbering boy inside.

"We'll each be doing roughly four hour shifts," Mint said. "Adults to take the night watches, I don't want the younger volunteers here too late. Who's going first?"

"If Kieron and Daniel do the first two, Gretta can watch before Trent and I take it in turns," Penny suggested. "It'll make travel arrangements easier for us."

"Anybody got any problem with that?" Mint asked. She glanced around to headshakes from all present. "Ok, it's agreed then. Kieron or Daniel first, your choice, boys."

"You go first, Kieron," Daniel said. "I don't mind stopping later - to help Gretta settle down."

"Kissy, kissy," Kieron mocked as he stepped into Gabriel's room, evading Daniel's punch to his shoulder.

"Whatever," Mint said, starting to walk away. "Trent or Penny, whoever's here last, let me know when you need me to take over. Roman, have you been working all night?"

"I've been at the station all night," he nodded. "Took a few more power naps. Aaron's been doing the same. We've sorted rotas and patrol patterns if you want to go home for a short break."

"I thought you said you didn't want my job," Mint teased him. "I'll go home, but for two hours max."

*

She had managed a brief forty minutes of Varla-haunted slumber, after a quick shower, when an incessant beeping from her command-pad woke her up. Mint knew it was an inbound call; the alarm she had set was a gentler tone. A brief fumble preceded her successful grip on the device.

She forced her eyes to open wide and fluttered her eyelids to clear sleep and a blurry film from her vision. It was Kieron Hall, calling from the hospital.

"Go ahead, Mr Hall," she said. "Sorry, I was sleeping."

"Gabriel's woken up," Kieron said, almost cut her off. "You need to hear what he's telling me."

"Ok," Mint looked at the time, 0930 hours. "I'll be there in fifteen minutes."

"Copy that, Sarge," Kieron answered. "I'm calling the Webster's here too."

Mint ignored the over-familiarity as she cut off the connection without further comment, and began to pull fresh items of uniform from her wardrobe. She shrugged into them clumsily, yawning uncontrollably. In the small kitchen, she hurriedly spread uneven layers of marmalade on a couple of slices of toast, put them on a plate and carried them out to her 4x4. She drove one-handed, glad that travel was restricted to authorised personnel only; she'd chided others for doing the same and didn't want to be spotted personally in contravention of that rule. Bites of toast were interspersed with perusal of the command-pad, attempting to get up-to-date, before she put a call through to her sister.

"Morning, Mint," Reid answered. "We're taking it in turns to try and sleep while Mikey's quiet."

"Sorry, I can't talk for long," Mint said, she had just entered the hospital grounds. "Thanks for the refreshments last night. Can you do the same at the station for lunchtime, today – I'll apply some station funds. I've also got a twenty-three hour watch on young Gabriel at the hospital: Kieron Hall, Daniel Reckhart and Gretta Webster in turns through the day. Trent and Penny Webster are covering nights with me. Can you put something together for that operation too, please?"

"No problem," Reid replied immediately. "Authorise our transport though, we were stopped endlessly yesterday. We'll both be glad to get out and about again and do something that feels useful."

"Thanks, Reid," Mint said with a pleased sigh. "I'll give you a special pass." She cut off the connection and pulled into an emergency services parking slot. A quick series of taps on the command-pad set up the vehicular movement authority for Java and Reid.

Doc Davidson was awaiting her arrival when she reached the entrance. He looked far more awake than she felt.

"First of all, my medical opinion is that Gabriel Parkes is on the mend. He's still in a bad way, quite weak, and needs a good deal of rest for his recuperation," Doc Davidson said. "On the reason for his early revival, I'll defer to the tough decision you made and say, reservedly, your instinct was correct. This is really quite remarkable."

Mint remained quiet as she walked alongside but regarded him with raised eyebrows. She had played that decision making process over and over so many times in her head she had nearly grown dizzy. In the end she found herself so wound up from the turmoil she had to forcibly stop, feeding Tiada Vejour was not her intention. Doc Davidson stopped her in the doorway to Gabriel's room with a hand on her shoulder.

"I'll tell you what I've told young Kieron Hall since my patient woke up," he said. "Gabriel still needs lots of sleep and bed rest. Don't keep him talking too long and definitely don't encourage or allow him to sit up. I'll trust you to pass that message on and leave you to it."

Mint watched him walk away. Their relationship had shifted since she had to make that call to Aaron; she didn't think her previously cosy working relationship with the Doctor would return anytime soon, if ever. With a heartfelt sigh, she opened the door and stepped in, a forced smile on her face. Gabriel was awake but Kieron's head had lolled back as he snoozed in the bedside seat. Mint walked as quietly as she could to Gabriel's bed and perched on the bottom corner. He was slightly propped up now, the head end of the bed on a shallow upward angle from his waist.

"Hello, Sergeant Harris," he said, his voice was quiet but stronger than

Mint had expected.

"Welcome back, Gabriel," Mint replied. "I'm glad to see you awake. You scared Roman and me half to death when you fell. It was lucky we were there. I'll not wake young Mr Hall just yet, but I hear he's also called the Webster's to the hospital. I guess you have something to tell us."

"I do, I ..." Gabriel started but Mint cut him off.

"No, I'll wait. Doc Davidson has issued orders not to over-exert you yet, I'm going to stick to his advice this time." Mint looked down once she'd finished, but quickly raised her head to smile reassuringly at the boy. She didn't want to pass on any of her burden.

They sat in silence for several minutes. Mint remembered watching the demise of his parents. She didn't know if Gabriel had been informed yet. The Webster's arrived just as it began to get uncomfortable. Kieron woke up as they all piled in.

"Oops, sorry," Kieron said. "Look, I can act a bit daft at times, but the Doctor's told me Gabriel shouldn't be pushed too hard and I intend to take that seriously. I'll tell you what I know and you can ask questions afterwards."

"That's very good, Kieron," Penny said, before Mint could open her mouth. "It's good to see you growing up, at last."

"Yeah, well ..." Kieron looked around with a blush at the expectant faces. "Ok," he continued. "That thing got into his head up on the hill, made him see and hear things, shadows among the trees. Then, it made him see a huge flying monster chase him; that's why he stumbled off the edge. Anyway, he heard from Bruce while he was in the coma. Bruce says he's held prisoner by Tiada Vejour and it's still connected to Gabriel but doesn't know. Bruce has found a way to get into Gabriel's head and can pass on information as long as he's careful. He says Tiada Vejour is growing stronger and it's been examining the space stations."

"Oh, no, poor Bruce, my poor dear," Penny wailed. Trent gathered her in his arms. Gretta leaned back against the wall, her eyes everywhere with tears welling.

"No, no, no," Mint said, thinking quickly. "This is actually good news. Through Gabriel we have a way to talk to Bruce, find out what he knows, a back door into Tiada Vejour's mind, however it works."

"You want to use our poor, lost boy as a spy?" Trent sounded incredulous as he spoke over Penny's sobs.

"Yes," Mint said. "Do you not see it, though? Bruce is finding out about the Varla. Your son has great intelligence, resourcefulness and creativity. That means he'll also be able to look for a way to get it out of his head and retrieve control of his own body."

"You think so?" Penny looked up with imploring eyes.

"This is more than I was hoping for, much more," Mint nodded. "I thought Gabriel was still connected to the Varla but I never dreamed Bruce would be able to make contact. This makes our constant vigil even more important. When Bruce feels safe to make contact again we might be able to talk directly with him, or, at the very least, draw up a list of questions for Gabriel to ask him. Are you strong enough for that, and, more importantly, happy to go along with us, Gabriel?"

"I am," Gabriel said. "He's been my best friend since forever; I know he'd do the same for me. Is anybody going to tell me why my parents aren't here?"

Kieron wasn't aware of their fate and looked around with a frown. Mint had been dreading this moment. The Webster's definitely knew but they were looking anywhere but at Gabriel. Mint cleared her throat and they all turned to stare at her.

"Have they been harmed by … it?" Gabriel asked.

"Umm," Mint began. "If Doc Davidson hasn't told you yet …"

"Has it killed them?" Gabriel cut her off with a high-pitched cry.

"Everybody out of the room," Mint ordered. "Not you, Penny - stay, please."

Mint walked to the head of the bed and took Gabriel's hand. Penny wiped her eyes and sniffed loudly as she walked to the other side and grasped Gabriel's other hand.

"They wanted to see where your accident happened," Mint began. "I was called there to bring them back to you but the Varla turned up. It was in Old Tom's body then and made your parents see demons. Your dad was magnificent, Gabriel. He faced up to that thing like a giant. But, none of us knew what we were dealing with, and we were all outmatched. I'm afraid they're gone, Gabriel."

*

Bruce watched in grim fascination as Tiada Vejour went about its work. Its powers and abilities far exceeded what Bruce thought he had discovered so far. This was way more than he ever thought possible. It took intense concentration for the Varla to achieve and Bruce realised now was his next perfect opportunity. He withdrew as carefully as he could and sat on his bed until he was certain the Varla hadn't detected him. He accessed his shortcut to Gabriel.

"Gabriel, it's me again," he began.

*

"He's here!" Gabriel tried to sit up.

"Oh, hell," Mint said. "Not now. Gabriel, you're too upset, ask Bruce to come back later."

*

Bruce couldn't believe it. He had heard Gabriel speak, followed by Sergeant Harris.

"What do they mean," he asked, "why not now?"

"Did Tiada Vejour kill my parents?" Gabriel asked in a voice full of anger.

"Gabriel, you must calm down, you'll attract the Varla," Bruce heard Sergeant Harris say. Yeah, he will, he thought and scanned back down his link to investigate. Nothing, that was lucky.

"Yes, it did," Bruce answered his friend. "It's also possessed my body. I'm a prisoner in my own brain, but it doesn't know about this link and you have to keep it that way. We can fight it and I can let people know what it's doing, but only as long as this link remains secret. I'm going now, tell them it's growing an army, I'll try to contact you again later."

*

"He's gone!" Gabriel sobbed.

"Damn it!" Mint said under her breath. "Gabriel, I am so sorry, that was horribly poor timing."

"It killed my mum and dad," Gabriel said in a cracked voice. "It tried to kill me, but I survived. It's possessed Bruce, my best friend. I hate it!" he stopped to look alternately at Penny and Mint. Penny had climbed onto the bed now and put her arm around him, drew him into her. "Bruce told me to tell you it's growing an army. He's going to come back later if he can," Gabriel snuggled into Penny and began to cry.

"Go," Penny said to Mint. "You have things to do. I'll be right here, waiting for my son."

Mint was speechless, she really had no words. She simply nodded and walked out. The others were waiting outside and crowded around her. Doc Davidson could be seen rushing towards the room.

"I saw the readouts," he said, once he was close enough. "What's happened, was he awake?"

"Yes," Mint nodded. She looked at Trent and Gretta. "It was Bruce," she announced. "He's found a way into Gabriel's head and can make contact when Tiada Vejour isn't aware. Unfortunately, he made contact when

Gabriel had just learned the dreadful truth about his parents and had to withdraw to prevent discovery. Penny's staying with him. It's up to you if you stay Kieron, but I think we'd best leave him now. I have to return to the station."

Mint pushed her way through the small crowd and deliberately didn't look back as she marched along the corridor. It wasn't until she was in the seat of her 4x4 that she thought about contacting Aaron. Mint raised the command-pad then changed her mind and placed it in the dashboard cradle; this news needed to be presented personally. She made excellent time through the virtually empty streets and hurried up the steps from the underground car park.

There was a shift changeover occurring in the main office; Mint let them get on with it and entered her office. Aaron was asleep with his head on her desk. She was about to kick the chair to wake him but changed her mind and gently shook his shoulder. He sprang up, awake but bleary.

"Sorry," she said, actually meaning it. "I've asked Java and Reid to provide more refreshments for the troops. You look like you could do with a strong one."

"I think I'm running on coffee at present, what time is it?" Aaron mumbled.

"Just gone 1030 hours," Mint advised. "I've been at the hospital, Gabriel's awake."

"Was it a good call?" Aaron asked, blinking his eyes and working his jaw muscles.

"Turns out it was, but I still feel guilty," Mint looked away. "Thanks for doing the deed."

"I told you, when it's deemed necessary I never hesitate to make the required orders," Aaron smiled the friendly smile at her again. "You'll get used to it. So, what did Gabriel Parkes have to say?"

"It appears Tiada Vejour isn't perfect," Mint said. "It left a connection open to Gabriel's brain; must've been when it was working Old Tom at New Cambridge, distracted. Anyway, Bruce is a prisoner in his own body but he's found this connection and can talk to Gabriel. He's watching what the Varla is up to and plans to pass on this intelligence when it's safe."

"Whoa!" Aaron sat back in the chair, heavily. He looked at Mint, perched on the corner of her desk and let out a long breath. "We're finally catching a break, a view into the enemy's thoughts, no less."

"Yeah, but don't get too excited," Mint shuffled uneasily. "Gabriel had just found out his parents were killed when Bruce connected, damned poor timing, but it can't be helped. Bruce didn't stay long, but he told Gabriel to let us know Tiada Vejour is growing an army."

"What," Aaron took to his feet, "an army of what?"

"That's all he could risk telling us," Mint said. "Gabriel was all fired up and likely to attract unwanted attention."

"Of course, I'm sorry," Aaron sat down again. "Bruce Webster, you little hero, it really couldn't have chosen a worse kid to possess. Ok, we know it's up to something, that's a positive. We just need to increase our knowledge base. I'm going to have to risk a reconnaissance mission."

*

"Yes, sir," Rick Gatiss said. "Message received and understood."

He lowered the data-pad and stood in thought for a moment. Other members of his squad gathered around to try and obtain the latest information. They were based at the original roadblock, looking out over the hills towards the distant forest.

"Ok," he finally became animated again. "Here's the deal. Apparently, there's a kid in hospital with some sort of link to the gribbly thing at ground zero. He says it's 'growing an army,' whatever the hell that means, and the boss wants visuals. We can't risk sending personnel and think a hover-jet will be too visible. We need options, people."

"It's got to be long distance remote viewing," Trooper Smith said. "A hover-jet might still attract its attention, but what about a drone?"

"Smith, you're a bloody genius," Rick burst out, "except for the long distance bit."

"Really?" Trooper Smith looked astounded.

"Boss, I've got a plan but I need your help," Rick announced over the data-pad.

*

Mint was still uncomfortable with being in the passenger seat but admitted, silently, she needed the downtime to recoup some energy while Aaron drove. It was just after midday but many curtains were drawn, blinds shuttered in the homes they drove past. It was a fairly primitive tactic as far as removing the hanging missile from your thoughts was concerned but Mint supposed it was effective. Strangely, the warning from Bruce Webster had unintentionally proved most successful at removing that concern from her mind. She was now consumed by thoughts about what sort of army he meant, how was it being grown, what exactly was the threat?

Gaining this intelligence had posed quite a thorny problem, but even Aaron's basic troopers were tested for high intelligence before being employed. This had the benefit of concentrating excellent problem solvers in Aaron's teams. Sending personnel was out of the question and hover-jets would be too obvious, Tiada Vejour would swiftly counter such approaches. It hadn't taken long for a proposal to emerge that seemed workable. The fields were full of automated agricultural machinery that had, so far, been ignored by the Varla. Aerial drones were also used by the agriculturists to map and survey their crops. It would be the work of a mere few minutes to place a new camera on a drone. This had been arranged with a minimum of fuss and effort and the drone had been airborne for twenty minutes now, following a prescribed route designed to look entirely ordinary and innocent.

"I don't know about you, but my heart rate is increasing the further we drive along this road," Aaron said.

"Small talk?" Mint took her eyes away from the outside to view the driver's profile.

"We're still alive and kicking aren't we?" Aaron countered. "We've just struck our first lucky break too. I'd say we should be able to swap small talk and carry on like normal people."

"Are you sure you're not schizophrenic? Sometimes I think I'm starting to figure you out, then you pop up with a surprise. Who is the real Aaron, is Aaron really your name?"

"I'm definitely not bipolar or anything similar," Aaron flashed a grin her way. "This is me, Aaron – actual name, no secrets there. I've told you before I have to compartmentalise, those compartments can open up as I get used to people and people get used to me. I thought we were getting used to each other?"

"I suppose so," Mint replied.

"I liked the refreshments idea. Good people management skills. Tiada Vejour tapped into my fear of drowning at the roadblock yesterday. I guess he showed you something to do with your parents. I can't imagine losing mine; they still work high admin positions in New Cambridge. It must have been hard for you and Java."

"How do you do it?" Mint shook her head. "I was on shift that day," she continued after a brief pause. "Got the call over the data-pads. Professionally, you're prepared to deal with incidents, except, it all falls down around your ears when it's your family involved. Suddenly it's personal, no longer a case or crime number, not statistics. I threw myself into work afterwards; Java took over management of the café, threw herself into Reid and settled down for the nuclear family."

"You're not family minded or involved?"

"Never really thought about it, my job takes up so much time anyway."

"Really? You aren't attracted to anyone; nobody's ever tried to get close?"

"No."

"What about Roman Reckhart?"

"What about him?"

"Oh, this is good. You really haven't noticed?"

"Noticed what?"

Aaron couldn't speak anymore. He pounded the steering wheel as he chuckled and pulled up a short distance from the roadblock.

"This isn't really funny, is it?" Mint shot daggers at him with her eyes.

"Spend some time with him. Go for a coffee together. His interest was obvious as soon as I started working with you."

"You're seeing things," Mint slammed the vehicle door. "Besides, there may not be a tomorrow."

"All the more reason to do it today," Aaron said over his shoulder. "Rick, how are we looking?"

"All systems are go," Rick Gatiss said. "The drone's been mapping and surveying for nearly half an hour, doesn't seem to have attracted any unwanted attention. Of course, if the … thing, can listen in it knows exactly what we're doing."

"We'll just have to take that risk," Aaron patted him on the shoulder. "Nothing we can do about it; Tiada Vejour holds far too many trump cards as it is. When do we enter the surveillance phase?"

"Two minutes," Rick replied. "I'll show you to the feed we're receiving."

"You've not had any fuzzing or blurring at all?" Mint asked when they stopped at a rugged transport case sat atop a makeshift table. Its lid was raised to reveal complex electronics and a screen, raised to a viewing angle. "How can you be sure you're receiving a real view, the Varla planted those demons on the media footage?"

"No unusual footage has come through, yet," Rick said. "We've embedded a ghost image into the live feed from the drone that software in here removes before it's shown on the screen. If anything tries to send us a false image without that ghost embedded, we'll know about it."

"Nice," Mint nodded in appreciation.

"It's starting the turn," a trooper called over.

The three crowded closer together to stare at the screen.

"The drone has just finished its scan of all the fields this side of the road," Rick explained. "It's going to gain altitude and fly along the treeline to begin scanning the fields on the other side. That's how it's supposed to look anyway. We've fixed a Bond class, model 4c, high power surveillance camera under the right wing. It'll be able to look right where we want it."

Mint watched as the footage stabilised into horizontal movement, indicating the drone had completed its turn, and waited nervously. It was imperative she and Aaron be here as they had first-hand knowledge of the target area. Aware she was holding her breath, Mint released it as the main road was crossed and the slip road fed onto the approach road.

"Trees are down," Aaron commented.

"It's widened the access road," Mint agreed. "But where are the trunks?"

"Never mind the trunks, what the fuck are they?" Aaron said.

The car park area was full of strange mounds, it was difficult to judge the scale, but Mint thought they looked about three metres tall and nearly two metres wide at the base. The mounds were bell shaped with strange striations that arose at the top to carry on down in regular intervals to ground level.

"I lost count at thirty," Mint admitted once the view swept on to display only the tree studded hillside.

"Doesn't matter," Rick said. "We've recorded the whole thing. Give me a second and I'll have a still shot for you."

"Is that the army Bruce was telling us about?" Aaron looked perplexed.

"I couldn't see anything else different," Mint said. "He was worried about discovery and couldn't risk staying longer than he did. We should be thankful he warned us in time to see whatever they are."

"Here you are," Rick announced.

A wide angle, still view of the car park area filled the screen. The chasm yawned to the left side; the car park with its strange mounds came next. They stretched all the way to the access road.

"Thirty-five," Aaron said. "Can you zoom in on one?"

"That one," Mint pointed at a mound on the extreme right of the view that looked slightly different.

Rick centred the crosshairs on the indicated mound and zoomed closer, dragged the zoom back a little as picture quality deteriorated. The striations on this mound seemed to be opening. Annoyingly, the inside was in deep shadow and failed to reveal any further details.

"It looks like there's a ring of tractable slats all around some central structure," Aaron noted. "They look quite rough in external texture."

"Bark!" Mint said. "That's why there are no trunks. It's widened the road by removing trees and built these mounds out of them. So, we know what they look like; what can they do?"

"That's a question for Gabriel," Aaron motioned for Mint to use her command-pad.

"I'm on it," Mint said as she raised the command-pad and began tapping out a message.

"We've got movement," Aaron's squad leader shouted.

Mint's head snapped round from the screen to follow the woman's pointed finger. She could just make out a speck on the distant road, where the slip road ran off.

"Get magnification on that," Aaron shouted. "Squaddie, form up defences and unload that laser cannon again."

Mint was impressed with the calm efficiency as orders were issued, called – not shouted. Firing positions were assumed along the roadblock and out into the fields where depressions had been dug. A high powered optical viewer was plugged into the screen in the transport case, showed a green blur as it swept along the treeline until the road appeared.

"Two of them," Aaron muttered.

Mint could clearly see two of the strange mounds on the road. Then, as if they had waited to be observed, they rose a further metre as four sturdy legs appeared to unfold below the outer curtain of slats. The legs were multiple jointed and provided a travelling gait similar to an insect as they began to approach.

"Let them know we mean business, squaddie," Aaron ordered. "Fire at will."

The tripod had been left bolted to the road surface. Mint saw Aaron's squad leader was already at the controls and zeroing in on the strange targets. A bright bluey-white beam spiked out to the mound on the left side, struck it squarely and faded. On the screen, Mint could see a direct hit, bits of bark flying from the impact point where a deep black scorch mark bruised the mound's exterior.

"Was that full power?" she asked. "Only asking 'cus that thing's still coming."

"It was," Aaron confirmed. "There's a fifteen second recharge required before we can take another shot. At the rate they're advancing we've got plenty more shots yet."

"Unless they start firing back," Mint observed.

"Good point. Squaddie, next shot to the top, let's see if we can't dislodge some of those slats and reveal what we're facing."

The next laser beam incised exactly where Aaron had requested, left smoking, cratered burn marks on a pair of the slats.

"Look at that," Rick Gatiss said.

Mint watched the screen in fascination as slats from the rear of the mound wrapped around to cover the wounded spot.

"If it can do that, this isn't going to work," she said. "Try the legs?"

"Go for the legs, squaddie," Aaron ordered.

"Do you have anything else able to hit them from this distance?" Mint asked.

"There's a spare laser cannon," Rick answered, looking up at Aaron. He received a silent nod in response. "Alright," Rick shouted, "Smith and Ellingham, get the second tripod bolted down on the other side of the road. Foster, reverse the weapons truck to them."

Mint watched the squad leader send a third beam at one of the mound's legs. To her untrained eyes it didn't seem to have had much of an effect.

"Concentrate your lasers on one spot," she suggested. "Do you have a target marker?"

"I'm on it," Aaron said. "Sergeant Harris, keep your eyes on that screen and call out damage reports, find us areas to target for maximum effect."

Mint watched Aaron dash away to the reversing truck and leap into its open rear storage area. He jumped out a few seconds later with a long rifle. It had a large targeting scope on the top and a laser range-finder slung underneath the barrel. Aaron dashed to the roadblock and rested the rifle on the top while he found a steady shooting position, braced himself against the barrier's bulk. Mint returned her eyes to the screen and saw a twinkling red spot moving down a slat.

"The legs are moving less at the top," she called over.

Aaron didn't reply but Mint saw the red spot move where she had advised.

"Call the shot, Sergeant," Aaron shouted.

"Ok," Mint replied. "Laser cannons, synchronised fire on the count of three: one, two, three."

Her eyes never strayed from the screen as she shouted out the order. Rick and squaddie synchronised perfectly as both beams spiked into the leg. Mint watched as it tried to use the leg but the combined laser power had seared deeply into the tough structure and it collapsed to hang limp, useless. For a few seconds it jerked along unsteadily on three legs until they folded down and it turned into a static mound. She turned her attention to the second mound and noted it had accelerated. Then she read the indicated range.

"The other one's moving quicker, now at a range of one mile and closing," she shouted. "Looks like you've immobilised your target. Wait a minute," Mint stared back at the screen. "The slats are folding back. I can see three, no, four arms. A big one and a small one on each side of a barrel body; looks like it has some sort of eye on a central stalk. The slats flow up and out from the top. What's it doing now?" She watched as the larger arms extended upwards and the mound seemed to settle onto the road behind it, brace itself. "I think it's going to shoot something out of the larger arms!"

As she spoke, a bright orange ball of energy was hurled out of each arm to arc into the air. Mint watched as they steadily rose, yellow bolts crackling around the main orange ball.

"Guide me onto the firing arms," Aaron yelled at her.

Mint snapped out of her fixation on the balls of energy and looked at the screen. It took huge force of will to concentrate on Aaron's laser pointer and ignore the approaching danger.

"Up, up, up," she shouted. "Left, no – too far, stop. Laser cannon, synchronise on three: one, two, three."

Mint jumped in excitement as she saw the largest left arm amputated by the precision firing. She landed with a shriek and rolled into a protective ball as the mound's energy shots impacted. There followed two large explosions and a shower of chippings from the fractured road surface.

"Shit," Mint complained as she unsteadily regained her feet and looked around to assess the damage.

Both balls of energy had been targeted on the first laser cannon. Small pieces of the weapon were strewn about. The severed power cable sparked and snaked about on the road surface next to the bent and twisted tripod legs. Mint had to look away when she saw the remains of Aaron's squad leader. She had taken the brunt of the blast on her front and her ruined body now laid several metres away, horribly burnt with deep incisions. Her lips had been peeled back to reveal a brown-toothed grin of death, her eyes had burst and melted, the orbits open, deep and dark.

"Get back in the game," Mint heard Aaron's shout through the ringing in her ears.

New sounds came to her as she swung back to the screen in slow motion. The troops had begun firing their assault rifles at the advancing mound. There were several distant booms as grenades from launchers slung beneath some of their barrels landed. Mint blinked at the screen, wafted away drifting smoke with her hands.

"More to the right," she shouted. "Stop! Laser cannon, fire."

Rick's shot was perfectly aimed. The remaining large arm was slung backwards by the energy of the laser but remained attached. Mint could see a blackened area with some large pits in the arm's structure.

"It's damaged," Mint shouted. "I don't know if it can shoot again."

"It already has," Aaron yelled back. "Take cover!"

Mint looked up as she dropped. Another ball of energy was falling out of the sky; it must have shot again while she was cowering earlier. She could see it was plummeting towards the second laser cannon, but her warning shout was lost in the explosion as the ball struck its target. Mint turned her back to the shower of debris, covered her head with her hands. She spun around and up as soon as the rain of particles had died down. The laser cannon was out of action, bent and crippled. Rick Gatiss had been blown clear and lay on his back unmoving, several metres away.

"Shit!" Mint shouted again. "Does that rifle have sufficient range?"

"We'll soon know," Aaron shouted back over the sound of intense gunfire. "Guide me on target."

"Up," Mint shouted. "To the right, again, stop – that's perfect."

Mint didn't hear Aaron's shot, lost in the cacophony. She saw it impact though and punched the air.

"Blew it clean off," she shouted. "That was more effective than the lasers."

She saw Aaron release the ammunition clip and examine its contents.

"No wonder," he shouted. "Armour piercing ammo."

Screams and shouts punctuated the constant chatter of full-automatic assault rifle fire. Aaron slammed the ammunition clip back into place and peered out to refocus on the firefight just beyond the roadblock. Mint saw him quickly duck down into cover and registered a slight shift in the structure. Something had struck it from the far side. With her stomach knotted in fear she edged around the table-top transport case and skittered across the road to the still body of Rick Gatiss. She could see he was still breathing as she skidded to her knees beside him, felt the burn of grazes. With shaking arms she lifted him up, ignored the low groan that elicited, and teased his assault rifle from his shoulder. Mint checked the weapon over; her expertise was hazy but she knew a safety catch when she saw one. Rick had extra ammunition clips in a bulging hip pouch. She pocketed two and dashed in a low crouch to the roadblock.

Aaron was still taking cover when she reached him.

"Three dead, two wounded," he informed her. "It's to the front and slightly right. Go on three: one, two, three."

Mint rose and pulled the assault rifles butt into her shoulder in a fluid movement. The mound was ten metres away, over three metres tall, its slats splayed, latticed, and rotating, the four arms deployed. She aimed the assault rifle and squeezed the trigger. A stream of bullets ripped through the air towards the mound. Mint was aiming for an arm. Slats whipped around to take the impacts, bark flying off as it was chipped away. Aaron fired the sniper rifle next to her and a slat fell to the ground. Mint ducked down, the assault rifle was clicking on empty. Aaron joined her a second later. Breath came to her in great heaving gasps as Mint glanced sideways at Aaron. He suggested another attack on the mound with a slight lift of his eyes; he was breathing heavily too.

Mint surged to her feet as a fresh burst of assault rifle fire started from one of the foxholes dug into the fields. She put her head above the roadblock in time to see the mound fire an energy ball from both large arms and a blur of projectiles shoot out of each smaller arm. Its attention was taken by the incoming fire from the flank and Mint intended to take full advantage. She squeezed the trigger and aimed for the large arm closest to her. Chips of wood and bark sprang off until the mound wrapped slats around to absorb her hail of fire. Mint noticed some of the slats were looking considerably pockmarked and tatty. Another slat fell free as Aaron expended another armour piercing round. They ducked as one as the mound turned their way. Mint looked up to see a line of sharp, wooden spikes fly through the air where they had just been.

"You do know that assault rifle has a grenade launcher, don't you?" Aaron panted.

Mint studied the assault rifle and spotted, indeed, a grenade launcher slung below the barrel.

"Is it loaded?" she asked.

"Looks like it," Aaron said after a moment's study. "Standard load is two grenades; pump it like a shotgun to load the second after you've used the first."

"Got it," she said. "Where do I aim?"

"Legs or arms," Aaron replied. "Wait a few seconds after my people engage it again."

Mint became acutely aware of her heavily beating heart as she crouched behind the defences waiting for the next firing opportunity. She wiped her brow, slick with sweat and noticed, with a bizarre casual interest, the streak of muck that the move left deposited on her forearm.

"Go!" Aaron yelled.

Mint reacted automatically, found herself in a firing position before she had time to think. The mound was firing its weapons into the field to their left side this time. Mint took a moment to study her target and noted a close collection of heavily damaged slats. She squeezed the trigger on the grenade launcher and ducked when a shower of wooden splinters came her way from the impact and detonation. Aaron didn't follow her down so she poked her head back up and gawked at what she had done. A swath of slats had fallen away to lie useless on the road and both arms were damaged. More importantly, the mound had been knocked over and was only just recovering.

"Again!" Aaron shouted.

Mint held the assault rifle tight and pumped the grenade launcher as she had been told. She felt a satisfying clunk and brought the weapon down to point at the same part of the mound. Finger on the trigger, squeeze. Mint lifted her head above the defences again to see a gaping hole where the arms had been and more slats settling to the ground.

"Concentrated fire, it's going down," Aaron yelled as loud as he could.

Mint didn't need inviting twice. She lined up on the mound's strange, stout legs and unloaded her clip into one. Aaron severed the eye stalk with a well-aimed round as the sound of running feet came to them. Mint was fumbling for another clip from her trouser pocket but Aaron placed his hand on the top of her assault rifle and pushed it down. He inclined his head over the defences where Mint saw four troops hacking at the mound's remaining pair of arms with their combat knives.

"Fuck me," Mint breathed as she slid down to sit on the roadblock step. "How many of those bastard things did we count?"

"Thirty-five, and I would if I wasn't married," Aaron said with a slight laugh. "We've killed one and immobilised another, blown off its larger arms. They've fucked over this squad though; we can't keep up that loss rate. A determined assault by four or more will finish us off, especially with the laser cannons out of action."

"Sir," Trooper Smith had appeared from the other side of the barrier. Several wooden spikes were lodged in his left thigh, little trickles of blood running down to his boots. "It's stopped moving. As far as we can tell, it's entirely wooden, fucking strange."

"Good job, Smith," Aaron said. "Get your leg sorted out."

"That's not all, sir," Smith looked uncomfortable. "We saw what looks like a whole troop of them up on the road."

"Everybody back behind the roadblock," Aaron shouted as Mint sprinted away from him.

She saw the table upended and feared the worst, but the screen was still functioning when she finally managed to haul the transport case the right way up. By then, Aaron and Smith had joined her and they all crowded round.

"They're forming a defensive perimeter along the treeline," Smith observed.

"Thank fuck they aren't headed our way," Aaron exclaimed.

"Yet," Mint added.

Aaron looked at her with hard eyes for a while then nodded. He fished his command-pad from his trouser pocket.

"All personnel, this is Aaron," he said. "We have just repelled an assault on the roadblock but suffered heavy casualties. I need medics and reinforcements. Leave the local police to patrol duties and report here, stat."

"Roman, come in, please," Mint had taken out her command-pad on a sudden thought.

"Sarge, are you ok?" his voice replied instantly. "I just heard Aaron's call."

"Ok? I'm still alive and moving, but I'm far from ok," Mint allowed. "This army Tiada Vejour has built is formidable and our strongest weapons have been destroyed. I want you to contact the heads of all the labs; find out which ones have lasers that can be portable, we need to use their ingenuity."

"I'm on it, boss," Roman cut the connection.

"Good thought," Aaron said. "You performed well in the firefight."

"I didn't have much choice, did I?" Mint shot back. "I was shit scared," she continued, softer.

"You rose above it," Aaron put a hand on her shoulder.

"Trooper Gatiss is still alive," Mint shrugged off his hand as she strode over to the still unconscious man.

Why had he found it necessary to reply to her vulgarity in the positive earlier? Mint busied herself checking Rick Gatiss for external injuries while she tried to force Aaron's face and that smile out of her mind.

*

Penny had noticed the increased level of activity in the hospital when the wounded arrived from the roadblock. Kieron Hall had soon abandoned her, eager to find out the details. She remained with Gabriel; he was spending longer periods of time awake between bouts of sleep. Daniel Reckhart had joined her an hour or so ago, escorted in by his father. Roman had told her about the dreadful firefight and asked if there had been any further contact from Bruce. Penny had shaken her head and watched him leave, obviously uncomfortable.

Daniel and Gabriel were talking quietly on the bed; Penny was sat in a chair against the wall. A beeping alarm came from the sensor suite connected to Gabriel by an abundance of pads. Penny was on her feet immediately and holding the youngster's hand.

"Is it Bruce?" she asked.

Gabriel nodded and furrowed his brow in concentration. Daniel slipped off the bed and came around to stand close at her side. He seemed a little unnerved by the experience.

"Tiada Vejour is still looking at the space stations but not as much. It's built its army and is pleased with the performance of the two it sent to attack the roadblock; fear has spiked since it happened, that's what it wanted. Bruce thinks it may be preparing to return to its own body. That's a major purpose of the army, protect it while it combines and re-emerges."

"Does Bruce know what will happen to him when that happens?" Penny asked.

"He thinks he'll get control of his body back but he'll still be a prisoner," Gabriel replied after a pause. "He's also sensing that it really doesn't want to drop the missile; I don't know what he means about a missile."

"I do," said Penny. "Bruce, you really must try to find a way to escape, we want you back with us, safe."

*

Bruce was finding it hard; he could hear his mother, like she was in the same room. He felt warm and comforted by her presence and began to feel upset, emotional. That couldn't be helpful, he knew, but he couldn't stop it, it was ingrained, love of family. He felt another presence starting to slide in and hastily withdrew from Gabriel.

*

"He's gone," Gabriel said sadly. "I felt something else beforehand; big, powerful."

"Did it find him with you?" Penny gasped, her hand shot over her mouth. "Is it in your head now?"

"No, I don't think so anyway," Gabriel said. "It was Bruce's choice, like he went away to prevent being found with me."

"Oh," Penny wailed. "I so wanted to talk with him, I miss him so much."

Daniel moved away from Mrs Webster as she collapsed on the bed and cried. He pulled out the data-pad and contacted Sergeant Harris.

*

"Thank you, Daniel," Mint said. "Was that all?"

"Bruce had to go, I think Tiada Vejour was coming to him," Daniel replied.

"Ok, good work, keep at it, you're all doing great," Mint cut the connection.

"He's working out well, as a spy," Aaron said beside her.

They were still at the roadblock, now considerably reinforced to form a more substantial barricade. The rest of Aaron's troopers had soon arrived when called upon and got to work straight away. Mint looked around at the defenders, into the distance at the far treeline, and then at the screen. It was elevated again on the old makeshift table, empty boxes rigged as a replacement leg.

"He's still protecting his best friend, too," Mint said. "Do you think Tiada Vejour may be vulnerable when it transitions back into its own body and rises from underground; otherwise, why the army? We were nearly taken apart by just two of those … tree soldiers. Thirty-odd seems like a big dose of overkill if they were simply supposed to scare us, I'd be worried about just a handful."

"He did say they were there to protect it while it recombines and emerges. Is the size of the army indicative of the time that's going to take? It's also just a major purpose of the army, he said. So, I have to assume there's a further use for them, afterwards. That ties in with Bruce's suspicion it no longer wants to drop the missile."

"Tiada Vejour still wants food," Mint picked up his thread. "It wants the population of Charlestown. Does that mean we can risk starting an evacuation?"

"I wouldn't like to," Aaron shook his head. "If it sees a threat to its plans it could still let it fall, annihilate the town and take that one, massive meal. It's got a planet full of people to attract it; the loss of seven thousand wouldn't worry it that much. At least, that's what I think. No, I have to keep it penned in here for as long as possible."

"You'd keep the population in Charlestown, as what – bait?" Mint squared up to him.

"If I have to," Aaron stared back at her, levelly. "To give the four million a fighting chance, yes I would."

Mint was lost for words. She turned and stomped away, leaned against his 4x4 to peer across the green fields at the distant hills. Her anger should be directed towards Tiada Vejour, she knew, but Aaron was always so bloody right, so clinical and analytical. He was thrust into this situation just the same as she had been. She couldn't fight and rail about the injustice of it all to Tiada Vejour, though. Aaron was the easy, close at hand alternative. Why did she have to find out he was married, a father? She could have coped with the level of attraction she felt towards him if he'd remained enigmatic and just disappeared back to New Cambridge when this was over, assuming they or anyone else survived. Now, she felt guilty, dirty, conflicted. And why did he have to point out the attention Roman Reckhart was paying her? Dammit to hell and back.

Mint watched Aaron wander away to chat lightly with some of his troops. She shook her head, unsure how he could continue to pull off the totally at ease attitude. Lifting her command-pad, she checked the disposition of her constables and sent a message for the nearest to drive by and pick her up.

Constable Pierce soon realised his boss was in no mood for idle chat or to discuss the battle at the roadblock. He simply drove the car after several failed attempts at conversation and snatched quick glances at her bedraggled appearance. Mint was aware of his interest and the furtive looks, felt a little guilty even, but she needed the down time; to relax, get her thoughts in order, and calm down after the excitement.

Mint had grown accustomed to the quiet, virtually empty roads of the last few days. It seemed strange now to join a stream of vehicles exiting the residential side roads to head towards town. Mint sat up to stare at them. Aware of her sudden wakefulness, Constable Pierce pointed at his dash-mounted data-pad.

"Roman's put out a list of vehicle authorisations," he said. "Your request for the lab boys to get to work on makeshift weapons, I believe."

"That's quite a response," Mint said, slumping back into the seat. "Look, I'm sorry, I know you're all working hard and want to know what's happening. I'm tired and a little scared to be honest. You'll get all the latest information once I've had chance to come down a bit and smarten up."

"Fair enough, boss," Constable Pierce said. "Some of us would like to be involved when these weapons get used, you know?"

"We'll have to see how it pans out," Mint looked at him, tried to judge his conviction. "I might need you all on traffic control if we have to evacuate."

"Won't that make it release the ..." he swallowed. "You know - the missile?"

"Honestly? We don't know. I get the impression Tiada Vejour is enjoying its meal of fear and terror too much to drop it though. People seem to be far more useful to it alive than dead. Twice it could have swatted me and it didn't; there's hope in that knowledge I take a crumb of comfort from."

"Here you are, boss, home sweet home," Constable Pierce announced as he pulled up outside the station's main entrance.

"Keep that happy tone going," Mint advised as she climbed out.

The building looked remarkably clean and peaceful to Mint's eyes. A far cry from the death, destruction, and debris she had just left behind. She needed that right now, an island of calm, comfort, familiarity.

Roman was still in his lab when Mint entered the main office. Constable Fletcher was sat at a screen, controlling the vehicular patrols. He looked over as he heard Mint enter and semi-rose before she waved him back to his seat.

"It's alright, I'm fine," Mint assured him. "How is it out there?"

"Nice and quiet," he replied. "We had some older teenagers and young adults get bored and wander out about an hour ago but they're all sorted now. Plenty of traffic just been authorised by Roman, headed for the lab zone."

"Yeah, I saw them," Mint nodded. "We're hoping they can supply some extra firepower. Tiada Vejour's tree soldiers don't go down easy."

"Tree soldiers?" Constable Fletcher asked to Mint's back.

"I'll tell you later," Mint said over her shoulder as she walked towards Roman's lab. "You've done well, Fletcher. After this is over we'll talk about the Sergeant's exam, ok?"

She didn't hear his answer as the lab door slid closed behind her. Roman was intent on his screen, strange geometric shapes filled it, similar to those Mint remembered from the rock wall. Aaron's observation jumped into her mind when the SOC constable glanced round, took a double take and rose to greet her.

"I'm alright," Mint held her hands up to keep him back. She recognised real concern and pain in his eyes, felt guilty that she couldn't return the feelings she could now plainly see he desired. "It got a little hairy but we've survived to fight again. I see you've had a good response from the lab workers."

"Once word got out, they seemed to all know something they could do to weaponise lab machinery," Roman said, still looking her up and down. "I think most of them were simply glad to have an excuse to leave their homes and get busy. There are still a good many stayed at home, family commitments and all that, but most of those are working remotely, sending ideas and instructions over data-pads."

"That's great," Mint clasped his upper arm. "Bruce Webster got in touch through Gabriel again. He thinks Tiada Vejour is working up to going back to its body soon. It's made the army for protection while it does that. I think your Daniel is at the hospital with Penny Webster at the moment, she won't leave now she knows she can contact Bruce."

"Dan's a good boy really," Roman nodded. "I think he's quite enamoured of Gretta Webster, there's an ulterior motive for definite."

"There always is," Mint looked into his eyes briefly. "What's all this?" she waved her hand at the symbols on the screen.

"I wish I knew," Roman retook his seat with a frown, whether at the symbols or her silent message, Mint couldn't guess. "These are from Starjump constructs. The form and structure are identical to those on the rock wall above Jaicon Hewson's corpse. I still can't get close to deciphering them, though. All I can confirm is that Tiada Vejour has either seen them and copied them for dramatic effect, or they are the Varla K'dyamon's written language and there's a message written on the rock we simply can't understand. Oh, speaking of dramatic effect, I extrapolated further from that old Earth demon connection I suggested. The pentagram, a five pointed star with the single point uppermost, was an ancient symbol of supernatural protection, amongst other meanings. We found an upside down pentagram, the single point downwards, on the wall. Most ancient references point to the pentagram in that orientation being symbolic of evil, satanic purpose or, most interestingly, demonic."

"Really?" Mint grasped his shoulder. "I wonder … no. Sorry, I'm thinking out loud. I was wondering if Tiada Vejour had maybe visited Earth in the past but I remember now it talked about having to learn how our bodies work when I tried to save Bruce Webster. If it had been to Earth it would surely be aware of our biology already; how then was it aware of the symbology to use?"

"Easily," Roman said. "Our fiction and history are full of it. I've read old classic novels, horror fiction they used to call it. Well, some modern authors still write in the genre. It has a fairly strong following. There'll be a handful or more people in Charlestown who've read some."

"Check Jaicon Hewson's media library," Mint suggested. "It's kind of a moot point now we know Tiada Vejour killed him. However, if it didn't get all its knowledge from Mr Hewson, it might give us an insight into how quickly it grew in power."

"I'll look into it, when time allows," Roman replied.

"I'm going to get changed while you do that," Mint said from the doorway. "I want everybody in tactical uniform from now onwards; get changed as soon as possible, Roman. That goes for you, too, Constable Fletcher. Rotate all constables back to the station to change into tactical wear and sign out heavier weaponry from the armoury."

"Wait a moment," Roman said. He fished about in a drawer and withdrew two small packets. "For your knees," he said, holding the medical plasters out to her. Mint took them without a word and walked out.

Mint stood in front of the heavy door, placed her hand on the security pad and leaned in close to allow her eye to be scanned by the optical security camera. A little buzz sounded and the door opened with a soft click. Mint pushed it wide and strolled in, motion activated lights pinging on as she did so. It wasn't a huge room, just big enough to accommodate the various racks bearing helmets, jackets and trousers. Boots were lined up at floor level. Uncaring, Mint stripped down to her undergarments. She found numerous small grazes and bruises she hadn't noticed before and applied the plasters to her knees. It was getting rough out there for sure. The trousers were lighter than she remembered; their strength came from modern technology, man-made fibres woven into a composite with tough threads made from graphene and other materials she didn't quite understand.

Once she was dressed, her attention turned to the weapons rack. Mint holstered a more powerful pistol than the one currently in her 4x4 and shouldered a rifle, not quite as powerful as the assault rifle she had fired at the roadblock; it also didn't have a grenade launcher attached. Grenades? She stared at the lines of smoke, concussion and high explosive grenades. Several tactical bags were sat empty on the floor. She swept up two of these and proceeded to fill them with grenades. Satisfied, she took hold of her helmet by its strap and dragged the tactical bags out to Roman's lab.

"Two bags full of grenades," she poked her head through the doorway. "Contact your labs and see if they can make them more effective. We definitely don't need the smoke or concussion ones."

She turned to walk away as Roman lifted his data-pad, paused, and then stuck her head through again.

"Get your tactical gear on and, while you're at it, find a set that will fit Aaron."

*

The fake emotional turmoil had soon disappeared after Tiada Vejour left Bruce alone. He could tell the alien was distracted and wanted to get back to important matters, so Bruce had given it no reason to remain in his mental prison. Whether he had portrayed a convincing tortured psyche, he didn't know, but it soon became plain the Varla had dismissed him from its thoughts as it concentrated on future plans.

Bruce didn't want to attempt contact with Gabriel and the others with him so soon, besides he didn't really have anything new to pass on. His mum had wanted him to find a way to escape, regain control of his body and get away from Tiada Vejour. He didn't think she was fully cognisant of the Varla K'dyamon's capabilities; mind you, Bruce wasn't sure he was. Maybe, that was the way forward; go much further backwards into Tiada Vejour's memories and learn as much as he could about it. A quick look out of his physical eyes showed his body was in the chasm, sheer rock walls fell away around him. Good, the Varla was fully engaged.

Bruce stepped into its memory well and surreptitiously began exploring. Keny-Thon, Moonquom, Tingold K'farlan, the Imperial G'frak Heirescence; Bruce's mind was suddenly awash with powerful memories. He swiftly backed out and found his psychic body sat on his bed. The power and strength of those memories was beyond anything he had ever encountered. He would need absolute control to filter through them.

"Arrogant human," Tiada Vejour roared at him. "So, you want to know about me, do you? Here, know my memories."

Bruce felt like his consciousness was dissolving as the memories poured into him. It hurt so bad, like an internal lightning storm. His tortured mind was caught in a torrent of space and time, washed away, uncontrolled, a witness to titanic events.

*

The barricade had been further reinforced, that was obvious as soon as Mint pulled up in her 4x4, happy to be behind the wheel and in control again. Most of the trucks had now been scavenged, panels taken off to be incorporated in the defences. She could see makeshift defensive walls around the foxholes in the fields to either side.

"You've been busy," Mint said to Aaron when he walked over to her. "Here, put these on," she tossed the tactical trousers and jacket to him. Boots followed quickly afterwards; several pairs, hoping to have stumbled on the right size.

"Thanks," Aaron smiled. "I must say your new uniform suits you." He dropped his trousers and began to pull on the new pair. "No movement

163

from our friends. They've set up their defensive line and haven't moved a jot since. I've fielded plenty of questions about laser power from Roman, fed to him by the scientists. I hear you've sent some grenades their way, too – looking for an upgrade?"

"The lasers did ok against the tree soldiers but armour piercing rounds and high explosives were more effective. I figured I'd try to even up the odds a little. Have you found more useful weapons?"

"You turn into quite a warrior queen when required," Aaron grinned as he fastened the tactical jacket. "We've changed to armour piercing and explosive tipped rounds where we can. I wish we had some old fashioned artillery, modern weapons are made for accuracy rather than the big boom required here."

"Tell Roman," Mint suggested. "He'll pass your request on to the scientists. They were eager to get to work doing something useful, make use of them."

"You do it for me?" Aaron asked. "I've got about eight boots to try on!"

Mint lifted her command-pad with a laugh and tapped in the request. She left Aaron examining boots next to her 4x4 and wandered over to the barricade. Troops were milling about comfortably on both sides and out of curiosity she made her way to the far side. The remnants of pine trees were still lying where they had fallen. Rick Gatiss smiled at her when he recognised the more militaristic looking Police Sergeant.

"Good work earlier," Rick said, extending a hand to shake. "I hear you turned into quite the Boadicea."

"It's good to see you're up and at it again," Mint didn't understand the reference but shook his hand anyway. "Have we learned anything from what's left?" she gestured at the disjointed carcass.

"They're wooden," Rick shrugged his shoulders. "Shaped pieces of pine tree, there's nothing special about them at all. Even the weapon arms we've managed to study are nothing more than tubes of wood."

"Shit," Mint looked down and kicked at a splinter. "I was hoping we'd discover more about what makes them tick."

"Wood doesn't tick," Aaron said, drawing up beside her. He did a quick spin to display his new tactical suit. Mint laughed, it wasn't a perfect fit. "We think they run off energy installed in the wood somehow by Tiada Vejour," he continued. "In a way I think that's good. They'll be finite; the Varla needs to conserve its energy reserves for flying and other tricks. Maybe a lot is needed to reanimate its body."

"Maybe," Mint agreed. "Hopefully."

"Hopefully," Aaron nodded. "Anything else from our little spy?"

"No," Mint replied. "That well's dry at the moment. We're on our own."

"I suppose no news could be good news." Aaron said. "Bruce is smart from what I've seen; he'll find a way to let us know when new things are afoot."

Mint nodded but didn't share his optimism. Bruce Webster was a teenager, unexpectedly thrown into possession and conflict. There was bound to be a limit to his ability to cope with all that.

*

If Bruce was in full possession of his physical body he would have described the searing pain as an explosion in his head, an over-inflated balloon exerting pressure on every square inch of his cranium. Except, Tiada Vejour had his body and Bruce was a castaway in some far, distant corner of a network of neurones and synapses. He had been taken unawares by the Varla, caught in the act of supposedly stealthy intelligence gathering. Bruce stretched out his imaginary body as he lay down on his imaginary bed, it brought no relief. What had Tiada Vejour done to him to make it hurt so badly?

As a wave of pain subsided a little he tried to think, remember something, the tiniest little nugget of what happened. It was useless, there was no control, no ability to form rational thoughts and order the operation of his mind. Bruce closed his eyes and rolled over with an imaginary groan.

*

Tedium, endless waiting and frustration; Mint was beginning to wonder whether she preferred it when events were rolling along at pace. The sun was very low in the sky, the day was dusking. Hours had dragged along interminably. She had spoken with Aaron several times; he seemed to relish the pause in activity by their adversary. It gave them time to catch up, to marshal their resources, he said. Mint couldn't help but worry what the Varla was doing while all that was accomplished. She had tried to break the boredom by cruising around town, checking up on her constables, giving pep talks and the like. Back at the station for a short visit, she had received an update on progress at the laboratories. The scientists and engineers had obviously been raring to go, get their hands and minds busy again. A number of portable lasers were being refitted and chemical specialists had begun brewing explosive concoctions. Mint had always been proud of human ingenuity and her species' technological advancement. This delight in creating the deadly weapons of war reminded her of the price paid over the centuries for those advances.

At present, she was in charge of the barricade whilst Aaron stretched out for some much needed sleep on the rear floor of a truck. The distant line of tree soldiers remained implacably in place. No movement had been observed since they assumed their positions. Mint couldn't help but feel that this was the calm before the storm; Tiada Vejour was preparing, completely unchallenged, maybe for the final play. She always tried to quell the unease that prospect generated, didn't want to add energy to their foe. She wasn't always successful. The troops around her seemed more at ease. They rotated lookout duties and took it in turns to snatch brief periods of sleep. How they did it was a mystery to Mint. They would come off watch, settle against a vehicle or defensive position, close their eyes and be asleep in moments.

"Still all quiet on the western front?" Aaron had joined her silently. The wooded area was on the south-southwest side of town so Mint was a little puzzled by the phrasing of his question.

"Yes," she said.

"Why don't you go home for a while?" Aaron suggested. "Rick Gatiss can work as my deputy and I promise to call you as soon as anything happens."

"I don't know," Mint said. "Although, I would like to check in on Gabriel, see how the vigil is going."

"Go on then," Aaron pulled her arm gently. "Don't come back without having slept."

Mint nodded silently as she trudged away and climbed into her 4x4. All the vehicles had been turned towards town a while ago, Mint's idea in case a hasty retreat was called for. Her eyes were weary as she stared out at the road forcing her to consciously ease off on the accelerator. It took over ten minutes to reach the hospital's emergency services parking spaces, by which time full night had fallen.

Only Trent Webster was visible through the door window when she arrived at Gabriel's room. She noticed Daniel and Gretta in the corner when she entered. They were sat cross-legged on the floor, heads close, whispering to each other, but raised a hand in greeting when she smiled their way.

"Finally persuaded Penny to go home?" she asked Trent when he turned to her. His eyes were baggy from lack of sleep.

"Mm-hmm," he nodded.

"Let me take over," Mint offered. "Go home and grab some shut eye."

"No," Trent shook his head. "Penny's gone home to do that, she took the vehicle. Gretta and I will go home when she returns in about three hours."

"Thanks for doing this," Mint placed a hand on his shoulder. "Has anything else happened?"

"Not a thing," Trent said. He stared at the slumbering form of Gabriel for a moment. "Gabriel tends to wake up for an hour then he's back to sleep for two. We always ask if he's heard from Bruce when he wakes but …"

"It'll come," Mint tried to sound reassuring. "I've got the labs working on makeshift weapons for the next attack by those tree soldiers."

"I know," Trent looked up at her. "Gretta came with me to the lab while Penny was here. I helped devise a new power coupling for the mobile lasers; everyone's pulling out all the stops at the labs, desperate to be useful. Mounting lasers on trucks would you believe, after they've dismantled the rear cargo holds. I think you'll be getting some long range grenade launchers too. Some faces lit up with anticipation when Roman delivered the grenades to my lab."

"Sounds great," Mint nodded as she stifled a yawn.

"You look more tired than me," Trent pointed out. "Leave us to it, we're ok here. Go home, get some sleep."

"Call me, I mean it, call me if anything happens," Mint retreated to the door. "Straight away, don't wait," she said from the threshold.

"Go," Trent laughed. "Of course we will."

Mint sat in her 4x4 and slowly sucked on a piece of chocolate, enjoyed the silky texture. She couldn't remember the last time she had eaten properly, probably late morning, when Reid brought coffee and sandwiches. Starting the engine, she reversed out and set course for her sister's home, arrived five minutes later.

Java ushered her in silently, indicating that Mikey was asleep and led her through to the kitchen.

"You look spent," Java said quietly, "how long since you ate or slept?"

"Hours since food," Mint admitted. "We've been napping in turns at the barricade."

"That's no good," Java shook her head and reached into a tall refrigerator, withdrew a wrapped package. "Here, have this sandwich while I warm up some stew from earlier."

Mint tucked into the sandwich hungrily while Java busied herself at the hob.

"I heard about the firefight," Java said. "Your constables were proud of you, eager to confirm you were ok."

"Thanks," Mint said after swallowing the last bite. "And thanks for running refreshments around. How are you bearing up?"

"I can't stop looking up at that missile," Java admitted. "Every time I'm out there driving I have to check it out, make sure it isn't moving, you know? Reid doesn't mention it but I think he's the same. Mikey is just Mikey, I think he's enjoying having Mummy and Daddy with him all the time."

"That's good," Mint said as her sister placed a steaming bowl in front of her. "Try and forget the missile, we don't think Tiada Vejour intends to drop it, the Varla seems to have other ideas."

"Eat up," Java said, walking away. "I'll get the guest bed made up for you."

Mint settled onto the comfortable bed ten minutes later. She left firm instructions to be awoken if any reports came through.

*

Bruce awoke. At least it felt like waking up, could he really sleep as a creature of thought with no body? The storm was no longer raging within him, which was good. He thought back to when Tiada Vejour found him invading his memories and shuddered. Thank goodness he had found Bruce there, not on the connection to Gabriel. The thought of his friend made his own memories resurface, but he felt a strange duality to them. There were memories of other events he knew he hadn't been involved in.

Bruce concentrated and understanding began to form. Tiada Vejour had flooded his mind with its own memories, planted them into his memory. He accessed the memory of killing Jaicon Hewson and recoiled from the violence immediately. It hadn't hurt, though. He could access the Varla's memories without pain. Tiada Vejour had inadvertently given Bruce a great gift, the background information he wanted so badly. In its arrogance and desire to inflict pain, the Varla had done his job for him. It really couldn't have any idea about the connection to Gabriel. Bruce lay back down on his bed and began to study the new memories he could access.

Day 5

Mint awoke to a stream of bright, morning light as Java opened the blinds in the guest room.

"Don't be angry," Java said defensively. "Aaron called here, traced your command-pad. He was very sweet. Told us to let you sleep undisturbed, everything was in order and you needed the rest."

"Dammit, Java," Mint rose quickly. She ached in a few places where her tactical suit had been rough. "I wanted news as soon as it happened."

"Don't shout at me," Java jumped.

"I'm sorry," Mint was instantly contrite. "I have to go though."

"Not before breakfast," Java winced, "Aaron's orders."

"I'm getting sick of Aaron's orders," Mint shook her clothes comfortable. "But, that synth-bacon does smell good. Maybe I'll roll with this one."

Mint was assaulted by an excited but heavy-eyed Mikey when she sat down in the kitchen. He sat on her knee as he munched his synth-bacon roll and Mint gobbled down hers.

"Wow, you were hungry," Reid said. "Want another?"

Mint's command-pad pinged before she could answer. She nodded as she withdrew the device from a pocket and looked at the screen. It was a message from Penny, at Gabriel's bedside: Get here, now!

"I've got to go, Bruce is in contact again, I think."

Reid handed her his own, untouched roll as Mint headed for the door. Java gave her a silent hug at the front door and watched as her twin sister rushed to the 4x4 and drove away.

Mint was at the hospital within five minutes. She had to admit the full night's sleep had done wonders for her clarity of thought and wakefulness. Damn that Aaron – right again. His 4x4 was parked in an emergency services space when she reached the car park; Penny must be excited by whatever was happening. Mint jogged all the way through silent corridors to Gabriel's room. Doc Davidson, Aaron and Penny were crowded around the bed upon which Gabriel was sat up.

"Hello, Sergeant Harris," Gabriel said.

"Hello, Gabriel, you're looking a lot better," Mint smiled back.

"It's me, Bruce, I'm talking through Gabriel."

Mint opened her mouth to speak but no words presented themselves. The voice was Gabriel's, she recognised it.

"Yeah, me too," Aaron chuckled. "Carry on, Bruce."

"As I said, Tiada Vejour has made a huge mistake," Bruce said through Gabriel's mouth. "It caught me trying to access its memories. It was angry at me, hurt me." Penny let out a whimper and gripped Gabriel's hand tighter in the clutch of both of hers. "It's ok Mum, I'm fine now. It fired its memories into me. It's so arrogant; it didn't see how I could possibly use them. Anyway, I've been accessing them to find out its capabilities and some of its history. It's an outcast; there was a war among the Varla K'dyamon after they destroyed the Imperial G'frak Heirescence. That's the alien race that created them. Tiada Vejour was leader of a faction that wanted control but a stronger faction fought them off; it fled here to hide and try to regain its power. It knew the Starjump constructs would be discovered by a young, spacefaring species and chose this planet as it bore primitive life and was close to one of the constructs. It was bound to attract visitors and, hopefully, colonists."

"Bruce, how long can you talk for?" Aaron asked. "Tell us vital information first, please."

"It's ok," Gabriel/Bruce replied. "I've used its memories to learn how to control this disembodied existence. I know exactly what it's doing now and have loads of time to withdraw from the connection. I've also hidden this pathway a lot better. I know how and when to get my body back and escape. Actually, Tiada Vejour will give me back my body. It has to when it migrates back to its body. That will be today, you need to prepare. I'll have a small portion of its energy still and know how to use it; I should be able to fly as far as the road."

"That's great, but those tree soldiers are lined up on the treeline," Mint said. "We had enough trouble fighting two; we can't get past that many to rescue you."

"You'll have a slight advantage," Bruce replied. "Tiada Vejour will be fully occupied when it transits into its body. Those tree soldiers aren't entirely autonomous, there's a degree of central control. When it makes the migration they'll be vulnerable, and they are all deployed along the treeline, there's no more."

"What about the missile and Tiada Vejour's physical form?" Aaron asked, leaning forward hungrily for the answer.

"It doesn't want to drop it but I can't access its actual plan, that's far too risky. The transition is the time to take back control or destroy the missile. As for fighting Tiada Vejour, forget it. It's way too powerful. It is physical; some sort of flesh, bone, and shell, but it has different organs. As you know, it feeds on energy so there's no digestive system. Hitting one of the storage bladders would definitely injure it badly but they're all located under a hard outer shell and it can manipulate energy to form a protective shield that would easily repel your weapons."

"You're saying we're beaten already?" Mint asked. "What's the point, then?"

"Tiada Vejour wants to reunite its faction, seek out its old allies. It needs energy to do that, your energy. It wants to keep people alive and harvest them. That's its plan for Charlestown. It will use the other towns and cities to feed its allies when they arrive here. Obsirion II will become its headquarters as it prepares to hunt out Moonquom and Keny-Thon. They're the leaders of the faction that defeated it before."

"Human slaves," Aaron muttered. "To be controlled by Tiada Vejour and fed whatever visions serve its hunger for energy."

"That's its plan," Bruce confirmed. "It can control minds, too; that's what happened to Jaicon Hewson and me. It plans to organise people, like a religion; it got the idea from Gabriel's parents, make people worship it, that will deliver energy, but it will also make them more willing to accept the visions and that'll increase the energy feed. It has people in town ready to help it but I don't recognise their faces. Wait, sorry, I have to withdraw now."

Gabriel's body slumped back and his eyes blinked rapidly. Penny Webster tended to him as she sobbed; Doc Davidson began a series of physical checks on his patient.

"It's going to set up a cult to worship it," Aaron stated. He turned to look sternly at Mint. "We have plans to make."

"I'm going after Bruce, don't try to stop me," Mint stated.

"You'll never get through," Aaron argued. "He can use residual energy to get to the road, let him make his own escape from there; he's shown he's capable."

"No," Mint stuck to her decision. "He'll be freshly back in his body and likely very confused, who knows how Tiada Vejour may leave him, anyway. No, he needs help and that's where I come in. I'll need a hover-jet."

"Ok, ok, let's see what we can plan," Aaron compromised. "What about these locals that Tiada Vejour's recruited, any ideas who they may be?"

"A few," Mint said after a moment. "I wouldn't worry; they're just disenchanted youths, harmless, with no access to weaponry."

*

Roman put the data-pad back in his pocket. It hadn't taken any thought to agree to accompany Mint and that made him feel guilty. Hannah and Daniel popped into his head, what would they do if he didn't return? But, they were growing up and becoming fine, capable human beings.

Besides, if the plan failed to deliver the desired result there wasn't a future for Charlestown and its citizens.

He powered down the desk screen, taking one last disparaging look at the indecipherable symbols before he did so. The tactical clothing felt stiff and uncomfortable as he walked out of the lab; it was designed for active wear, not sitting at a desk. There was plenty of activity on his personal horizon so he was sure it wouldn't bother him for long. It wasn't until he reached the underground car park that he remembered his SOC truck had been at the hydrogen fuel plant when Tiada Vejour destroyed it. Looking around, he found the area empty of police vehicles; Constable Fletcher must have taken the last one when he left ten minutes ago. Roman's eyes settled on Jaicon Hewson's vehicle, still parked in the far corner. He just hoped it still had liquid hydrogen fuel in the tank.

The late Mr Hewson had been shorter than Roman; he took some time to make the necessary seating adjustments to assume a comfortable position. Despite his concern, the engine fired up easily enough and the tank read half full. The station soon receded behind him. He ignored the traffic control lights at the central crossroads, waved at one of the weapons specialists busily unloading boxes from their truck. Roman hoped they had a foolproof plan to neutralise the missile. He adjusted a mirror to glare at the hanging danger above town then shook his head and drove on.

Weapons were suddenly raised as he approached the barricade. Roman slowed down and leaned out of the window so he could be identified. He'd forgotten he was in a civilian vehicle and understood the reaction; he chided himself for the slip. Mint and Aaron dashed over to him when he pulled up.

"Why?" Mint asked.

"Only vehicle left in the garage, Fletcher took the last one," Roman explained.

"This is Jaicon Hewson's?" Mint stared at the vehicle.

"No other choice, sorry."

"He's here," Aaron butted in. "That's what matters. Get going or timing will be shot to shit."

Mint turned to say goodbye but couldn't summon the right words now the time had finally arrived. Aaron held his hand out but Mint leaned in and wrapped her arms around his neck.

"See you on the other side," she said when she released him and stalked to the passenger door, climbed in next to Roman.

"Take care and good luck," Aaron called after her.

Roman noticed the look on Mint's face and quelled bitter disappointment. Silently, he made a three point turn and retraced his recent drive from the crossroads, carrying straight on this time.

This end of town mirrored the opposite side. They exited the central administrative and shopping zone and passed through a wide spread of residences. Greenhouses followed in their regular band, sharply changing to agricultural fields, although algae ponds were also present in their recognisable grid patterns. The forest afterwards was not as hilly as it was on the far side. Laboratory buildings were visible within the trees, a multitude of coloured vehicles gathered in their car parks. Roman checked his rear-view mirror and smiled satisfactorily when he saw a police vehicle not too far behind, leading a convoy of personal vehicles. The slowly staged evacuation to the laboratories had begun. It wasn't the ideal area to move Charlestown's population to, but it was furthest from Tiada Vejour and his small army.

Roman parked at the second laboratory and walked in to the reception area with his boss, both had shouldered police issue rifles. Ancillary staff had stayed away so nobody was there to guide them. He pulled out his data-pad and messaged Trent Webster. They only had to wait a few minutes for Trent to appear and wave them through a side door. Bruce's father was tight-lipped and focussed. Roman could understand that. They walked along a corridor in silence, through an engineering workshop and out into a loading bay. Roman stopped and stared when he saw the truck. It was a rugged six wheeler, off-road capable, with what had once been a double cabin and cargo section at the rear. The interior was open to the elements now, except for a section above the driver and passenger seats. A generator and fuel tank were bolted to the rear superstructure, surrounded by protective metal grating. A tripod mount arose a short distance behind the front seats with a three metre long industrial laser attached on a swivel joint. There was a sling and footplate system rigged up to hold the weapon's operator.

"What do you think?" Trent asked.

"I think you guys have a dangerous streak running through you," Mint said. "Have you test driven it?"

"I took it for its first spin after we got your message. It's a little heavy in the steering but handles fine. Come on over, Roman, I'll show you how the laser works."

Mint climbed up to the driver's seat and familiarised herself with the controls; they weren't dissimilar to those in her 4x4. She could hear Trent and Roman talking behind her and detected the distant sound of a hover-jet.

"Transport's inbound," she turned and said. "Make it quick Trent; we'll be leaving as soon as it gets here."

"I'm coming with you," Trent turned his determined eyes on her.

"No way," Mint shook her head, "no civilians."

"I am Bruce's father," Trent announced slowly. "You are not fucking keeping me away."

"Trent, Mint's right," Roman said with a hand on his shoulder.

"No, I'm going with you," Trent was obstinate, shook off the hand. "Anyway, you'll need a third pair of hands when you pick up my son, and an engineer in case this goes wrong." He patted the laser.

The hover-jet was much closer now, swinging round to land just outside a pair of nearby gates. Two crew members jumped out and beckoned them over. Mint swore loudly and colourfully and brought the truck's engine to life. She drove angrily and hit the brakes hard, made Roman and Trent stumble in the back.

"You stubborn son of a bitch," Mint shouted at Trent. "You will do exactly what we tell you to do – understand?"

Trent stood with his chin defiantly raised and nodded. Another hover-jet crew member ushered them into the crew compartment while the other two unrolled a large net and drove the truck onto it. Mint was directed to the window seat and looked out at the loading activity as her harness buckles were fastened and checked. She watched as the net was gathered atop the truck and attached to a short, stout length of winch cable. The hover-jet lifted into the air and drifted over the load. Mint heard a loud clunk followed by a whirring sound she assumed was the winch motor. The crew member had finished buckling in Roman and Trent and opened the door on the far side of the compartment. He lowered a winch and swiftly lifted the two crew members. Once they were safely inside and the door was fastened, the hover-jet started forward in a shallow ascent.

Mint could understand Trent's need to accompany them. It hadn't been considered in mission planning though; it was supposed to be Mint and Roman making a lightning dash to rescue Bruce and join up with Aaron at the barricade. She hoped it was the one and only mission upset.

Her eyes drifted to the outside view. They were quite high now, several hundred metres at least and she could see Charlestown and its environs spread out below in concentric rings. A convoy of vehicles was snaking along the road towards the labs, another forming up in the nearest residential area. Mint changed her perspective to take in the missile. It was still hanging above town and she thought she could make out the weapons specialist team working on a rooftop. So much revolved around their successful destruction of that weapon; if Tiada Vejour detonated it in town the whole mission was pointless.

A vehicle moving in the hospital grounds caught her attention. It was her 4x4; she knew it would be without examination. Thankfully, she hadn't been forced to rely on Aaron's authority to convince Doc Davidson to play his essential role; Penny had been there when she outlined the plan and her motherly persuasiveness had been utilised instead. She would be sat in the driver's seat, Gabriel and the Doc would be on the back seats with the mobile medical equipment. If he could persuade one, Doc Davidson had promised to have a paramedic in the front passenger seat.

Town was slipping past much quicker now as the hover-jet accelerated. It was headed directly towards New Cambridge.

*

Bruce could feel the tension rising in Tiada Vejour. It was excited, anxious to begin. He smiled; his body would be his own again very soon. He only hoped Sergeant Harris and the tall man in black clothing had a good plan to snatch him away from recapture.

Tiada Vejour tensed and Bruce felt a rising power. Was this it? He sat on his imaginary bed and tapped into the Varla, just in time to feel a great outrushing of terror.

*

Aaron gripped his head as the wave of fright washed over him. He sank to his knees, aware of many others doing the same. It took a good deal of willpower to rise up and stare at the screen on the makeshift table, still displaying the optical sensor's view of the distant treeline. The tree soldiers were advancing.

*

This wasn't right, Bruce knew instantly. He hadn't sensed any hint of this in Tiada Vejour's planning. A sneering sensation washed over him.

'One last meal before I return to a proper, powerful body," the Varla's voice was painful. "You will then witness the true might of a Varla K'dyamon, and cower, as you should."

*

Penny had slammed her foot on the brake as soon as she felt the terror. Screaming had filled the inside of the 4x4 as they all cried out in fear.

She awoke, slumped forward on the steering wheel. The 4x4 had veered off the road and crashed into a greenhouse. As Penny raised her aching head she saw the vehicle was half inside, fruit was smashed and smeared on the bonnet. Plant stems and pieces of greenhouse structure dangled off the vehicle. The paramedic in the passenger seat gave her a half-hearted thumbs up gesture and a quick peer into the back confirmed Doc Davidson was ok; he was studying readouts on the mobile medical equipment and gave her a perfunctory nod. Penny fired up the engine and engaged reverse gear. For a dreadful moment she thought the 4x4 was stuck, pushed down harder on the accelerator. With a screech and rending sound as greenhouse support struts scratched and tore along its flanks the 4x4 backed out onto the road surface.

*

A convoy of evacuating civilian vehicles was passing by below the weapons specialist team when the wave of terror reached them. Vehicles had slammed into walls below as control was lost, raising a clamour of building and vehicle alarms. One member of the team rolled from his knees as his head swam and fell from the fourth storey roof. His ruined body was visible on a caved in vehicle roof below. The police constable from the head of the convoy was still shaking her head clear as she tried to reorganise the evacuees, discover which vehicles were still mobile.

The leader of the military team looked at the missile just as it began to move.

"Get the rocket launcher!" he roared.

His remaining team member grabbed the launcher and rested it on his shoulder as the leader reached for the laser targeting pistol and aimed. By this time the missile had dropped several metres but almost completed a turn to aim upwards.

"Don't wait, fire the bloody thing."

A rocket leapt out of the launch tube as internal air cylinders decompressed. After it had travelled five metres, the main rocket engine flared, and it accelerated towards the laser designated target.

However, the missile had now begun to rise. Its engine was starting to apply power but the team leader knew its movement must be due to external influences, it was so fast. His helmet microphone had a direct link to Aaron, which he triggered.

"The missile's turned 180 degrees and is rising. We've fired the rocket but I don't think we're going to hit it," he reported.

"Try remote detonation of your rocket," Aaron replied. "Hope for a shrapnel hit."

The team leader punched the self-destruct button, looked up, and shook his head. The rocket had exploded in a spectacular fireball but the missile was beyond its influence, still accelerating.

"The missile's gone ballistic, it has not been destroyed."

*

"Shit!" Aaron barked.

"What?" Rick Gatiss shouted over from the barricade.

"The missile," Aaron called back. "It's turned and gone ballistic. We failed to destroy it."

"What's it going to do?" Rick yelled. "Gain height and come back down?"

"No, I don't think so," Aaron shook his head. Then it hit him and he quickly tapped buttons on his command-pad.

"Patch me through to Space Station 1, stat," he said.

"This is spa ..."

"You have a missile inbound," Aaron cut off the response. "Launch the Lightning and defend the station."

*

Clouds of chaff floated away in the vacuum outside Space Station 1. The Lightning was away quickly, the crew were prepping for flight when the frantic call came from flight control. They ditched the remaining procedures and made an emergency detach. Manoeuvring thrusters pushed the boxy spaceship away from its launch platform to join the floating, radar reflective cloud of foil pieces. The weapons officer pointed to a rapidly approaching flash of bright light as the pilot engaged the main thruster and the crew were all pushed back into their flight seats by the acceleration.

In a flash, the Varla guided missile streaked past the Lightning, through the useless chaff and slammed into the space station. A powerful blast wave caught up with the spaceship thirty seconds later, pummelled it with debris. Warning lights began to flash on the control consoles.

*

Aaron hung his head. The expression on his contact's face clearly told him the space station had been hit. The command-pad began to shake in his trembling hand. He took a double handed hold of it and watched as the man's face tried to regain a professional attitude.

"Did the Lightning get away in time?" Aaron asked.

"We … we received separation confirmation before Space Station 1 went offline. We are attempting to establish a link with Space Stations 2 and 3, and the Lightning."

Aaron stared impatiently at the screen, he hated waiting. He heard calm, forceful orders from the barricade and knew the advancing tree soldiers had entered the effective range of the new weapons.

"Ok, sorry for the wait, sir," the New Cambridge contact finally spoke again. "Space Stations 1 and 3 have been destroyed. We have a weak signal from station 2 but they're about to evacuate in the lifepods. The Lightning is still operational but has sustained engine damage. ETA over target area is forty-three minutes."

"Thank you," Aaron said as he cut the connection. "Shit!"

The dull thud and boom of grenade explosions reached him from beyond the barricade and he sprinted over to the screen to establish situational awareness. The screen was split into six separate views to guard against total loss of feed. Each view showed advancing tree soldiers. They had deployed the slats in an umbrella formation, responding to the threat from the lobbed grenades. The scientists and engineers had already delivered one batch of scratch-built mortars; another was due, hopefully soon.

"Use the sniper rifles with AP," Aaron shouted to Rick.

"One step ahead of you," Rick yelled back. "Get the rest of the artillery here."

Aaron was lifting his command-pad as he noticed something strange on one of the screens. Six of the tree soldiers had gathered together, two in the middle with four spread evenly around them. As he watched, the outer four lowered the slats in the middle, and the inner two's large arms pumped out balls of energy. The slats raised again in defence.

"Incoming!" Aaron screamed. "Rick they're forming fire groups, sniper priority."

An overhead defensive plate had been erected above the screen but Aaron still crouched as low as he dared while still keeping a good view on the screen. He hastily fitted the helmet over his head; it had been casually left on the ground nearby. Eighteen of the tree soldiers had now formed into three fire groups, another fifteen were still advancing.

*

Bruce watched the tree soldiers form up as Tiada Vejour had ordered. He had thought about making contact through Gabriel when the Varla had sent the missile against the space station but knew such a warning would be too late. No, he needed to wait until he was certain transition was close. It didn't feel like that was imminent but it must be soon.

*

Kris's group had received a warning to become active about a quarter of an hour before the wave of terror was unleashed. Tiada Vejour had only told him what it wanted at the initial contact; detailed planning was entrusted to him. The hurried organisation of evacuation convoys had given his group the opportunity it needed to congregate and sneak into the town centre.

Kris' grin had been fierce when he saw the trooper's body fall onto the vehicle below the weapons specialist team's rooftop position. He had quickly despatched a couple of his people to relieve the body of its gun and ammunition and bring them back to him. It also left a smaller contingent to be dealt with on the roof. He had already sent a group of six tough lads to sort them out.

The feel of the assault rifle in his hands gave him an immense feeling of pleasure and excitement. He had interrogated the knowledge database thoroughly in the time available and knew, in theory, how to use it. His eyes were fixed on the rooftop over the street from his temporary base of operations in a small clothes shop. On the other side of the road, the hateful bitch of a female police constable, who had arrested him for shoplifting a year ago, was gathering the survivors of the crashed vehicles and organising them to clear the obstructed road. He watched as her head lifted and then caught the shouts and sounds of a struggle from the roof. A body crashed to the pavement. It wasn't a soldier; it was Grant, his youngest follower. Cursing, Kris rose and made for the door.

The constable must have caught his movement because she was looking his way as he exited the shop. It didn't matter; he had the assault rifle ready, her hands were empty. His first shot impacted her shoulder and spun her around. The next two punched into her back. She collapsed onto the road and lay still in a spreading pool of blood.

Screams sounded all around him. Kris held the gun aloft and fired off another three round burst.

"Shut the fuck up," he roared. "Soldiers on the roof – put your guns down or I start killing civilians."

It was quiet for a moment. Kris was about to shout again, his gun aimed at a cowering child when the sound of two shots echoed down from the rooftop. The bodies of the other two soldiers plummeted to the ground immediately afterwards.

"We've got their guns," Harald Jones shouted down to him.

"Get your arses down here," Kris shouted. "Fuck ups, have to do everything myself," he said quietly to himself.

Kris' eyes panned around the street. People were staring at him, terrified. He liked it, this fired his blood.

"Shut up," he shouted at a whimpering family group. "No evacuation for you. Round them up!"

The rest of his group had followed him from the shop and began to throw their weight about, corralled people into a tight knot. Harald and the remaining four walked out of the building opposite and sauntered over to Kris, brandishing the weapons they had appropriated.

"A rocket launcher, nice!" Kris' eyes lit up. "Time to kill more of the fuzz."

*

Penny had stopped the 4x4 a good one hundred and fifty metres away from the roadblock. She could feel Doc Davidson leaning through the gap between the front seats to stare at the spectacle ahead. The troops were spread in a wide line along the barricade and into the fields, and had started to lob grenades from long tubular structures soon after they had parked up. The return fire had made them gasp when the sparking, orange balls of energy began to loop though the air. Apart from the constant worry about her son, all Penny could think was how lovely a day it was for such violence to be perpetrated. The odd thought also ran through her mind that one hundred and fifty metres separation from the maelstrom may not be sufficient.

"They're going to need me soon, I need to get closer," the paramedic stated as she climbed out.

Penny remained silent and watched her jog away.

"She's a brave girl," Doc Davidson whispered next to her ear. "Don't get any ideas about driving closer, I can see perfectly well from here."

"Are you reading my mind?" Penny tried to smile. "Don't worry, there's no danger of that happening. How's Gabriel?"

"I'm good, Mrs Webster," the boy's thin voice piped up.

"It's a strain on you, take it easy," Doc Davidson ordered.

"No contact from Bruce yet?" Penny asked.

"No, Mrs Webster."

Penny pursed her lips and stared out of the windscreen again, flinched as another ball of energy hit the barricade.

*

"Time to commit the mobile lasers," Rick Gatiss yelled at Aaron from the barricade.

The gunners and drivers must have heard, they were already revving for action when Aaron looked their way and nodded. Three modified all terrain trucks had been delivered to the barricade forces so far. Of the rest, Mint had appropriated one for her mission, and another three were supposed to be on the verge of completion. Aaron hoped they were rushing with those and the other weapons due to be delivered, he wasn't optimistic about their chances of holding off this full frontal attack without them. In truth, he wasn't too optimistic even when he factored them in.

Another energetic blast sounded from the barricade. It was taking a real pounding from the fire groups the tree soldiers had set up. They were a problem he hoped the mobile lasers could solve. The armour piercing sniper rounds were effective against the enemy but they were tough targets; they also kept swapping roles, so a shielding tree soldier one minute may rotate with another to be one of the firing pair the next.

The improvised mortar artillery, provided by the scientists and engineers, had proved quite effective. It didn't have the range to accurately target the fire groups; however, there were plenty of tree soldiers advancing down the road and through the fields which were much closer. Two had been taken out of the game so far and Aaron needed to analyse damage to a third.

The trucks raised fountains of soil as they left the road and entered the fields. Aaron watched them for a few seconds then returned his attention to the screen. No, the third tree soldier was heavily damaged but remained operational. Great, he still had thirty-one to worry about, thirteen of which continued a relentless advance. So far, there had not been any casualties amongst Aaron's defenders. He wasn't complacent, that situation would not last. As if sensing his thoughts, a paramedic bundled under his defensive shield.

"Anybody need me yet?" the paramedic asked, breathing heavily.

"Stay here and wait for the screams, then you'll know when and where you're needed," Aaron answered with a shake of his head. "Rick," he shouted. "Concentrate sniper fire on the same targets as the mobile lasers."

Rick Gatiss gave him a quick salute in acknowledgement and shouted out his orders. Looking back at the screens, Aaron spotted the trucks bumping across the fields. Suddenly, they all braked hard and came to an abrupt stop. Three modified lasers swung on target, there was a brief pause as targeting was fine-tuned then they fired simultaneously. Aaron cast his eyes back onto the screen to analyse their effectiveness, and punched the air when he saw a shielding tree soldier shedding slats at a prodigious rate. Just as the trucks recommenced their crazy romp across the fields he caught the sound of a mass volley of sniper rifles and looked back at the relevant fire group in time to see the tree soldier's demise. This was more like it; his people were working well as a team.

As if in response to the destruction of one of their own, the tree soldiers fired en masse. All of the incoming balls of energy appeared to be aimed at one point on the barricade, the far right side. Aaron cupped his hands to his mouth to shout out a warning but it was too late. The bolts of energy fired by the advancing tree soldiers impacted much earlier than those from the fire groups and blew a hole in the defensive structure. It began to lose structural integrity and sagged dangerously as Aaron watched. Two of his troopers were lying on the ground nearby, flung away from their positions by the blast. The paramedic started to move.

"Not yet," Aaron grabbed her shoulder firmly. His finger pointed into the sky where another group of energy balls could be seen descending. They landed with fresh explosive percussion and completed the process of dismantling that three metre width of defences.

"Go now," Aaron shouted at the paramedic. "Keep low and drag them out of the way; that breach will attract more incoming fire."

*

Constable Fletcher revved the big truck's engine and followed the leading all-terrain truck out of the laboratory's car park. Instinctively, he'd lifted his data-pad before setting off, intended to inform his boss of the current situation. He had blushed slightly when he remembered Sergeant Harris was not to be contacted; she was on a separate, more dangerous mission. Fletcher shifted in the seat, his crotch uncomfortably pinched. He'd never worn the tactical clothing outside of training and exercises, and now here he was, about to enter a warzone with a convoy of weaponry. Well, he always strove to excel in his daily work and wanted to follow a career path up the police rank structure. He would work damned hard to ensure he impressed in this unusual duty.

The lead truck set off at pace when they turned onto the main road and soon left him behind. Fletcher remembered the warning from the scientists; some of the explosive munitions he carried may be less stable than others so he wasn't to jostle them too much. He drove at a steadier speed. He could see the other two all-terrain trucks with their rear mounted lasers in his wing mirrors. Apart from a few constables who were still on convoy escort duty, this small convoy amounted to the bulk of Charlestown's police contingent. Some were more excited about the pending conflict than others.

Fletcher frowned when he looked further along the road and saw a lone vehicle approaching the lead truck. It was a police vehicle but where was the convoy of civilian traffic? As he watched, the police vehicle slewed sideways and stopped in a cloud of dust. A figure stepped out on the far side and rested something long and cylindrical on the roof. Realisation dawned when a plume of smoke shot from the back of it and something rocketed forwards, aimed at the lead truck.

His foot found the brakes and pushed down hard. The wheels locked and the big truck skidded as the truck ahead was consumed by a ball of flames. Debris clattered down onto the road about fifty metres in front of him, the chassis of the truck could be seen within the inferno, black smoke rising from it in a roiling pillar. The trucks from the rear drew alongside his truck and stopped, Fletcher could see the constables leaping out of the passenger side doors to take charge of the top mounted lasers.

"Fletcher to Aaron," the data-pad was instinctively in his hands. "Weapons convoy is under attack."

"What?" Aaron's reply was shouted, there was a lot of noise in the background. "All the tree soldiers are here, who is attacking you?"

"I don't kn …" Fletcher stopped abruptly when he saw the long cylinder again, held aloft by two men this time. "Oh shit!" he slammed the truck into reverse and hammered his foot down on the accelerator.

It was already too late. The rocket flew out of the launcher and covered the intervening distance in two seconds. Fletcher was killed instantly when it penetrated the windscreen and punched through the superstructure to the rear cargo compartment. Loaded with an assortment of jury-rigged launchers and projectile ammunition, Kristopher Manson could not have selected a worse target for his second rocket. The explosion was sufficiently violent to knock him from his feet and totally obliterated the three trucks. No reinforcements would reach the barricade defences.

*

Aaron turned on the spot and peered back towards Charlestown. He didn't know which part of the route Fletcher had called from but his eyes were instantly drawn to two distant plumes of smoke on the far side of town. He snatched a pair of optical viewers from the table and stared at the rising smoke with a sinking feeling. One plume was considerably larger than the other; both were black as night and billowing explosively.

"Constable Fletcher," he dropped the viewers and lifted his command-pad. "Constable Fletcher, I need a sit-rep. What is your current condition?"

No answer came.

"Shit!" he shouted and kicked at the ground.

"Boss?" Rick Gatiss had stepped down from the barricade to call to him.

"We have unidentified bad guys to the rear," Aaron spat back at him. "It seems they may have destroyed our reinforcements, so much for Mint calling them harmless."

"Boss, we're outgunned here as it is," Rick shouted back. "I can't spare any bodies to watch our backs."

"Keep firing, I'm on it," Aaron turned and sprinted away from the screens he was monitoring.

*

"What's he doing?" Doc Davidson suddenly asked.

Penny looked up to see a man in tactical uniform dashing towards the 4x4. Anger flared and she dropped the window, leaned out.

"Coward, get back to the fight," she shouted.

"I'm not running away, Mrs Webster," Aaron skidded to a halt, slamming his palms on the bonnet of the 4x4. "It's me, Aaron, but there's no time for this. I've lost contact with our reinforcements and munitions convoy. Their last call mentioned being under attack. I need to know what's occurring back there and have no troops to spare."

"We can't go ..." Doc Davidson started talking but was silenced by Penny's raised hand.

"Let me try Java," she said, raising her data-pad to her mouth. "Java, this is Penny Webster. We have reports of enemy presence behind us, in Charlestown. Do you know anything?"

"It's Kristopher Manson he's go ..." the frantic reply was cut short.

Penny stared at her data-pad in disbelief; she didn't know what to say.

"No!" Aaron grabbed her hand as she lifted the device to speak again. "Who is Kristopher Manson?"

"He works refuse collection in town, mid-twenties, bit of a bad boy," Doc Davidson advised as Aaron tapped away on his command-pad.

"Looks like he's what goes for public enemy number one in this town," Aaron frowned at the personal record on his command-pad. "What's his part in this?"

"Bruce," Gabriel said. They all turned to look at him. "Bruce, can you hear me?"

"Don't try to contact him now," Aaron hissed. "You could blow his advantage. Can you even make contact this way?"

Gabriel's monitor bleeped and his eyes fluttered, his thin body stiffened and twitched for a moment.

"What happened?" Aaron demanded as soon as the boy's eyes popped open.

"Bruce, he answered," Gabriel looked around at the three faces staring at him.

"What about the Varla?" Aaron asked urgently.

"No, just Bruce," Gabriel shook his head weakly. "He didn't know about the missile or the wave of terror and knows nothing about Kristopher. He thinks Tiada Vejour has made secret plans even he hasn't got access to."

"Great," Aaron slammed his hand onto the 4x4s bonnet. "Are you still in touch, when is transition?"

"No, but he's certain its due any time now."

"What are you going to do?" Penny asked. "We're trapped if there are unfriendly forces behind."

"Let me think," Aaron paced away from the vehicle, his head often lifting to stare at the ongoing battle. Several times he turned then paced away again.

"We haven't got time for this," Penny shouted at him. "My Bruce is counting on us."

"No, you're right," Aaron finally returned to the 4x4. "We stay here and continue the fight. Destroying the Varla is top priority."

Penny watched with her mouth open as Aaron ran back towards the barricade.

"What about Bruce?" she shouted after him.

Her words were lost, swallowed amidst the sounds of conflict.

*

Aaron tried to quell the worry by immersing himself in the battle. The screens showed one fire group had been negated; three tree soldiers had been rendered harmless, the other three were advancing now they could no longer use that tactic. A quick glance showed the paramedic had now dragged three bodies from the barricade to dubious safety further back. She was working on one of his people; another had been ominously covered up from head to toe. The third was sat with her back against a truck wheel.

He knew his options had all been bad. To continue the combat here condemned most, if not all, of his fighting force to death. Retreating to deal with the threat behind would likely save his people and most of the town's population - but at what cost? He wouldn't have proper control over the attempted destruction of Tiada Vejour from a distance and that made an already risky plan even more likely to fail. Mint and Roman would be isolated in their insane dash to try and rescue Bruce Webster. Aaron was quite certain now that Tiada Vejour had recruited, or taken control of, Kristopher Manson to subvert the evacuation. If, by some miracle, they managed to destroy the Varla, he would immediately have a dangerous hostage situation on his hands. Aaron knew it was more likely he would fail to destroy the alien and have to make a hasty withdrawal; would that be under fire? So, this unexpected move by Tiada Vejour had ruined all their planning for every eventuality; would they fail to save a portion of the population, and if so, how many?

Aaron balled his fists in impotent frustration. He knew no plan survived first contact with the enemy but it seemed all the worst case scenarios he'd considered hadn't been worst case enough. A small part of him enjoyed the dark humour that he needed more pessimistic people on his planning teams.

The three trucks were still charging around in the fields; too fast for the tree soldiers to bring accurate fire against. That cheered him slightly. He could see they were still combining with the snipers and working to disrupt the second fire group. As he watched the screen they came to a stop again and fired their lasers at a fresh target. A volley of sniper rifle fire followed and another tree soldier was disposed of. However, the move had been anticipated and a rapid response ensued. Multiple balls of energy hammered into the barricade where a pair of snipers was positioned. They were knocked backwards and only one got back to his feet.

Aaron ran to the scene, arriving at the same time as the paramedic. She took one look at the man and shook her head. Aaron's decision was made for him. He relieved the dead trooper of his ammunition bandolier and picked up the sniper rifle.

"Gather all the wounded's weapons and ammunition," he said to the paramedic as she began to drag the body out of the way. "We're going to need it."

He didn't wait for a reply and climbed onto the defensive bulwark. A quick peer over the top set his heart racing faster. There were a dozen tree soldiers close to the defenders, one full strength fire group, and one down to four members. He raised his head again and concentrated on the advancing tree soldiers. The closest were no more than one hundred metres away but they seemed to have settled down into mounds and were no longer approaching. Ok, so Tiada Vejour wanted to hold them; but was that a sign that a rear attack was incoming or was transition close and it simply needed enough of a buffer?

There's not much I can do in either case he decided, raised the sniper rifle and took a firing stance.

*

Java's face stung from the slap. She didn't know the identities of the two youths holding them captive but she had heard them talking to Kristopher Manson over their data-pads. That brief contact from Penny Webster had resulted in her data-pad being stamped on hard, several times. It still lay at her feet, totally wrecked.

Mikey was cradled to her chest; Reid had wrapped his arms around both of them. Gretta Webster was close but Java had been careful to hide their connection to her. Penny had entrusted her daughter to them while she and Trent worked to get Bruce back. Reid would have a black eye after the solid punch that had knocked him from his feet when he reacted to the assault on his wife. Their captors had laughed afterwards, enjoyed the sight of the cowering townspeople before them. They were being held in the underground car park below the police station. Java found no amusement in the irony.

They had been part of a convoy when crashed vehicles in the centre of town had brought them to a sudden stop. The police constable at the head of the convoy had ushered everyone out of their vehicles to help clear the obstacles. The ambush had played out perfectly. A single shot to the head had killed the constable and brought about a number of screams. They had soon stopped when the young thugs emerged from the surrounding buildings and rounded them all up.

Java hugged Mikey tight while she looked sideways at the thugs. There were only two exits from the car park: the ramp and the doorway at the top of the stairs. The grinning, armed youths had both covered. Java moved one arm surreptitiously, reached to tap on Reid's chest.

"Data-pad," she whispered from the corner of her mouth. "Where is it?"

"Trouser pocket," he replied under his breath. "Give me a minute."

They both watched their captors, waited for the opportunity. The young men were taking their jobs seriously, watching their captives like hawks. One sneered at Java when he saw her eyes on him but kept his eyes moving over the group, eager to spot any signs of sedition. Reid dropped one arm when he was temporarily unobserved but had to stop as the eyes swung back his way.

There was a sudden commotion as an elderly captive stumbled and people milled about. Several jumped to his assistance. The stairway guard shouted at them but they persisted in helping the man to a wall where they sat him down and let him rest his back. By the time the group was rounded back into the huddle, Java and Reid had worked their way to the middle, the data-pad was on Mikey's chest.

Java pretended to play with Mikey as she tapped out a message.

*

Bruce had to be honest with himself and admit he was worried. After the surprise of discovering that Gabriel could instigate contact with him, he had mulled over the information his friend had provided. Bruce had kept the contact as short as possible; he didn't know if Tiada Vejour would have detected Gabriel's incoming call. So far, it appeared not. However, Gabriel had told Bruce about another development he hadn't known about in the Varla's plans. That was the root of his current unease and concern. Tiada Vejour had made detailed plans for the transition and some of the actions and components had completely evaded Bruce's detection.

At present, the Varla was forming its forward shield with the army. It was surprised by the ability of the defenders to destroy a number of its tree soldiers but had a sense of assuredness that, once they formed the forward line, they would be less vulnerable. It had formed the fire groups to counter the advancing tree soldiers' susceptibility to targeted attacks when moving. Once the line was formed, it would leave them to autonomous sentry duties; nothing was to get beyond them. Bruce also knew it was infuriated by the trucks with rear mounted lasers. Did it have a plan to eradicate them? So far, they had proved far too quick and agile for it to target accurately.

Bruce made up his mind and surged along the link to Gabriel.

"Don't reply, just listen," he said. "I have to make this quick. The tree soldiers will form a forward line and cease their advance. Once they're all lined up as a defensive wall, Tiada Vejour plans to commence transition. Its only concern is the trucks. I think it has a plan to deal with them but I don't know what it is. That's all for now, I'll be back later."

*

Penny had been staring at her data-pad with a hand over her mouth when the medical monitors began beeping urgently. She had turned to see Doc Davidson fussing over Gabriel as the boy sat unmoving, his eyes closed. Suddenly, the beeping ceased and Gabriel's eyes snapped open.

"Tree soldiers will stop to form a defensive wall," Gabriel said. "That's when transition will commence. It has to deal with the trucks first and has a plan, but Bruce doesn't know what it is."

"Thank you, Gabriel," Penny said. "How is Bruce?" She couldn't yet face the worry that Gretta was also in danger now.

"He didn't have time, Mrs Webster," Gabriel looked down. "I'm sorry."

"Don't worry, sweetheart," Penny said, although her heart had just sunk a little further. "Aaron, come in, Aaron," she called over the data-pad.

There was no response. Penny leaned out of the vehicle's door and stared along the cluttered road. She could just make out the table she had watched Aaron return to after his recent visit. He wasn't there. She lifted the data-pad and sent a text message: Urgent, contact Penny.

Again, she waited. There was no response. With a deep intake of breath she opened the door and stepped out.

"What are you doing?" Doc Davidson called to her.

"I have to tell them," Penny looked back with frightened eyes. "Aaron won't answer his command-pad."

She faintly heard a shouted reply from the medic but couldn't make out any words. She was forcing her feet forwards, towards the violent maelstrom ahead. To one side of the barricade she spotted three trucks bouncing at speed across the field. A few balls of energy were landing close to them but not near enough to cause any damage. More energy balls must be hitting the barricade; she could see the explosions and flying debris quite clearly.

"Mrs Webster," she heard her name shouted from quite close by.

Penny stopped and looked this way and that, finally spotted the paramedic waving frantically from next to a truck.

"Mrs Webster, come over here, get in cover," the paramedic waved urgently, beckoned her into some small semblance of safety.

Penny ran over, ducking and flinching with each loud bang and explosion. The paramedic was on the near side of the truck with four other people, all troopers. Two were obviously deceased, covered up. Of the others, one was unconscious, the other awake and moaning feebly.

"What are you doing here, get back to safety," the paramedic berated her.

"I can't," Penny shook her head vigorously. "I have a message for Aaron, from Bruce. He doesn't respond to his command-pad."

"Shit!" said the paramedic. She leaned out from behind the cover of the truck and stared along the defensive barricade. "There he is, near the middle."

Penny looked. Sure enough, there was Aaron, right in the thick of the fight. He fired his sniper rifle and immediately ducked down to reload, turned slightly her way.

"Aaron!" Penny shouted, "Aaron, over here."

He didn't hear and stood up again, his back to her. Penny took a deep breath, counted to three in her head and dashed forward. The paramedic lunged to stop her but failed. Debris fell and fluttered from the air all around her as Penny charged forward. She wasn't thinking. Her determination was set on reaching Aaron and passing on the message. An energy ball overshot the defensive wall and hit the ground eight metres away. Penny was lifted from her feet and flung forwards to crash dazed, bruised and filthy against the barricade. Her ears rang and she hurt all over but she lifted her torso up on her elbows and tried to look up. There was a boot a short distance above her, within reach. She stretched out a hand to it. The leg flinched in surprise at her touch and she felt a body drop to the ground beside her. Hands slid under her armpits and lifted her to sit with her back against the defences.

"Who are you?" Trooper Smith demanded.

"Aaron," Penny managed to stammer, "must get message to Aaron."

The trooper stood for a moment then crouched in front of her again. Aaron appeared alongside him.

"Smith, take this," Aaron handed him the sniper rifle. "Mrs Webster, what the fuck are you doing here?"

Penny coughed and spat. "Sorry," she said. "Message for you, couldn't raise you on the command-pad."

"My turn to be sorry," Aaron berated himself, casting his eyes temporarily skyward in self-recrimination. "They're unstoppable out there; I thought I was best used on the frontline. I was wrong."

"Java has sent me a text message," Penny told him. "She's being held prisoner, with other citizens, by armed youths. They're in the police station car park but she thinks other thugs have gone to the laboratories."

"Hostages," Aaron nodded. "Ok, at least I know for definite now. The chances of us being attacked from behind are low. Now, get back to the 4x4, it isn't safe for you here."

"No," Penny shook her head. "Bruce sent a message, too. He says the Varla intends to form a wall in front of you and stop you getting beyond them. Once the wall is fully formed transition will begin. Before that, though, it has to eliminate the trucks. Bruce doesn't know how it plans to do that but I think it will be soon."

"Ok," Aaron helped Penny to her feet. "Come on, let's get you safe."

He put an arm around her shoulders and ushered her away from the barricade in a half crouched run.

"You'll be safe now," he assured her once they had covered thirty metres. "Any more messages, send a text, I'll put my command-pad on vibrate. Good work, Mrs Webster. That was very brave."

Penny couldn't help but smile as she dashed back to the 4x4, eager to leave the violence.

*

Aaron watched her run away and shook his head. How could he have been so stupid? Caught up in the adrenaline and fog of war he'd forgotten his vital communication links. He stabbed his fingers at the command-pad in anger at his careless mistake, and set it to vibration alert.

Glancing around, he spotted the pile of weapons the paramedic had assembled on his request and trotted over to it. He selected an assault rifle with an underslung grenade launcher and filled all available pockets with grenades and ammunition clips. His run back to the barricade was somewhat slower with the added weight.

Aaron angled to the right side of the barricade; that was the side the trucks were currently operating on. It was a shame Bruce couldn't identify Tiada Vejour's plan to deal with them, but any forewarning was welcome. He jumped up to a firing step and gazed across the road and fields beyond to catch sight of the mobile laser platforms. They were attracting a torrent of energy balls but evading them quite easily. What is your plan?

There was a sudden ceasefire from the tree soldiers as they all settled into mounds with slats wrapped around to the front for maximum protection against incoming fire.

"Hammer them," Aaron shouted, immediately ceasing the opportunity. However, something told him this was seriously wrong.

His eyes roved over the battleground in front of him as his mind raced. What was happening here? The tree soldiers aren't fully autonomous, there's an element of Varla control. That was it! Tiada Vejour had withdrawn from the tree soldiers, but why? The defensive wall wasn't fully formed so it couldn't be transition.

A new wave of terror washed over him without warning. All along the barricade, troopers fell to the ground, some writhing, others screaming in pain and anguish. Aaron found himself on all fours, staring at the road surface. It's not real he told himself as the water washed over him, entered his mouth, his lungs. IT'S NOT REAL. He was choking and hacking as the feelings departed his tortured mind. Groggily, he regained his feet and heard Rick Gatiss bellowing out orders further along the barricade, urging his troopers back into action. Aaron unsteadily stepped back to his firing position and stared out at the fields.

He was just in time to see one of the lasers lance into another truck. Realisation dawned as Aaron looked on in fury. The tree soldiers were still locked down as defensive mounds. Tiada Vejour had entered the minds of the crew firing the laser. He ground his teeth as the targeted truck exploded and scattered debris across the field. The command-pad flew to Aaron's mouth.

"Everybody, target that truck," he yelled. "The Varla is in their heads."

It was already too late. The other truck, seeing what had happened, hadn't waited for Aaron's order and had fired on their former colleagues. The Varla K'dyamon exercised its newly regained power and annulled the laser with a defensive force-shield. Simultaneously, it made the driver under its control ram the other vehicle. The trucks hit in a glancing head on crash and jumped into the air. Both crashed back to the ground heavily, raised great fountains of soil. The laser gunners had been thrown clear to lie unmoving in the churned up loam. A fire sprang into life and quickly spread to engulf both wrecks.

Aaron looked down and kicked the barricade in anger.

"Heads up, they're active again," Rick Gatiss' shout pierced his blazing rage.

Sure enough, the tree soldiers were in motion again when Aaron looked out. Tiada Vejour had done its worst. Aaron's mobile weaponry had been negated. He opened fire at the closest target as he noticed the farthest ten tree soldiers disband their fire groups and commence a quick approach. His command-pad vibrated in his pocket.

Aaron retrieved it with trepidation; he didn't need more bad news. It was a text message from New Cambridge. The Lightning had just assumed geosynchronous orbit above the battlefield. He only hoped he was still around to order the missile strike at the critical time.

*

Java stared at the dead body; blood had welled more slowly out of the bullet holes in Kieron Hall's body as his breathing became ever shallower. Eventually his chest ceased its painful rise and fall and the pooled blood began to soak into his t-shirt. His mother had screamed and tried to comfort her dying son but the angry young thug responsible for his murder had swung at her with the rifle's butt and threatened to shoot her too, if she didn't back up.

The wave of terror had caught everybody by surprise, even the thugs holding them captive. Kieron had responded quickly to the snap opportunity once it had passed. The thug from the stairway was still on his back where he had toppled down the flight of steps; his rifle lay on the floor beside his prostrate body. Kieron had so nearly got hands on it first, if only he hadn't half tripped on a dizzy-headed citizen still struggling to his feet. He had stumbled into the half risen thug who had pushed the teenager away with strong arms and grabbed for his gun. Kieron had righted himself and charged back at his adversary, only to be gunned down mercilessly. Another brave citizen had charged at the thug guarding the ramp. She had stopped upon hearing gunfire across the car park and been clubbed down with the butt end of a gun.

This is deadly real, Java thought. She felt a tremble deep inside and began to breathe more deeply and steadily to quell her rising panic. How her twin sister did her job with this kind of threat she had no idea. A new found respect for Mint built in her consciousness. With a final look at the tragic scene, she lightened her iron grip on Mikey and began to surreptitiously tap away at the command-pad again. Potential rescuers had to be warned the thugs were trigger happy.

*

Mint sat next to Trent and marvelled at his calm demeanour. He had never backtracked from his assertion that he was an essential addition to the mission and had carefully followed all of Mint's orders. She was feeling a little more comfortable now with the last-minute change to her plan.

Roman had been behind her, strapped to the laser weapon, since they had been dropped off by the hover-jet. It had taken them twenty miles away from Charlestown on a direct bearing for New Cambridge before it turned in a wide arc and deposited them on a road that connected to the main route back to Charlestown, past the site of the former hydrogen fuel plant. They were taking no chances that Tiada Vejour was totally unaware of their plan, therefore, crewing of their offensive weaponry was deemed essential. Mint had driven to a point two miles short of the forest that encircled Charlestown and stopped to wait. On this side of the forested ring around the town, imported vegetation from Earth was gradually starting to win the battle against local plant life, with a lot of help from biological scientists.

They were in a communications blackout but Mint's command-pad had now vibrated three times in its cradle mount. She stared at it, fully aware that Aaron's 'mission go' order would be hacked through her pad's standby mode. Therefore, the messages, or attempts at direct contact, had definitely not come from him. Nobody else was supposed to attempt any type of contact with her. With a heavy sigh she reached for the device but hesitated when it came to bringing it back online.

"You said you were going to ignore it," Trent pointed out.

"I know," Mint agreed. "Something inside tells me it's important I check, though."

The device screen lit up as Mint activated it and stared at the message icons; one from Penny, two from Java. Java's first message was the earliest so she tapped that one. Mint's free hand clamped over her mouth as she read.

"What's wrong?" Trent asked.

"We never planned for this," Mint whispered. "Armed youths have taken citizens hostage; they've got Java, Reid, Mikey, and Gretta, along with many more, in the police station car park. Others have headed for the laboratories to take more hostages."

"Armed youths?" Trent's eyes were wide. "How? Where did they get weapons from?"

"I've not had any contact from Aaron so it can't have been from the defensive barricade," Mint said quietly. "Oh, Java, how do we get you out of there? The only other weapons in town would be with the weapons specialist team, we've cleared out the station armoury."

Mint's finger hovered over the icon for Penny's message, she made to tap it several times but pulled back before she fully steeled herself for more bad news and stabbed at it.

"Bruce made contact," she told Trent. "Passed on some tactical information he'd picked up. Looks like the laser armed trucks have been causing Tiada Vejour some problems."

Trent managed a tight smile at that news. He didn't want to appear too pleased to have heard from his son when his daughter and Mint's family were now hostages too.

"Oh shit, no," Mint had not hesitated to press the second message icon from Java. She turned tear-filled eyes on Trent. "Kieron Hall was a hostage in the car park. He tried to get the gun from one of the thugs after some sort of disruption. They shot him, he's dead."

Trent's mouth flopped open but he couldn't find any words. He looked down and shook his head several times before staring out of the window with a blank expression.

Mint turned to look at Roman.

"What?" he asked.

"Do you know which convoy Hayley and Daniel were due to evacuate in?"

Roman swallowed and looked away.

"Roman?" Mint said.

"I …" Roman swallowed again. "I told them to stay home. We agreed I'd pick them up if we pull this off, otherwise …"

"Oh, Roman," Mint cocked her head to one side and stared at him. "You might have just saved them."

"Eh?" Roman swung around on the tripod mount, eager to hear more.

"Citizens have been taken hostage by armed thugs. Kristopher Manson and his gang, I would have to guess. They're holding a group, including Java and her family in the police station car park. Kieron Hall was there, tried to be a hero – they shot him, Roman, he's dead."

"No," Roman shook his head. "Why? What for?"

"I can only guess," Mint shrugged. "Some plan by Tiada Vejour to prevent an evacuation, keep people in the town for its plans. Java tells me Kieron tried to grab a gun from one of the thugs. You have to contact Hayley and Daniel, make sure they hide and stay hidden."

*

Another grenade hit the ground next to a tree soldier. It excavated a shallow crater when it exploded and hurled out metal fragments in a circular blast pattern. Many slats were severed and shrapnel penetrated through to the tree soldier's legs. It sagged to lean precariously to one side before it folded its good pair of legs and assumed position as a static mound. Aaron pumped the grenade launcher underneath his rifle barrel and shot his own grenade at the sitting target. He had to duck down to avoid an incoming ball of energy and didn't see the result. His grenade struck at the domed top of the mound and severed the vast majority of its remaining slats. It didn't take long for another grenade to slam into the mound and destroy it; splinters of wood flew in all directions.

Aaron peered over the rim of the barricade and made a quick scan of the scene beyond. The forward line of tree soldiers was taking shape. Twenty-one of them were still active; he was impressed his small force had destroyed twelve of the deadly foe but knew they were still facing defeat in this tactical situation. He had started with a force of twenty-four troops, himself included. Only eleven remained fighting fit and several of those were walking wounded. The laser armed trucks had been essential in mounting the heavy toll of destroyed tree soldiers and they were gone now. On top of that, grenades were running low. Things looked decidedly bleak. Aaron emptied his clip of ammunition into the closest enemy and jumped down from the barricade. Ducking as low as was practical he raced over to the paramedic.

"It's time you moved further back," he told her. "Doc Davidson is still in the police 4x4 down the road. Ferry the wounded back to him in my 4x4, there are trucks for them to get into. Load the dead into a separate truck."

The paramedic looked at him with eyes that had seen too much. Her face was streaked with blood and dirt, her hands were trembling slightly, but her expression was surprisingly calm.

"Go," Aaron urged her on. "You've been amazing, but it's time you pulled out now."

He watched as she slowly gained her feet and helped a wounded trooper stand, started to guide him towards the 4x4. Aaron refilled his pockets with ammunition and reloaded the assault rifle. With a heavy sigh he turned and dashed back to the barricade.

"The line's almost formed," Rick Gatiss shouted over to him.

Aaron acknowledged his update with a raised finger. Rick turned back to the fight. His face was bloody from a graze to his scalp where a wooden dart had nearly killed him. He was also singed and burnt to one side of his face from ducking an energy ball too late. Aaron considered it extremely fortunate he hadn't sustained any injuries and wondered how much longer that would last.

*

Kris punched the wall in frustration. The capture of the evacuees had gone without a hitch after the extremely lucky despatch of the remaining fuzz with just one rocket. That had been a sight to behold, once he'd picked himself up anyway. It had taken an annoying length of time for the blaze to diminish sufficiently to clear the wreckage from the road so he could continue towards the laboratories with his little armed group.

One of the scientists had actually thrown an improvised grenade at them when they pulled up at the entrance. His capture and eventual death in front of the others had cowed the rest of the evacuated citizens. Kris had set his people to work on locating the chief police bitch's twin sister and family but they weren't here. That was the source of his current anger. He was so hoping to have some fun at their expense.

"Harald," he shouted into his data-pad.

"Had to kill a hostage," Harald replied. "Tiada sent another terror wave out, knocked us off. One little fucker thought he'd try and get my gun."

"Never mind that," Kris hissed. "Check your hostages, is Java there?"

There was a brief pause.

"She's here; I'm looking right at her."

"Good," Kris grinned. "I'm sending a couple of lads to collect her."

*

Penny and Doc Davidson had jumped out of Mint's 4x4 when the first group of wounded troopers was ferried back to them by the paramedic. The doctor fussed over their wounds but could find nothing wrong with the field dressings the paramedic had applied. Penny kept close to the 4x4 and looked back at regular intervals to check on Gabriel.

Aaron's 4x4 pulled up again to the sound of crushed debris and the paramedic jumped out. Penny wasn't sure where the paramedic's energy was coming from; the dash to give Aaron the message and return to Mint's 4x4 had left her worn out.

"Gotta be quick," the paramedic announced, "the tree soldiers are almost formed up and the barricade's taking a pounding. Just pulled another dead body away; there's only ten of our guys left. I'm sure they can't last much longer."

Penny was already helping a female trooper out of the 4x4 but paused on hearing that statement. If the tree soldiers were almost formed up, transition must be close. She guided the trooper to a ramp and into the back of a truck. Once she was seated, Penny dashed back to Mint's 4x4 and looked keenly at Gabriel.

"Anything?" she asked.

Gabriel shook his head. Penny could see he was tired. "Stay awake, Gabriel," she gently shook his shoulder. "The critical point is approaching; Bruce will be in contact soon."

"He's here now," Gabriel lifted his head. "He says it's time, transition is starting."

Penny almost danced on the spot as she grabbed her data-pad.

*

Java didn't like the look of this. Another pair of thugs had arrived, pulled up on the ramp in a stolen vehicle. They had whooped and swapped high-fives with the ramp guard before sauntering over to the stairway guard. She looked away as their eyes began to scan the cluster of hostages.

"There she is, in the middle," the stairway guard called.

Java couldn't help looking and felt a surge of fear when she saw a finger pointed straight at her. She began to fumble with Reid's data-pad as the two new arrivals elbowed and shoved their way through to her.

"You're coming with us," the taller of the two sneered, "Kris has plans for you."

"What have you got there?" the shorter one rushed forward.

He almost knocked Mikey from her arms as he roughly grabbed the data-pad and held it aloft.

"Fucking spy bitch," he shouted, dropped the device and stamped on it.

"Idiot!" stairway guard shouted. "Is it broken?"

"Yeah, why?"

"Who did you contact, what did you tell them?" stairway guard roared at Java.

Java returned his glare with an impudent smile. Smaller thug was infuriated by that; he crashed a stinging back slap across her face. Reid grabbed Mikey as Java staggered and dropped him.

"Enough!" stairway guard bellowed. "Kris'll want her unspoiled. Take 'em."

Java hawked bloody spit at short thug as he took her arm in a rough, vice-like grip. He shook her roughly and marched her after Reid and Mikey who were being led away by tall thug. Anxious faces swept by in a blur as she was dragged past them, out of the tight knot of hostages. At least Gretta hadn't been taken, but Java felt deeply guilty at the failure to fulfil her promise to Penny.

Java held her head aloft as she was manhandled to the waiting vehicle. Mint would soon be back from the mission to deal with this band of misfits. She was damned if she was going to give them any sport in the intervening time.

*

Bruce had acted suitably horrified and surprised when Tiada Vejour forced him to witness events at the defensive barricade. He had noticed the tree soldiers had formed their forward line and knew transition must be close; it would not be a good time to lose concentration and betray the depth of his penetration of the Varla's powers and abilities. He had recognised the tall man in black clothing amongst the small group of defenders and allowed a small grin of satisfaction when he saw the carcasses of destroyed tree soldiers.

"False hope, Bruce Webster," Tiada Vejour had intoned. "These rude constructs are expendable but entirely capable of holding back this pitiful force when I regain my body. You shall be present to witness my return to the light; I may even allow you to live afterwards, though I have other disciples now."

Bruce had remained silent as the Varla gloated. He felt its focus moving away from the barricade and found himself back in his facsimile bedroom. Tentatively he had reached out and felt the Varla distracted. It had taken a mere three seconds to contact Gabriel and pass on the message that transition was commencing.

Now, Bruce was impatient. He reached out to see what Tiada Vejour was doing and watched bare rock walls pass by as his body floated down to the gloomy depths of the chasm and landed next to the Varla's physical body. It was slumped, seemingly dead or deep in slumber, the hard shell-like carapaces uppermost. A long, spidery limb flexed and reached out.

For a moment, Bruce thought it was going to strike his body but it swept slightly beyond and to one side. Instead, a tentacle unwrapped from around the barrel of the leg and curled several times around his body's waist. Bruce inadvertently gasped.

"What?" Tiada Vejour whispered to him in a menacing tone. "You think I am unaware of your little spying activity, your hope to escape once you are returned to your body?"

Bruce had nothing to say, his mind raced for a plan to overcome this disaster. Nothing came to him.

*

"Here we go," Mint called as she hit the accelerator.

She looked at Trent to her left. He remained calm and focussed, the police issue assault rifle laid on his lap. Mint had given him a lightning lesson in its use and watched him load and reload multiple times. She doubted it would be much use in a firefight against the Varla K'dyamon but accepted that something was better than nothing.

Roman was strapped to the laser weapon behind her, swinging alternatively to the left and right.

"How's the charge for the laser?" she asked Trent.

He looked at the relevant readout on his data-pad then held it up for her to see. 100% charge, it displayed. Trent had informed her full charge was sufficient for four good shots and the generator was set for continuous recharge. In the worst case scenario of full charge depletion, it would take ten seconds to build up adequate charge for another shot. Secretly, Mint considered if they reached that situation it was over. She tried to remain optimistic and hopeful for a fast drive through the forest, collect Bruce, and blast out the other side to connect with Aaron and his people. Like the others, this truck was off-road capable, which was essential to bypass the inevitable surviving tree soldiers.

The dashboard readout showed their velocity sneaking past sixty miles per hour. Mint eased back on the acceleration and kept to that speed, aware of mission plan timings. Ahead, the wall of pine trees was fast approaching. She had two miles of forest to drive through to reach the access road where they should rendezvous with Bruce.

*

"Transition!" Aaron shouted to his people.

He was crouched with his back to the barricade, the command-pad in his hands. He'd already sent the 'mission go' message to Mint. Without further delay, he commenced the countdown; Mint had five minutes before he sent the release order to the Lightning in orbit above.

"They're all covering up," he heard Rick Gatiss shout.

Sure enough, when Aaron stood up and looked over the top of the battered barricade, all the tree soldiers had assumed mound position, no weapon arms were deployed.

"Tiada Vejour is disconnecting from them," Aaron called. "Grenades now, let's seize this opportunity."

He aimed and fired from his rifle's grenade launcher, pumped it and fired again at the same target. Explosions rippled along the extended line of tree soldiers but not nearly as many as Aaron had hoped for. He risked reloading the grenade launcher whilst still standing but kept glancing to see if any of the tree soldiers were preparing to take offensive action. They remained locked down, so Aaron aimed at a new target and squeezed the trigger. As soon as the grenade detonated, a tree soldier nearby quickly deployed its arms and released two balls of energy and a stream of wooden darts at Aaron. He ducked down just in time. The impact of the balls of energy against the barricade knocked Aaron from his perch; he tumbled onto the littered road surface below.

As he began to pick himself up, he spotted Trooper Smith fire his sniper rifle. There must have been an immediate reply as Smith instantly took cover and the barricade rocked from more impacts. A thought came to him.

"Everybody, cease fire," Aaron shouted as he stepped back onto the barricade. "Rick, watch what happens."

Aaron popped his head up and saw that all the tree soldiers were locked down. He checked the grenade launcher was armed and slowly stood. The tree soldiers made no reaction to his appearance. Aaron aimed carefully and placed his finger on the trigger. He tensed, ready for his next action, and counted down from three in his head. Squeeze. As soon as the grenade left the barrel he stepped back and dropped to the road. Aaron nodded in understanding as he saw the barricade shake alarmingly from several fresh impacts.

"Two of 'em fired back at you," Rick shouted from atop the defences.

"They're autonomous now," Aaron shouted to all his troops. "They'll only respond when fired upon."

Aaron's eyes took in the condition of the barricade. It was shorter now than when the tree soldiers' assault had begun. Sections at either end had collapsed and large holes were evident all along its length. His troopers were positioned where the barricade remained most intact. That feeling of safety was quite illusory, he realised. He could pinpoint far too many places where the multi-layered panels had shifted to reveal dangerous weaknesses and loss of structural integrity.

"Stand down, everybody," Aaron called. "Smith, I want you on the screen watching those bastard things. Sergeant Harris has begun her run, we'll conserve our remaining ammunition until she needs covering fire to get clear. Unless I order otherwise, we only open fire now if fired upon."

Aaron took a couple of minutes to walk amongst his people and praise their efforts, offer a few comforting words. There were many faces he failed to immediately recognise, such was the accumulation of dirt and blood. Many other faces he dearly wanted to see were missing. Department 44's field personnel had taken a battering today.

He walked to the table top screen with Rick, noticed his second in command was limping and slowed to match his pace.

"Thanks," Rick said to him. "Landed badly when I was knocked off, sprained my ankle."

"You've all performed magnificently," Aaron clamped his hand on the man's shoulder. "Especially you - forced into the lead role. For what it's worth, I'm giving you a battlefield promotion. Congratulations, squaddie."

Rick forced a tired smile in reply and looked at the screen. The tree soldiers were all still locked down as mounds.

"How long?" Rick asked.

Aaron raised his command-pad and checked the time. "They should be nearly at the approach road now," he said.

*

Bruce felt a sudden surge of expectation and excitement from the Varla.

Transition was here.

The facsimile bedroom began to fade. Panic gripped him as he realised the tentacle remained taut around his physical body. Would he have sufficient remaining energy to break loose and fly to the main road? He had no idea, but that addition to his original plan was his only option.

The Varla K'dyamon's body quivered as its legs started to unfold one by one and reach for secure purchase on the rock walls. Multiple tentacles uncurled on each leg to strengthen the vast body's grasp and it began to rise, slowly to begin with, but with gathering pace.

Not yet, Bruce told himself. The bedroom had not yet fully faded, he couldn't feel his body. The Varla was fully committed now and he knew he was unmonitored. Frustration tore through his thoughts at the slow progress.

*

The approach road junction was visible ahead. Mint had to fight the curiosity that urged her to look through the trees and keep her attention on the road. Roman was still tracking left and right with the laser but he remained on the right side for longer. Beside her, Trent had the assault rifle in both hands; his head turned her way to look for any sign of his son. Mint's foot lifted from the accelerator pedal and applied slight pressure on the brakes. She increased the braking rate as the approach road loomed. Roman and Trent gasped loudly as the truck came to a complete halt in the middle of the junction. Mint turned her head and felt her own gasp escape.

Trees had been stripped from alongside the approach road to create the tree soldiers. This made for a broad avenue, a little over two hundred metres in length, terminating at the broad chasm. Five, long black legs could be seen reaching upwards from within the gulf. There seemed to be something, or a number of things, wriggling along the last section of each leg. Mint reached for the optical viewers in her driver's door pocket and peered through them.

She could see now that three tentacles were arranged around the end portion of each leg. There was no accurate way to judge scale but the legs looked quite thick. They thickened towards the, yet to be revealed, body within the chasm. The legs articulated, the tips bending down to the ground. Mint watched as the tentacles stretched out to feel for the ground. Once the end of the leg touched the surface, the tentacles seemed to search for additional anchor points, strengthen its grip.

More legs began to emerge as the initial cluster gained stable purchase. Mint swung the viewers to cover the entire chasm and saw that a ring of legs had appeared all around it. She counted twelve in total. Suddenly, she stiffened. Could it be? Mint increased magnification on the viewers and stared at the sight that unfolded. One of the legs was only using two tentacles to secure its footing. The other was holding Bruce Webster.

"I see Bruce," she said, handing the viewers to Trent. "Check out the left side leg closest to us."

"Bloody hell!" Trent exclaimed. "It's holding him tight, but Bruce isn't moving."

*

Suddenly, Bruce was in his body. The tentacle was squeezed tight around his waist. His first physical act was to gasp at the pain of it but he knew he had no time to lose. Feeling the residual power available to him, he blasted a portion into the grasping appendage. It loosened and he prepared to leap. Another tentacle wrapped its tip around his throat.

"Foolish human," Tiada Vejour intoned in his head. "Did you really expect me to allow you to fly away to your waiting rescuers? I have been aware of your plans, activities and hopes from the very beginning. You were a quick learner, I will acknowledge that, but I have inhabited this body and used these powers for millions of your years. You cannot hope to defeat me."

Bruce slumped and prepared to send a last desperate message to Gabriel.

"Send your message," Tiada Vejour mocked. "It will be amusing, and sate a small part of my growing appetite, to feel your friends' response."

Bruce was actually pushed along the pathway to Gabriel's mind.

*

"There's another tentacle around Bruce's neck," Trent shouted.

"Calm down, relax," Mint said. "Has Bruce made any move yet?"

"There was something," Trent said, quieter. "The original tentacle flexed as though in pain, then the other wrapped around his throat. Wait - all of the legs are flexing. The body's emerging, looks like domed shells."

Mint snatched the viewers from the startled man and put them to her face. Trent was correct; she could see seven domed shells rising out of the chasm. They were mostly dull browns and greys but glinted in places. Mint magnified the view and saw the shell structure was an odd mishmash mosaic of rock, crystal and metal. She could also see their overall structure more clearly now. Six sided, they were more conical than domed, and looked like they were evenly hexagonal in shape. Six arranged around a central one.

The body heaved upwards and free of the chasm, settled to squat on the twelve legs. Mint could now see the legs were connected to the body on the outside angles of the outer hexagons. The body beneath the shells was bloated and seemed to pulse in places. Mint could not identify anything that resembled a conventional mouth or eyes. More tentacles and antennae sprouted, seemingly at random, from the main body, some moving, others remained static. Mint wordlessly handed the viewers back to Trent. He gasped when he looked down the road at the alien being.

"I've got a great shot," Roman called.

"Not yet," Mint said. "Come on, Bruce – you've got to do it now."

*

Bruce realised he was altogether beaten and out-manoeuvred, and felt the rage build in his breast. No, he couldn't allow the Varla to get the final victory over him. He wouldn't be held for its dubious pleasure, feeding and amusement. He had valuable information in his head that must get out to Sergeant Harris and the tall man. Tiada Vejour laughed inside his head at the impotent rage it felt in its captive human.

Bruce lashed out with his powers. He severed the link from Gabriel to the Varla and felt the last sensations from his physical body desert him. The howl of the frustrated Varla receded as he tried to hold his being together inside his friend's mind. Bruce could still vaguely sense the activity within Gabriel's brain and searched desperately for somewhere to settle and anchor himself. He identified a damaged section from the Varla's attack and swam to it. He could feel a little residual power still available to his call and directed it into the cells, synapses and neurones. The patch of brain matter was still glowing faintly to his perception as he insinuated his consciousness into the living substance.

*

Gabriel's scream carried out of the open 4x4 door. Penny landed on her backside; she had instinctively retreated from the agonised yell. As she pushed her body up she could hear Doc Davidson calling from behind,

Aaron shouting from a distance, the sound of running feet.

Gabriel's eyes were wide, the whites showing around each iris. Tears were rolling down each cheek, past nostrils from which thin streams of blood were leaking. His body was leaning forward, straining against the safety harness. Penny stared silently, her own tears rising, the sound of running steps getting ever closer. Doc Davidson rushed up to the boy and attempted to push him against the seat.

"Gabriel, relax," he said. "Gabriel, please, relax."

There was no reaction from the boy. Doc Davidson huffed and began to dash around the 4x4, leaned in through the far-side rear door to examine the medical monitor. He stared at it dumbfounded; he couldn't understand the sudden flood of activity.

"What's happened?" Aaron puffed as he skidded to a halt beside Penny.

"I have no idea," Penny admitted.

Suddenly Gabriel slumped back into the seat. He looked to his left at Doc Davidson, then to the right at Penny and Aaron.

"Gabriel, what happened?" Penny asked quietly. "Was it Bruce?"

The boy nodded slightly then sucked in a deep breath.

"It was me, mum," Gabriel's voice said. "It went wrong. Tiada Vejour knew all along and disabled my body. I'm trapped inside Gabriel's head now."

"No!" Penny screamed herself into a dead faint.

Aaron caught her before she hit the ground and lowered her gently.

"You must tell Sergeant Harris to get away," Gabriel's voice said weakly. "It'll be too strong soon."

Aaron reached for his command-pad.

*

"It's stopped moving," Mint said. "What is it doing?"

Through the magnified viewers she watched as the body of Bruce Webster was shaken by the tentacles holding it then dropped to the ground. The leg lifted then stabbed down at the defenceless form below. Finally, a tentacle picked up Bruce's body and casually flung it into the chasm.

A bellowing roar of pain and anguish confirmed Trent had seen the grisly spectacle. He was already out of the truck's door when Mint turned to him.

"Stop!" she shouted, but he ignored her and charged around the front of the vehicle.

Mint reached for the door handle and flung it wide. Trent sidestepped it and charged onto the access road, Mint in hot pursuit. A beam flashed next to her as Roman finally opened fire on the Varla K'dyamon.

"Mint, get out of there, now!" Aaron's voice blasted out of the dashboard mounted command-pad. "Lightning strike is imminent."

"Come back," Roman shouted after her. "Mint, it's begun – you can't stop him, he's beyond your help."

Mint stopped and looked back at the truck twenty metres away. Her feet danced in agitation as she looked forward again to see Trent still sprinting, fifteen metres ahead of her now. She balled her fists and raised them above her head, emitted a scream of hatred, frustration and anger.

"Get – back – here – now," Roman roared at her.

Another sustained flash of laser energy fizzled past Mint as she ran back to the truck. She slammed her door with enough power to shake the entire vehicle. Mint gunned the engine as she took a last look at the still charging figure of Trent Webster. She could hear the chatter of his assault rifle and muffled screaming from Roman behind. Her left hand shifted the engine into gear and wheels span, spitting gravel, as she pressed the accelerator hard.

Trent's data-pad was on his empty seat. It displayed 8% laser charge available.

*

Rage.

Fury.

Wrath.

Revenge.

Those were the only words in Trent Webster's mind as he forced his leaden legs to carry him onwards. The initial, uncontrolled release of energy had been too much; he was a distance runner, not a powerful sprinter. His finger clicked the trigger on empty again. Without slowing his more measured advance toward the enormous alien monster, his left hand released the ammunition clip. It dropped to the ground as he snatched another from his trouser pocket and slammed it home. The trigger finger squeezed once more. His shots were aimless, all over the place, most impacting the ground below the Varla K'dyamon.

"You killed my son," he screamed as he approached to within ten metres of the monster.

A single leg lifted and swatted him in a fluid motion, much faster than they had moved during the laboured climb out of the chasm.

"I am complete," Tiada Vejour boomed inside Trent's head. "You cannot touch me now."

Trent rolled into a foetal heap as he screamed and clawed at his head, the gun abandoned.

*

"Keep going," Roman shouted. "Charge is up to 15%, Trent must be delaying it, there's no sign of pursuit."

Mint watched her speed accelerate beyond sixty miles per hour and kept

219

her foot hard down. The truck rushed past the final trees and into brighter daylight. She could see the barricade a couple of miles distant and a line of mounds ranged in front of it. She couldn't see any explosions or signs of combat. That puzzled her; she had heard Aaron's voice loud and clear. Defenders were still alive, so why weren't they firing?

"Floor it Mint, you have ten seconds," Aaron's voice erupted from the command-pad as though she had summoned it.

She felt a pressure on the back of her seat and guessed Roman was bracing himself for the missile's impact.

*

Trent's fingers gripped tight to the grenade in his pocket. He hadn't told anybody how he lifted it from an ammunition crate he passed by lucky fortune. Just in case the worst happens, he had told himself. It was more to provide a quick and blissful end for his remaining family if they failed to beat the Varla, but this situation would serve as well. He would miss Penny and his children. They were the last thought in his mind as he spotted the missile streaking down, pushed the impact activation button on the little bomb, and flung it as hard as he could at the alien.

The Varla's horrible grating laugh was the last thing he heard when it ground him into the road surface with one of its legs. It had concentrated its defensive shield around the grenade and left only a cursory protection around its body. The undetected missile hit between two of the outer hexagon shaped shells and achieved slight penetration prior to warhead detonation.

All twelve legs collapsed as the blast forced the Varla K'dyamon downwards. It emitted a psychic shriek of pain as the explosion tore into it. Trees were flattened for hundreds of metres by the blast wave. A churning ball of yellow, orange and red flames arose skyward, accompanied by billows of deep black smoke.

Intense pain pulsed through Tiada Vejour. How was this possible? How could it have suffered damage from their weapons? Anger and rage swelled and it swept out with a wave of terror. But, something was horribly amiss. The wave was much weaker than it had intended. The humans must have damaged a major storage bladder.

Tiada Vejour screamed inside and crawled backwards, each metre covered causing fresh agony as the damaged area dragged along the ground, two legs trailing along uselessly. Upon reaching the chasm, it rotated until the damaged body segments hung over the drop, the legs dangled and swung. The pain decreased dramatically and Tiada manipulated an energetic field to gently hold the damaged body segments in place.

Once achieved, it compartmentalised that continuous action and raised as powerful a force shield as it could currently manage in a dome above and around itself. Next, it reached out to the tree soldiers.

*

"Huge explosion," Roman shouted, barely audible above the thunderous sound.

Mint eased off on the accelerator pedal and twisted her neck to glance over her right shoulder. She watched as the outer fringe of pine trees swayed crazily from the powerful blast wave. Only the thinnest veneer of forestation remained standing at the field edges, trunks could be seen lying flat, pointed towards Charlestown, the odd splintered trunk still standing defiantly a mere few metres tall.

Mint's right foot found the brake pedal and she eased the truck down to a dawdling ten miles per hour.

"Did we actually do it?" she asked in the sudden silence.

A feeling of fear arose and the truck veered off course as she lifted both hands to her face.

"Not if that's any indication," Roman replied, his face slightly pale.

"No," Mint chewed her lower lip, steering back on course. "Not very strong though, was it?"

"I can't see anything back there," Roman mused. "Best floor it and put some distance between us and it."

"One step ahead of you," Mint said. "Face forward and have that laser ready."

The truck accelerated rapidly. Mint's attention was grabbed by a series of flashes in the distance. The tree soldiers were active again.

"Incoming!" Roman shouted.

Mint risked a lightning quick look at Trent's data-pad on the passenger seat, it displayed 55%. Laser recharge wasn't as quick as she'd like but there was nothing to do about that. Next, she peered into the sky and counted sixteen balls of energy heading their way.

"They've opened up against the barricade and us," Roman called to her. "I'm not going to waste laser charge at this range. It'll be more use up close and personal."

"Good call," Mint agreed. "Those energy bolts will trash the road surface. Hang on tight, I'm going off-road."

*

"Back to the barricade, weapons free," Rick Gatiss shouted.

Aaron watched his people dash to their positions as he ran carefully back from Mint's 4x4. He held the command-pad flat in one hand, a video connection open to his contact in New Cambridge.

"Come on," he muttered. "Come on, come on, come on."

"Real-time images received," his contact said. "I'm sending them to you now."

Aaron ducked behind a truck for shelter. He could see the barricade shaking and rocking dangerously, panels were falling away at a rapid rate under the concerted assault. Other balls of energy were arcing over to fall behind the structure. With pride that drew a lump to his throat, he saw his troopers bravely returning fire.

Aaron's eyes dropped to the command-pad, his finger pressed the new icon. The first image displayed a creature of alien design at the end of the access road. It was mostly dark grey and brown in colouration with a spattering of sparkles. From this overhead angle, the hexagonal structure was plain to see, one central surrounded by six outer hexagons, with twelve legs sticking outwards.

"You are one big son-of-a-bitch," Aaron whispered; he estimated it was fifty metres across, if not more.

The next image showed a huge explosion, obscured the alien from view. Aaron quickly scrolled through two more images that still showed the explosive conflagration. The next series of images made him sag backwards to sit on the road, his head shaking slowly. He initially thought the Varla was dead when he saw the two shattered shell carapaces, a gaping wound on the back of the alien. Then it had obviously moved and repositioned itself next to the chasm.

"We've hurt you, you big bastard," Aaron said out loud.

"Go for second strike," he ordered after toggling back to his live video link.

"Copy that, sir," his contact replied and cut the link.

"Fall back," Aaron shouted as loud as he could, "rolling retreat."

He stood and moved to the truck's bonnet, rested his assault rifle on the vehicle and took a firing stance. His eyes, however, ranged beyond the rapidly failing barricade to search for any sign of Mint's vehicle.

*

"You'll have to slow right down for me to get a targeted shot," Roman shouted as the truck thumped heavily down in the rutted field.

"I know, I know," Mint called back. "Once this next salvo lands, ok?"

She didn't hear Roman's reply as she turned sharply and bumped once more. Ahead she could see the wreckage of three trucks, all burnt out. The latest salvo of energy bolts impacted a safe distance away and Mint hit the brakes hard.

"Go, you're at 70%," Mint shouted.

A loud hum sounded behind her, held for a moment.

"Scratch one tree soldier," Roman shouted, "move!"

The truck bogged down for a frightening few seconds. Mint growled as she lifted and dropped her right foot, gunning the accelerator. Finally, the wheels stopped spinning, gained some grip and the vehicle lurched forwards. Mint turned back towards the road and picked up speed. A very quick look told her the laser had 27% charge available. Although Roman had managed to destroy a tree soldier with a sustained shot it had depleted the charge and she knew the numbers for such a tactic were stacked against their favour. There were still far too many of the deadly enemy ahead of them.

"What's happening at the barricade?" she shouted to Roman.

"What barricade, it's almost gone," Roman yelled back. "It looks like they're being forced back."

"Tiada Vejour is still alive," Mint realised. "It's controlling this fight."
She turned her head to look at the forest just in time to see a silver streak lance down from the sky.

"Hold on," she screamed at Roman, "second missile strike!"

Mint jerked the steering wheel to the right; she didn't want the blast wave to strike the truck side on, that would be calamitous. Her eyes found the mirror then her eyebrows shot up upon seeing the great inferno amongst the trees. Surely, Tiada Vejour couldn't survive such violence.

*

The horseshoe shape cut into the hillside was very evident now the trees that once surrounded it had been felled by the mighty blasts. The Varla's body shook from the immense force of the second strike. Within its defensive shield, the Varla K'dyamon worked frantically to manipulate its defences. It came to a painful decision and sacrificed the two already wounded body segments in order to fully protect the other five. As the explosion began to fade, it stabilised the force shield and began to suck the energy into its extraction organs to chemically hoard in its remaining storage bladders. Next it extracted heat energy from the surrounding air. Frost began to form in a halo all around the vast body.

Tiada Vejour was disabled, badly wounded and depleted; but most of all, it was insanely furious and wanted revenge.

*

Explosions and the persistent rattle of gunfire filled Aaron's ears. He could no longer talk to his contact and had to resort to text messages. A new icon appeared on his command-pad's screen, more images from the Lightning orbiting above. He prodded it with his finger and flicked through the new package. His head hung low at the end. The Varla was still alive; two orbital missile strikes had failed. Initially, he felt jubilant as he saw the two wounded body segments destroyed. Then he saw the frost formation and knew what it represented. The Varla had sucked heat energy out of the surrounding air. It was still alive. His head snapped up. If it had to resort to that level of energy harvest it must be depleted. He tapped out a fresh message, ordering a third strike.

*

The truck had presented its rear end to the blast wave just in time. Mint had struggled to retain control as it bucked about. She had judged that the latest salvo of energy bolts would land behind them. Unfortunately, the blast wave had affected their angle of descent and they landed far too close for comfort. The left side front quarter panel had absorbed a near miss and fell away to lay smoking in the field as the truck careened onwards. Mint was desperate to know if the front left wheel had been buckled or otherwise damaged. She slowed down to a crawl.

"Fire," she shouted. "You have 33%."

"Done, move!" Roman called back.

Mint accelerated and felt the steering wheel judder alarmingly. Then it calmed and she sighed with relief. For a terrifying moment she had thought the front left wheel was responsible.

"They're starting to move," Roman called.

Mint's head snapped round to take in the location of the enemy mounds. Sure enough, ten tree soldiers were making for the barricade. The remaining ten were facing her way and advancing. A glance at Trent's data-pad showed 10% charge.

"Time we left," she shouted back to Roman.

Mint accelerated to the fastest speed she felt safe to bump across the field at. Space began to open between the truck and the pursuing tree soldiers, although she was heading away from Aaron and the road into town. She scanned the field ahead and looked left to the long line of greenhouses. Would the truck fit in the spaces between them? Only one way to find out, she decided. A quick glance back to the forest showed no activity in that direction. Mint lifted her foot off the accelerator pedal slightly and made a sharp left turn, floored the pedal again. Energy bolts landed harmlessly behind them.

*

The weapons officer acknowledged the order and loaded the target coordinates into the last remaining missile. The weapon ready light illuminated green and she pressed the weapon launch button.

The pylon on the slab side of the spaceship had already rotated to point the missile at the blue, brown and green world below. Clamps released the weapon and pushed it slightly away. Its rocket ignited and began to glow a fierce, fiery red. Then it exploded.

Shrapnel ripped into the already damaged Lightning. A large piece ripped through a liquid propellant tank. The flash was brief and bright as the spaceship was torn asunder.

*

Satisfaction - Tiada Vejour had cause for celebration at last. It had so wanted to pour all its available energy and anger into the humans fighting the tree soldiers but knew the orbital threat could yet prove fatal. A great proportion of available energy had been used to affect the human weapon, the distance was so great, and it begrudged the lack of capability it was left with to do anything more than control some of the remaining tree soldiers.

Tiada Vejour reached out to Charlestown and felt the hostages in the police station car park, then out at the cluster of laboratories. A plan began to form and it sent a message to the human minion to create fear. Next, it concentrated on the tree soldiers. Tiada Vejour selected the ten least damaged and shut down the others, drew their energy back. The feelings of fear and hate began to reach it and it supplemented the energy gain by sucking heat from the air once more.

Yes, now it had sufficient. It reached back to the ten active tree soldiers and took direct control, lifted them airborne.

*

Glass panels flashed by with centimetres to spare on each side as Mint screamed out loud, half in fear, half in relief and joy. The truck ceased its bumpy, jolting passage as it drove over a paved surface at last. Mint didn't dare increase speed; the passageway was just too narrow. She knew there were regular gaps leading back to the main road and intended to turn, somehow, onto one of those.

"What the fuck?" Roman's shout surprised her.

"What?" Mint could see nothing in the mirrors.

"They're, err, flying!" Roman stated.

"Shit!" Mint swore.

This move into the greenhouses seemed like a bad idea now. Their route would be obvious, funnelled along the grid pattern of pathways. She looked at the data-pad – 21%.

"Can you fire upwards?" she asked.

"Only a little," Roman replied. "One's going to fly directly above us; they're going at some speed."

"Shoot it," Mint decided they had no option but to drain the energy banks.

*

Aaron pocketed the data-pad and cursed his luck. New Cambridge had confirmed destruction of the Lightning; his last shot had not got away and he had lost overhead reconnaissance.

"Boss," Rick Gatiss shouted. "Boss, quick, something's happening."

Aaron looked over at his newly promoted squad leader, crouched in cover behind a burnt out truck. Rick was pointing back at the barricade. Aaron followed his indication to see a tree soldier fall apart. Another pile of wood next to it showed the demise of another.

"What did we do?" Aaron called.

"Nothing," Rick shouted back. "It just happened. Hang on – what the fuck?"

Aaron tracked his amazed stare. Two tree soldiers had soared upwards. Taking a huge risk, Aaron stepped out from cover and scanned around. He counted ten airborne tree soldiers before he ducked back behind the truck again. His mind was working overtime. Tiada Vejour must be consolidating its remaining power and capabilities, he decided. That means we must have hurt it badly. It didn't have the available energy to control all the tree soldiers, so it had concentrated on ten; the ten least damaged, no doubt. What would its plan be? Containment of hostages would be my choice, he decided.

"Everybody, concentrated fire on the nearest target," he shouted as he raised the assault rifle.

Seven assault rifles fired in unison, rounds poured into a tree soldier. Chips of wood and sections of slats began to pour down to the road below. Aaron's gun clicked on empty. He released the empty clip and pressed another one home. His eyes rose in time to see a hail of wooden darts and energy bolts raining down from airborne tree soldiers. Darts clattered off his helmet as he ducked and a sharp fire was lit in his left shoulder. An energy bolt crashed into the truck he was using for cover and he was flung onto his back. Aaron rolled over to cover his face as it exploded, felt the heat wash over him.

He heard Rick shouting when he lifted his head and the chatter of a handful of assault rifles. Aaron forced his attention skyward. He smiled grimly when he saw a dismantling tree soldier plummet to crash through a greenhouse roof. Pain radiated out from his shoulder and he lifted his right hand to it as he turned to survey the injury. A wooden dart had pierced the tough police armoured jacket, half of it was embedded in him. He prepared to tug it out then decided against the move. Climbing to his feet clumsily, he shrugged the assault rifle to hang by its strap from his right shoulder. Flying tree soldiers could be seen receding into the distance. His hunch had been correct; Tiada Vejour was sending sentries to guard the hostages.

"Shit, shit, shit!" Rick Gatiss shouted nearby.

Aaron looked his way. He was relieved to see the new squaddie wasn't further injured and began to survey his surroundings. Most vehicles were destroyed and smoking, the road surface cratered like a moon. Worst of all, besides squaddie and himself, only two troopers were visible: Smith and Laghari.

"The others?" Aaron asked, his voice breaking.

"All gone," Rick shook his head.

Aaron hung his head for a moment then looked further along the road, remembering the wounded, the medics, Penny and Gabriel. He heaved a huge sigh of relief when he saw some people stood in the road, the vehicles untouched. His force had taken the brunt of the Varla's aerial onslaught.

"Leave the dead," Aaron said with deep regret. "We aren't finished yet."

He began a slow jog along the road, his pace judged for the limping squaddie, although Laghari was also struggling to move and Smith, his helmet gone, was bleeding from a nasty gash to his head.

*

"They've gone," Mint said, "headed for town."

She put her hands down carefully; glass shards covered the ground. She heard clinking, the grinding of glass as Roman began to rise behind her. The energy bolt had hit the ground just in front of the truck and barrelled into the engine. Mint's warning shout had given Roman just enough time to detach from the laser and drop to cover behind her seat. The truck had died instantly and veered off into a greenhouse on the left. Mint had flung herself out of the driver's door and heard Roman impact the ground behind her as the truck ploughed on, flames taking hold.

Mint turned to look at Roman once she was upright and breathed out when she saw he was largely unharmed. A few spots of blood showed where glass had scratched his hands and forehead. He looked back at her in concern.

"Hold still," he said.

Roman's hands reached up to her face. One held her head steady with a grip on her helmet, the other reached for her right cheek. He pulled out a ten centimetre long shard of glass, dropped it immediately. Fumbling in his tactical cargo pockets, he withdrew a medical patch and ripped the sachet open. With great care he lifted the patch to her cheek and pressed it home. Mint hadn't felt anything until he applied pressure, she was now acutely aware of the pain. Their eyes met and held for long seconds.

"The bleeding's stopping now," Roman looked away first. "Place your hand on the patch and keep up the pressure.

Mint's hand brushed Roman's as she reached for the patch.

"Thank you," she said softly. "Don't worry, we'll find another vehicle to collect Hayley and Daniel."

"We'd best get moving, then," Roman said without looking at her.

Mint followed Roman as he stepped out of the shattered remains of the greenhouse and began to jog down a line between the structures, towards the main road. Mint followed him, her emotions in turmoil.

The battered police 4x4 screeched to a halt when they dashed out from between two greenhouses. A truck came to a more sedate stop behind. Mint looked through the window, straight into a pair of piercing, ice blue eyes. A broad smile lit up Aaron's streaked face as he opened the door.

"No," Mint held her left hand out to halt him, noticed the bandage around his shoulder. "No hugging."

Their eyes met and they seemed to understand each other. Mint thought she detected a hint of regret from Aaron and forcefully ignored it.

"Roman," Aaron turned to her companion. "Nice work, but we have other developments to sort out."

"I know," Mint said. "I lost my command-pad when the truck was destroyed. We'll have to use yours to access the security system in the police station. The sensors are discreet, I doubt if they'll have found them."

The paramedic appeared at Mint's side and gently removed her hand from the medical patch on her cheek. Mint smiled then winced when it was removed.

"That's gonna need stitches," the paramedic said. "I'll apply some gel and cover it up for now."

Mint let her work as she looked at Aaron's command-pad. As expected, he had accessed the system in a matter of seconds.

"That's Harald Jones on the stairway," Roman stated.

"Mo Abbas on the ramp," Mint added. "Looks like just the two. I can't see Java or Reid in the crowd, but she sent the message from there. Check the other rooms and corridors. As long as they're the only ones in the building we'll be able to mount a simultaneous raid from the stairway door and top of the ramp."

"I tried to connect to Trent Webster in the labs using Penny's data-pad, didn't get a reply," Aaron said as he skipped through the different security sensors. "There's nobody else in the building."

"No, you wouldn't," Mint replied. "Trent came with us, wouldn't take no for an answer. He said we'd need an engineer if the laser broke. I lost him when the Varla killed Bruce; he charged off to confront it. Trent Webster is dead."

"Shit," Aaron said. "But, Bruce isn't dead, not quite, anyway."

"Don't tell me that," Mint drew up to him. "I saw it pound his poor body and throw him down the chasm. Bruce Webster is dead, Aaron."

"He's inside Gabriel," Aaron stared straight at her.

"What?" Roman exclaimed.

"Don't ask me how, but Bruce transferred his consciousness into Gabriel Parkes," Aaron said, his hand wiped at his forehead. "He made that announcement then fell asleep, hasn't woken since. Penny had to be sedated from the shock."

"Penny," Mint said, as though just remembering her, "how the hell do I tell her about Trent, especially now?"

"One thing at a time," Aaron put the command-pad back in his pocket. "Tiada Vejour looks badly injured but still alive. Those tree soldiers will be guarding the hostages. We have more work to do yet and not many bodies to do it."

Mint looked around and saw Rick Gatiss, medical plasters all over his face, along with another trooper, this one with a well-bandaged head, looking out of the truck's front window. There was another in the passenger seat of Mint's 4x4.

"How many in the back of the truck?" Mint asked.

"Eight, all wounded and out of the fight," Aaron replied. "With you and Roman we now have six combat capable."

"That's not enough," Mint said with a frown.

"No," Aaron agreed. "I saw ten tree soldiers take to the air. We got one; did you manage to destroy any?" Roman shook his head. "Ok, so nine tree soldiers. There aren't more than one hundred or so hostages in the car park. Unless there are other concentrations of hostages dispersed around Charlestown, that means the majority are at the laboratories. That's where all or most of the tree soldiers will be."

"Use the pad again, access traffic control sensors around the station," Mint said. "The labs will all have car park, interior and exterior sensors."

Aaron looked skyward, berated himself for not thinking about that. He withdrew the device from his pocket. Twenty seconds later they were staring at a single tree soldier at the top of the car park ramp.

"Should be eight at the labs," Aaron muttered as he accessed their systems.

It took a couple of minutes to access all the sensors but, eventually, they located all eight remaining tree soldiers at the labs. Aaron tapped into a different system and studied the readout.

"Twenty hover-jets are still holding at altitude, fifteen miles out," he said.

"Are any of those armed?" Roman asked.

"The rear crew members all have assault rifles," Aaron nodded.

"Ok, so we use them to destroy the tree soldiers from the air," Mint said, suddenly animated.

"No," Aaron shook his head. "We can't risk the air assets."

"Alright," Mint was thinking as quickly as she could. "We land the hover-jets and gather those armed crew members. There were three in our hover-jet, so that would be sixty more people to fight the tree soldiers. That'd be enough, surely?"

"No," Aaron shook his head again, slowly. "They're barely trained to use the guns, not even close to your level. They certainly aren't trained for full scale combat. Anyway, they don't have grenades or the armour piercing ammunition."

"What do we do, then?" Mint held her hands up. "How do we rescue those people?"

Aaron stared at her and Mint began to shake her head. "No, no, no," she said. "You cannot leave them. There are thousands of hostages; my sister and her family, other families."

"Your sister messaged us from the car park," Aaron said quietly. "We can mount a snatch and grab raid on the police station but the labs are too well protected. They're beyond our ability to save them."

"My children are at home," Roman butted in when Mint turned and stalked away, her head in her hands. "If it all ended badly, you know ..."

"Which side of town?" Aaron asked.

"This side," Roman brightened.

"We'll go pick them up, then," Aaron clapped a hand on his arm. "You take the passenger seat in the 4x4. Mint can drive, take her mind off it. I'll be in the truck behind. We don't want both leaders in one vehicle."

Mint turned in time to see Aaron lead the limping Trooper Laghari to the truck. Roman was stood on the passenger side door frame of her 4x4, staring at her. He beckoned her over. Mint knew, deep inside, Aaron was making the right call. The empathy she had built for her people, her Charlestown citizens, was strong, deeply embedded and it tugged at her feelings. She felt like an imposter, a betrayer, abandoning them and their trust. Her feet had moved automatically and she found herself at the driver's door.

"Let's go get Hayley and Daniel," Roman said.

Mint nodded as she sat in her seat and looked in the mirror. Doc Davidson was in the middle of the back seat, Gabriel and Penny on either side of him, both unconscious. Nobody said a word as Mint fired up the engine and set off along the road. Her mind was blank; she drove on autopilot to Roman's house and didn't say a word even when Rick Gatiss took her passenger seat. Roman had guided his children to the rear of the truck after a brief conversation with Aaron.

"The crossroads at the centre of town are fouled up with crashed vehicles," Rick told her. "You need to take us a different route, but don't go too close to the police station."

"How do we get the people to the hover-jets?" Mint asked quietly, finally roused.

"The truck will take the wounded to a rendezvous point before we start the raid, the science team is already there," Rick said. "We go in on foot. The 4x4 will be close by for any wounded. The rest are on foot."

Mint nodded. She could see the sense in the plan. "Who's going in?" she asked.

"Aaron, Smith and me," Rick replied.

"No," Mint stared at him. "You can't move fast enough, I've seen your limp. I know the layout, I should go."

"Aaron doesn't want you," Rick shook his head. "You're too emotionally involved."

"Too fucking right I am," Mint exploded. "Am I the only one? No, fuck Aaron and his orders – I'm going in, discussion over."

Mint slammed the brakes on hard and was out of the door as soon as the vehicle came to a halt. The truck pulled up sedately, close to the rear rack.

"Get out, Aaron," Mint shouted.

"Calm down," Aaron said as he jumped down. "What is ..."

"Enough, enough of your cold, passionless plans and orders," Mint shrieked at him. "Rick is too slow with his limp. I'm going in. I know the station, it makes sense. That's it, done. No argument."

Mint turned before Aaron could utter a reply and slammed the driver's door closed. In the mirror, she saw Doc Davidson avoid her eyes to hastily check Penny and Gabriel as she started driving again. The air was thick with tension inside the 4x4 and nobody spoke until Mint stopped outside a large office building.

"We need to get you three in the truck for evacuation," Mint said, looking pointedly at Doc Davidson.

He nodded but kept quiet, indicating his inability to move. Rick stepped out and called Smith and Laghari over. They gently eased Penny out and carried her to the rear of the truck. Doc Davidson clambered out, as ungainly as his ample frame would suggest. Rick carried Gabriel's inert body to him and handed him over. Then, he turned to Mint.

"Here, you'll need this," he held out his assault rifle.

Mint took it and hung it from her shoulder.

"That's a fresh clip and there are a couple of grenades in the tube," he added as he passed over a spare. "Sorry, not a lot left. I'm still coming, though. I'll drive the 4x4."

"I'm sorry," Mint said, placing a hand on his shoulder.

"I understand," Rick looked away. "In your place, I'd be the same."

"No time like the present," Aaron said from next to Mint's left ear. She did well not to jump, his approach had been stealthy. "Ok," he nodded. Mint got the distinct impression he had crept up on her purely to test her nerves and mental state. "It's your station, your family below. What's your plan?"

Mint had been considering all the points she could raise to pick fault with

Aaron's plan to assault the station. Unexpectedly given the task, she gave him a hard stare to disguise her quick mental jigsaw puzzle as she pieced her sections together.

"The tree soldier is at the top of the ramp," she stated. "It wasn't patrolling the area so I can only assume that situation will continue and work around it. We cross this road and work our way around to the school. The school's access road is next to the station although, unfortunately, there isn't a side door. We'll have to hug the wall as tightly as possible and make for the main entrance. The ramp gives a good field of vision but there will be a blind spot, not a wide one, but it should be enough. It's the only way we can gain entry without alerting the inside guards by fighting the tree soldier. The young thugs are the weak link; they're untested and inexperienced in anything but petty crime. Once we're at the stairway door, we check the security sensors again and pick our time. We have to take out the two thugs as quickly as possible, no disabling shots – kill them. The tree soldiers don't move too quickly, we can use grenades as it comes down the ramp."

"Not bad at all," Aaron nodded in admiration.

"It's simple and straightforward," Rick said. "That makes it obvious, too. You'll need to be on your toes and ready for the unexpected. Call me in just before you commit to the final assault. If I make an appearance at the same time you attack, it should distract the tree soldier long enough to gain a real advantage."

"Ok, I like it," Aaron started across the road. "Move, before we overthink it."

Mint had to run to catch up with Aaron and Smith as they reached the far pavement. The school was close and they soon turned off to the left. Rick edged the 4x4 along the road as quietly as possible. It seemed even more eerie to Mint, passing through entirely silent, abandoned streets, all too aware of the fate of her citizens.

"There's my office window," Mint pointed from the corner of a school building. "Check the sensors on your command-pad, Aaron.

"All clear, no observation," Aaron told her after a brief pause.

"Go!" Mint ordered.

They dashed around the corner and across the road to put their backs against the police station's side wall, and then worked their way to the front corner. Aaron made some hand signals to Smith. Mint watched as the trooper dropped to all fours and leaned forwards. As close to the ground as possible, he poked his head out and withdrew.

"Can't see it from here," he whispered.

"This is the last point we can safely abandon the mission," Aaron said. "Lean further out, see what our coverage is."

Mint held her breath as Smith crawled forwards. He stopped suddenly and skittered backwards.

"Half a meter at most," he said, climbing back to his feet.

"Did it see you?" Mint asked.

Smith shook his head. Aaron raised his right fist and extended three fingers. He folded one finger, then another. Finally he dropped his forearm to the horizontal in a 'go' signal. Smith seemed to be magnetically attached to the wall as he slid around the corner. Aaron moved to allow Mint to follow the trooper.

She breathed in a great gulp of air and moved. Mint tried to copy Smith's motion as closely as possible and kept her back pressed against the wall. The corner was a tricky prospect, pivoting her body. Her eyes snapped to the left, to where the ramp rose to street level. There was no sign of the tree soldier. Smith was already at the entrance, slightly recessed. He beckoned her over urgently. Mint commenced a fast, sideways motion, hugging the wall. She was out of breath when she reached Smith, didn't realise she had been so tense. Smith dragged her into the building as Aaron arrived.

"Phase one complete," Aaron said into his command-pad. "We're in."

"Copy that, boss," Rick replied. "Be advised, I am in position and await the go order."

"Follow me," Mint said.

She led them through the reception area and stopped at the door to the main office. Mint pointed at Aaron's command-pad; she didn't want to risk speaking in case the room was occupied.

"Clear," Aaron whispered. "Uh oh, we have a problem."

"What?" Mint hissed.

Aaron showed her the sensor view on the command-pad. Mint cursed inwardly. It displayed a sensor feed from the car park and clearly showed the two thugs chatting at the bottom of the stairway. The tree soldier was at the bottom of the ramp.

"Do we wait?" Mint asked. "See if it goes back up?"

"Negative," Aaron shook his head. "We have to assume they're expecting something. We're committed; if we turn back we could have company waiting at the front and be trapped inside. No, we use Rick, he's our outside eyes." Aaron raised the device and touched the screen several times. "Rick, respond," he said.

"Here, boss, go ahead."

"The tree soldier has descended the ramp. We need eyes on the front entrance, have we been rumbled?"

"I'm moving, hold on. Negative, I can see the main entrance," Rick said, "no bad guys and nothing airborne."

"Copy that, remain in your current position and await further orders," Aaron gave a tight smile. "Tiada Vejour is keeping his strength at the labs and only threatening the hostages here, hoping we'll pull back."

"We're still going in?" Mint asked.

"Smith and me first," Aaron nodded, "we're the best shots. We go first and despatch the two thugs. You follow straight away and grenade that walking pine tree. Rick will distract it."

Mint swallowed, nodded her assent and agreement. Aaron made more hand signals for Smith and followed him through the door into the main office. Mint tiptoed as quietly as she could behind. Smith stopped just short of the door to the stairwell. Aaron and Mint crouched beside him.

"I'll deploy Rick, and then give a three finger countdown," Aaron said. "Everybody know their role?"

Mint nodded, saw Smith do likewise, and then watched Aaron raise the command-pad.

"Rick," he whispered. "We need a diversion, hit the top of that ramp."

"I'm ready, boss," Rick replied. "Go on your signal."

"Go," Aaron ordered. He dropped the command-pad and raised three fingers, counted them down slowly.

Aaron and Smith moved like lightning. Smith shoulder-barged the door, they rushed through without stopping and Mint heard two shots before she was through.

"Everybody down!" she shouted as soon as she was on the top platform.

The assault rifle was comfortable in her grip now. Her finger squeezed the trigger and she was already pumping to reload the grenade launcher as she watched the flight of the first. Her aim was good, she knew. Full automatic fire from Aaron and Smith's rifles kicked in as she launched the second grenade and changed her grip to take control of the main weapon.

The tree soldier was facing away from her with wooden darts spearing out of its smaller arms at the out of sight 4x4. The larger arms had been unleashing bolts of energy when she launched the first grenade. Both of her grenades impacted the tree soldier on its right side and gouged a deep hole, severed both weapons arms. Their combined assault rifle fire was chewing through slats but the left side arms were still firing. Mint heard a screech of tyres as another energy bolt was fired. Her gun clicked on empty as full beam headlights illuminated the underground garage. The 4x4 charged down the ramp and collected the tree soldier on its front end. Rick kept the accelerator hard down and slammed into the far wall. The rear wheels rose from the floor as the 4x4 came to an abrupt halt. Smoke rose from the 4x4's bodywork and engine. The tree soldier was disassembled.

"Mint, hold the door," Aaron's shout cut through her temporary paralysis.

Mint took several backwards steps as she watched Aaron and Smith descend the steps at pace. Her eyes scanned the cowering crowd of citizens and caught a hint of movement. It was Harald Jones; he wasn't dead and still had his gun. Mint started to aim with the rifle but remembered it was empty. She dropped it and reached for her hip holster. It was all happening in slow motion; Harald rising to his knees with the assault rifle while Aaron slowly turned to face the threat. More movement registered as Mint fumbled with the catch on her holster, finally freed it. Harald was about to fire when a charging body knocked him over. Mint had the revolver in a two-handed grip and fired. The shot caught Harald in his shoulder and flung him onto his back. The other figure lunged for his assault rifle.

"Put it down!" Mint shouted.

The figure ignored her, stood over Harald and fired.

The assault rifle was set to full automatic and Kieron Hall's father didn't release the trigger until the ammo clip was empty. Aaron relieved him of the weapon then collected the other rifle and ammunition from the corpse of Mo Abbas.

"Everybody up!" Aaron shouted, pushing Mr Hall in front of him. "Go! Up the stairs, now! Mint, lead them out."

Mint watched as the frightened crowd of people took to their feet and streamed towards the stairs. Smith was supporting Rick Gatiss who looked badly wounded. They were already half way up the stairs. Mint was anxious to spot Java, Reid and Mikey but withdrew into the main office. She saw many darts poking out of Rick's upper body; blood flowing freely, and more scorch marks on his face. He was going to need urgent attention from the paramedic. Smith dragged him to a chair and Rick collapsed into it. Mint guided the surge of citizens into the room.

"Gather in the clear space," she repeated over and over.

Mint watched for familiar faces, saw Gretta Webster rush past her. Then, Mr Hall dashed through and Aaron followed.

"Where are they?" Mint asked, panic taking hold. "Where's my sister?"

"This is all of them," Aaron said, he had spun around to check the stairs but already knew the garage had been empty when he started up the stairway.

"Where are they?" Mint screamed, breaking out in tears and sinking to her knees.

"They were taken," Gretta Webster stepped forward and put her arms around Mint. "About twenty minutes ago, two more armed men came and took them to the labs."

"We have to move," Aaron shouted, hating himself, but aware they had to go. "Come on," he hauled Mint to her feet. "This isn't over, save it for later – we need you."

Mint stumbled to her feet and swiped at her eyes with her sleeve. She watched Aaron run forward to take the lead as she removed her tactical helmet and hurled it at a wall as she released a further scream of utter despair. People were filing after Aaron as she turned and saw Smith step away from Rick Gatiss. Smith had laid him out on the floor and closed his unseeing eyes. Mint became aware of a tug on her arm and looked down with blurry eyes to see Gretta trying to tow her to the door. She raised one foot and began to follow.

Tears for her family, and all of the fallen, were still streaming down her face when Gretta led her out into daylight. Mint stopped and dropped her rifle, hands on her knees. She retched and heaved up bile, spat it onto the pavement. She straightened with difficulty and wiped her eyes dry. With a last look at her police station, Sergeant Mint Harris collected her gun and abandoned her post. She took Gretta's hand and began to run; the line of rescued evacuees had disappeared around the corner.

They soon caught up with Smith at the tail end. He nodded at her and sprinted forwards to take up position half way along the snaking line, blood had leaked through the bandage on his head. Mint's mind was empty; she simply followed the people in front. Aaron had his command-pad. He could navigate with that and call in the hover-jets to the rendezvous. She suddenly became aware of a figure running alongside. It was Aaron.

"Don't worry," he said. "I've called in the airlift and your people know where to go. How are you?"

Mint couldn't answer. Her chest ached, there was a lump in her throat, and a void deep inside where her sister belonged.

"Ok, just keep moving," Aaron said softly. "I've got the rear."

Mint moved mechanically for the next ten minutes, kept pace with the person in front. Gretta maintained a tight grip on her hand and Mint noticed her look up to check on her many times. Behind, she heard Aaron stop several times then pounding feet as he caught up again and slowed to match their pace. After a circuitous route through office buildings and residential areas, they stopped on the main road out of town that eventually led to New Cambridge.

Several hover jets had just taken to the air and were climbing away steadily. Two more were swooping in to land.

"Smith, start loading," Aaron shouted above the roar of engines, "women and children first."

Trooper Smith raised his arm and began to organise the puffing and panting crowd. Aaron turned to Gretta.

"I've got her now," he said gently. "You go to Trooper Smith and get on a hover-jet."

Mint reluctantly released her hand and turned to look back at Charlestown.

"Nothing followed," Aaron told her. "The pilots tell me they can see tree soldiers hovering over the labs but they're letting us go. Talk to me, please."

Mint couldn't, she shook her head and stared into the distance. Aaron nodded once in understanding then put an arm around her shoulder and led her to the front of the queue. Mint bordered the hover-jet and didn't look back.

Day 6

All evacuees spent the night hooked up to medical monitors at the main hospital in New Cambridge. That included all of the surviving Department 44 personnel, Mint and Roman. No risks were being taken.

A nurse led Mint to a top floor conference room at 0900 hours and advised her to go in. She managed to smile when Roman rushed over to greet her and even returned his embrace. He guided her to a seat next to his own, opposite Aaron, Inspector Pete Fields and several others Mint didn't know. There were many more vacant chairs than those in use.

"Welcome, Sergeant Harris," an older gentleman said. Mint thought he looked about sixty. "My name is Edward, this is my wife Charlotte. You already know our son, Aaron," he continued. "I was the overseer's deputy. Unfortunately, Elizabeth was on Space Station 1 when Tiada Vejour destroyed it. Therefore, I am now the overseer, Charlotte is my deputy. Owing to my wife's promotion, Aaron is now in charge of Department 44's operation on Obsirion II. Inspector Field is the new liaison officer for Forty-four's smooth communication with regular police forces. Your former colleague, Roman Reckhart, has already agreed to join the department. We want you to join, too. Your experience is invaluable and you have already proved yourself in field operations."

Mint looked around at the gathered faces. Pete Field offered a tired smile, Aaron stared at her eagerly. Roman took her hand and squeezed. Mint squeezed back.

"Ok," Mint said. "On one condition, I get to destroy that bastard thing and free my family."

"We are many years away from practical help and on our own against this 'bastard thing' as you call it," Edward smiled at her. "I assure you, your condition is our desire."

"Excuse me," Charlotte stood and gathered her things. "I wanted to meet you all and show my face. Thank you, Sergeant Harris for agreeing so readily, it frees me up for other priorities. We still have numerous assets in space; transport ships, ore carriers and the like. I have another meeting to chair to work out how we will deal with that situation."

"So much to deal with," Edward shook his head. He watched his wife place a hand on Aaron's shoulder then disappear through the door. It closed behind her with an audible click. "This room is now secure," he continued. "Let us begin the mission debrief."

Doc Davidson joined them after half an hour and they halted an hour later for a refreshment break. Mint chatted lightly with Roman as they sipped at cups of coffee. Not as good as Java's, the loss still hurt. Aaron caught her eye and she excused herself from Roman, wandered over to him.

"Quite a family you have," Mint started. "What's your wife's job, planetary treasurer?"

"No," Aaron laughed. "She doesn't work, full time mum. It's good to see you and Roman, you know …"

"Early days, Aaron" Mint smiled, a slight flush blossoming. "Things are still too raw and painful, but I need a shoulder to cry on."

"Of course you do, excuse me," Aaron's command-pad had just buzzed. "Ok," he said. "Bring him in."

Mint cocked her head at him.

"Gabriel," Aaron raised his eyebrows. "Well, Gabriel and Bruce Webster's consciousness."

Everybody turned when the door opened and Penny Webster walked in, her hand in Gabriel's. The boy looked at them all then at a wall screen, currently showing some of the geometric symbols from the Jaicon Hewson murder scene.

"The Imperial G'frak Heirescence," Gabriel/Bruce said. "Tiada Vejour knew we hadn't fully deciphered G'frak symbology and used those, with the upside down pentagram, to suggest demonic practices were behind the murder. It instantly caught the connection between our word demon and Varla K'dyamon. It knows its kind has visited Earth."

"You can read the symbols?" Aaron asked. His face was aglow with excitement and expectation.

"Oh yes," Gabriel/Bruce replied. "I can read their language; it's the G'frak language actually. They created the Varla K'dyamon. What a big mistake that was. I still have Tiada Vejour's memories. You want to fight it – I can help."

ABOUT THE AUTHOR

Steve P Lee is a science fiction writer from Newark-on-Trent. He worked for HM Government for 23 years, in the Inland Revenue and Ministry of Defence, before taking voluntary redundancy and striking out in the private sector. Recent health issues have restricted his ability to work, prompting a final attempt to realise his youthful ambition to become a successful author.

Other Authors With Green Cat Books

Lisa J Rivers –

Why I Have So Many Cats

Winding Down

Searching (Coming 2018)

Luna Felis –

Life Well Lived

Gabriel Eziorobo –

Words Of My Mouth

The Brain Behind Freelance Writing

Mike Herring –

Nature Boy

Glyn Roberts & David Smith –

Prince Porrig And The Calamitous Carbuncle

Peach Berry –

A Bag of Souls

Elijah Barns –

The Witch and Jet Splinters: Part 1. A Bustle In The Hedgerow

The Witch and Jet Splinters: Part 2. The Shadow Cutters (coming 2018)

Michelle DuVal –

The Coach

Sean P Gaughan –

And God For His Own

David Rollins –

Haiku From The Asylum

Horsey (coming 2018)

Brian N Sigauke –

The Power Of Collectivity

Bridgette Hamilton –

The Break The Crave System…7 Steps to Effortless Lifelong WeightLoss

Michael Keene –

For The Love Of Tom

Richard Tyndall –

The Aldwark Tales

Truth C Matters –

I Rest My Case

Jon Carvell –

Chaos In Camelot

Deborah Carnelley –

Milo

Zapher Iqbal –

Lucy At The Snake Sanctuary

ARE YOU A WRITER?

We are looking for writers to send in their manuscripts.

If you would like to submit your work, please send a small sample, along with a synopsis ,to

books@green-cat.co

GREEN CAT BOOKS

www.green-cat.co/books

89950663R00155

Made in the USA
Columbia, SC
05 March 2018